Unholy Choices
By
David Dwyer

Unholy Choices is a work of fiction. Any resemblance to persons living or dead, with the exception of historical figures, is coincidental. However, the named establishments in Minnesota are real. Go visit them and say hello from me. The Second World War was real, The Holocaust was real, German POWs lived in Minnesota, and Max Chayka approves this disclaimer.

Front cover art by Joan Frenz of Turnpike Designs. Back cover design by Dana Holmay. Back cover written by Dan Holmay. Author photograph by Angela Beth.

For more information please visit www.unholychoices.com

ISBN-13: 978-1542790260
ISBN-10: 1542790263

Printed in the United States of America

Dedication

Find that sweet spot where your passions and talents intersect.
It's a fun place to live.

Acknowledgements:
Bob Gust for your editing skills. Debbie Batjer for a great developmental edit. John and Sheila Scates for smart thoughts and unending love. James and Jan Dwyer for the gift of your presence. Sandra Reynolds for supporting this crazy idea. Mark Dwyer for your support and smart feedback. Grant Anderson for actually reading my stuff. Todd Weisjahn for your insight and wisdom. Emily Brecht for reading my messy first edition. Dan Holmay for your excellent garage advice. Jeff Carlson for being the original beta reader. Steve Erickson for reading early edition and still believing in my skills. Dan and Kory Bengtson for your kindness and support. Steven Dwyer for helping shape narrative. Charles Jensen for your Duluth smarts. Ziv and Tali Liberman for your friendship and help. Elmer Trousdale for your intelligent review. Dan Klis for your eagle eye. To all not mentioned that have been kind and loyal to me over the years – thank you.

Special Acknowledgements:
To my entire wonderful family, I am indeed lucky. Barbara Dwyer, without you, I would be nothing. Angela Dwyer, the draw and center of my life. Michael Dwyer, I hope you would be proud. Jacob, Mikayla and Trey; never let anyone or anything stand in the way of your dreams. Always overcome. I love you all.

,

Chapter 1

June 1941

Kiev, Soviet Socialist Republic of Ukraine

Seventeen-year-old Vlad Chayka was invited to a Kiev hotel bar by friends with connections to local Communist Party bosses. The bar and hotel were reserved for the well-connected, select members of the Communist Party, and wealthy foreign travelers. The windows were open, and a warm June evening breeze flowed through the hotel lobby and bar. Those permitted to be there enjoyed a nice respite from the brutal winters everyone endured in Ukraine.

At the center of the bar stood his three brothers, surrounded by a group of good looking women. Vlad didn't recognize the ladies, which made him happy. Many people were half joking when they said a person couldn't swing a dead cat by the tail, and not hit a woman enticed by one of the Chayka brothers. They were considered gentlemen, but with an uncanny ability to tempt women. An almost empty bottle of vodka and loud laughter were positive indicators of a successful night ahead.

Mikhail held court as usual. He was by far the funniest and kept all entertained with quick humor. He possessed a skill many men lack and most women admire. "Tonight will be good," Vlad thought as he approached. Vlad's next oldest brother, Timor, greeted him with a bear hug and a shot of vodka.

"Vlad, this is great, beautiful ladies lured to our Chayka charm." Vlad downed the shot, and Timor gave him a forceful kiss on the cheek. Timor loved getting drunk. His propensity to drink and get in fisticuffs was legendary in Kiev.

Vlad's youngest brother Stepan leaned in and made the introductions. "Vlad these fine ladies are down from Minsk on government business and have invited us back tomorrow morning for a weekend of fun. They even have official papers allowing each a companion and assure us proper travel passes for the return trip. What do you say, my brother?"

Vlad needed no further persuasion, plus he had never been to Minsk. It was a ten-hour train ride north, but to an unexplored city with beautiful new friends. Typical needs for a handsome 17-year-old kid trying to navigate his way in a harsh Soviet world. Although Vlad would miss the secret Catholic Mass on Sunday, he figured it was worth it. He often struggled with teachings of the Church versus the realities of being desired by attractive young women. It was his cross to bear, he joked to himself.

The next morning Vlad, his brothers, and their lady friends boarded a train to Minsk. They spent a few hours sleeping off the previous night's vodka and then proceeded to start eating and drinking again while the train rolled north through the countryside. The brothers sat together in the dining car, and the ladies excused themselves to get a fresh round of cocktails from the bar.

"Minsk in 15 minutes" the conductor announced.

The ladies returned, and everybody downed their drinks. A night of brotherly carousing in a new town with fresh faces lay ahead. "I am blessed," Vlad said under his breath as they disembarked the train. He did his usual ladies first and let them pass before him.

The following morning, Vlad woke to complete chaos in the streets below his fifth-floor hotel room in downtown Minsk. He rolled out of bed with a screaming hangover, and the girl who spent the night was gone, as was cash from his wallet.

"She robbed me" he muttered to himself. "Or did she take what was rightfully hers? Did I just sleep with a prostitute? What the hell happened last night?"

Vlad fell twice while attempting to put on his pants. He steadied himself and walked down five flights of stairs because the elevators were out of service, which Vlad attributed to a power outage or something of that nature. The stairwell was chaotic as patrons and staff passed by him. He entered the lobby, and the usual light breakfast with coffee was unavailable. His brothers gathered with others trying to determine the situation.

Vlad walked up to the group ready to relate the story of his missing cash when he noticed a worried look on all of their faces. Vlad stepped away and walked outside. Police vehicles, fire trucks, and a few military transports raced through the streets. People scurried about and darted from corner to corner trying to find the latest news. Shops closed when they should be open, sirens wailed, and a tension hung in the air.

Vlad turned back to the hotel and grabbed Stepan, "What the hell is going on? It looks like the end of the world out there." Stepan gave Vlad a serious look and told him Nazi Germany had just invaded the Soviet

Union. Vlad couldn't believe the news. "Bullshit. They are our allies. Dad told us about the non-aggression pact Stalin and Hitler signed. I remember how relieved he was that war with Germany was off the table." Mikhail walked into the conversation. Vlad never saw such a horrified look on his quick-witted oldest brother.

"Brothers, this is not good. Hitler invaded this morning using the same Blitzkrieg tactics that caused Poland and France to roll over and surrender. They are headed directly this way, and nobody seems to be in charge or knows what's happening. I've checked on the train, and it is not moving. We are stuck here."

Timor spoke up "Let's get to the armory and see what's going on. Maybe we can get out of here and back to Kiev." All nodded in agreement, and they left the hotel without settling the bill. The staff had abandoned their jobs, and there was nobody to pay. As the brothers hurried to the armory, the street was even more chaotic. People wandered about as though they had no idea what to do or to whom to turn. The nervous energy and fear pulsing through Minsk were as real as a thunderstorm, but invisible.

Vlad spotted a formation of airplanes on the Western horizon headed towards the city. "God I hope they are ours," Vlad thought out loud. The planes were the feared Stuka dive bombers, famous for generating a distinct loud howling noise when in attack mode. Vlad saw them in newsreels at the local cinema during Germany's invasions of Poland, France, Holland, and Belgium. The planes banked hard right, and one by one nose-dived at incredible speeds toward the center of Minsk. The brothers stood in awe as the Stuka's screamed in, strafed with machine guns on full automatic, and dropped bombs with remarkable precision.

One of the lead planes made a direct hit on a natural gas main. The entire center of the city heaved with a titanic explosion that knocked Vlad and his brothers off their feet. Vlad never felt such a powerful concussion. The shockwave left him disoriented and unable to hear out of his right ear. Vlad witnessed the dive bombers coming in waves hitting factories, the train station, the airport, government buildings, hotels, and anything that moved. The Stukas attacked at will. No anti-aircraft defenses or heavy machine guns were in place to fend off the attack. Due to poor leadership by Stalin and Red Army purges, Minsk was a city at the mercy of an enemy that would show none.

During the fourth wave, a bomb hit and destroyed the Minsk water works. All water pressure was lost and the ability to fight fires extinguished. The Germans used special incendiary weapons meant to destroy the target and ignite firestorms. Minsk became engulfed in flames within minutes of the attack. The heat and smoke overwhelmed all, especially the old and young. The smells, sights, and sounds were something Vlad and his brothers never experienced. This was total war. It came with unexpected violence and sudden fury.

Vlad, Mikhail, Timor, and Stepan made their way to the armory, which was damaged and smoke filled, but still functioning. "What the hell is going on?" Mikhail asked a bewildered Red Army Captain wandering near the entrance.

The Captain regained his composure and blurted, "The Germans launched a surprise attack this morning. Grab what you can and come help us." There was no military command and control, junior officers desperately asked enlisted men what to do, and pure chaos reigned. Vlad and his brothers took the initiative to scavenge inside for anything useful.

They found parts of uniforms. A jacket here, some pants in the corner, and a few belts hanging on hooks. Combat boots of non-matching sizes were strewn about and smashed medical kits littered the floor. They could only locate three rifles with limited ammunition between the four of them. All of the brothers had attended quasi-military summer camps and were proficient with firearms. Vlad even earned a marksmanship medal the previous year. Vlad and his brothers gathered what they could while navigating the darkened armory through thick smoke.

The heat from the fires was becoming unbearable, "We need to get to the edge of town, or we will die here" Timor shouted. All brothers nodded in agreement. Timor led them out of the armory with their meager supply of weapons and ammunition. As they exited the building, the roof thunderously collapsed killing all who remained inside.

"Holy shit!" Stepan exclaimed to his older brothers. "This is insane. We need to get home and find mom and dad." Timor gave Stepan an older-brother look as if to say 'don't concern yourself about mom and dad, but get your ass in gear and follow me.' Timor led his brothers through the streets, tripping over dead bodies and debris as they headed west. Fires spread unabated from building to building, and Vlad saw people in flames rolling on the ground attempting to put themselves out. What was unthinkable last night became a brutal reality this morning. Minsk was ablaze, under attack, full of death, and in complete pandemonium.

Chapter 2
June 1941
Minsk, Soviet Socialist Republic of Belarus

As they reached the western edge of Minsk, Timor saw an old friend from grade school who was now a junior officer in the Red Army. The officer confirmed Germany attacked in three different areas along the border; North, Center, and South. They were in direct path of Army Group Center, and legendary German Panzer tank commander Heinz Guderian. Timor's friend complained about the lack of command. Any defense against the invaders turned into a disorganized free for all. The group decided to stay together and walk another mile west, in hopes of joining some organized resistance.

They made it a few miles west of Minsk and could see the city completely on fire. The sun shined fully overhead but was hard to see through acrid smoke from the burning ruins. A Russian troop transport truck sat abandoned on the side of the road, Vlad checked in the back and found four jugs of water. They were all incredibly thirsty and took a few minutes to hydrate and rest. Timor jumped into the front driver's seat and pushed the ignition button. The engine turned over but did not start. The gas gauge read full, so he popped open the hood to check the motor. The threat from German planes had subsided, but the brothers remained unsure if the Stukas were bombing other places or had gone to refuel and return. "Get this truck started," Stepan said, "Not sure how long until those bastards come back and use us for target practice."

They worked on the truck for thirty minutes, but could not get it started. Nobody had tools, none were trained mechanics, and they could only do so much. As Mikhail and Timor discussed the next move for the group, a column of German infantry and tanks appeared over a ridge. The Germans were a half mile away, and rapidly advancing towards them.

Another two companies of mechanized light infantry, accompanied by tanks, approached on their right and left. It was a classic pincer move the German Wehrmacht employed many times with great success. Suddenly a shell from a German tank landed and exploded precariously close to Vlad. The Germans were giving the hands up gesture to the brothers. "What do we do?" Stepan nervously asked.

Timor responded, "Put your rifles on the ground and hands in the air, or all of us are going to get killed." Everyone nodded in agreement and followed Timor's command.

The Germans advanced quickly upon them, and orders were given in German which none of them understood. Two German soldiers stepped out of the ranks and approached Timor's Red Army Officer friend. The more muscular German soldier grabbed him by the shirt collar with one hand and smashed him with a pair of brass knuckles in the head using the other. Blood shot out of his temple in pulsating spurts as he dropped to the ground with both legs convulsing. The German spoke to the brothers in broken Russian

"You pieces of shit come with me and join the other Russian pussy's we are holding in the rear. I could kill you without any recourse because your rotten lives mean nothing to me. My commander wants you pigs brought to the holding area, and upon my return, I will rejoin my unit to rape and beat to death some women in Minsk tonight."

Vlad, Timor, Mikhail, and Stepan walked away from Minsk in shocked defeat with the two guards, as thousands of spiteful German soldiers descended upon the city.

It was late afternoon when Vlad and his brothers approached a large open field strewn with circular strands of barbed wire, creating a makeshift perimeter. A few thousand Russian soldiers and male civilians stood inside the wire. A small entrance guarded by German soldiers and two heavy machine guns opened up for them.

"Get in there with the other Russian dogs," the muscular German soldier said. "I will now return to Minsk with my victorious brothers and have some fun with your women. I will personally penetrate and murder four Soviet whores tonight, one for each of you. Hopefully, your mother and sister are in the bunch." The two Germans shoved the brothers inside and laughed as they headed east towards Minsk.

Defeated men continued to pour into the make-shift prison camp as dusk fell. Another few thousand prisoners crammed into the open space. It was still hot and standing room only with no water, no food, and no toilet. The Germans parked five of Guderian's Panzer tanks outside the wire with cannons pointed inside at the POWs. German guards armed with automatic weapons and grenades patrolled the perimeter. German soldiers were eating, drinking, dancing, laughing and singing songs by the bonfires burning outside the camp. The aura of arrogant invincibility was most apparent among the conquering troops.

Inside the wire, Vlad, Mikhail, Timor, and Stepan stood together speaking with Russian soldiers and male civilians the Germans had captured. Rumors swirled about the mighty Red Army, but little solid information was available. Most complained bitterly about the complete breakdown of Soviet defenses and lack of preparation by the chain of command. Others were preoccupied with their women and children left in town, now at the total mercy of a menacing enemy.

As the night wore on and the guards got drunk, they started shooting rifles into the air. Some took pot shots into the crowded field of captives for sport. "We need to stick together," Mikhail said, "All we can do is depend on each other. Don't plan on being rescued by the mighty Red Army anytime soon."

Stepan being the youngest started to cry. "Mom and Dad are back in Kiev. They must be worried sick about us. Plus I am starved, thirsty, and my whole body hurts."

"Stepan, Brother Mikhail is right. We need to stick together and be here for each other. You sit down next to Timor and me, rest your back against ours, and get some sleep. We'll talk in the morning." Vlad put his arm around the youngest brother as Stepan cried himself to sleep in the overcrowded dusty field.

The brothers awoke at daybreak to German shouts of "Raus, schnell." All of the prisoners were being moved out of the field and farther to the rear. The effects of sleeping on the ground, which none of them were used to, showed on everyone. Timor was the slowest to get up, stretching his back in an attempt to recover from the primitive sleeping conditions. His mood showed it.

"These goddamned German Krauts are like locusts. They are a plague upon all of us. Stalin is evil, but Hitler is far worse. These people are lower than animals, and are happily carrying out the wishes of that maniac."

The brothers and thousands of POWs assembled in long columns on a winding dirt road and began their march deeper into the newly conquered Nazi territory. The columns stretched to the horizon and extended 30 men wide. Thousands of male Soviet soldiers and civilians walked away in defeat from the fight, while thousands of German Soldiers walked confidently towards it. They passed each other all day, with the Germans hurling insults and sneers at the prisoners as they advanced.

During the march, German soldiers wearing different uniforms started to appear from time to time. Some uniforms were black with red swastika armbands and hats bearing the emblem of skull and crossbones. Most of these black-clad Germans wore black leather riding boots and displayed an even bigger swagger than regular Wehrmacht soldiers. Vlad assumed they were SS. He read about them in newspapers and saw their exploits in newsreels.

Anyone living in Europe knew the SS served as Hitler's personal army. The SS were fanatical believers in Nazi racial ideology and fierce fighters who showed no mercy to their enemies. Above all, the SS fervently believed in Hitler's directive of ruthless destruction of all inferior races. This included Soviets, Poles, Gypsies, and especially Jews.

The column marched towards their destination, and a few SS men joined the German guards. Vlad, Mikhail, Timor, and Stepan marched together under the hot sun with no food or water for twenty-four hours. They were herded like and treated worse than cattle. The Germans gave no consideration to their physical well-being or state of mind. Timor, being the most sarcastic of the brothers, suddenly let out a loud "moo" as if imitating a cow. He didn't realize an SS man was within earshot. It was a mistake that would cost him dearly.

"Who is the stupid Russian pig that just did that?" the SS man screamed. "I swear to God; I will kill ten of you shit eating dogs right now if you don't identify yourself," Timor said nothing as the column continued to march. Everyone in the immediate vicinity knew it was Timor, but none wanted to betray him. The SS man started to count off as he pointed to individual prisoners. "One, two, three" he pointed to Stepan, "four" he continued to count, "five." Timor suddenly stepped out of line and eyeballed the SS man.

"I said it."

The SS man quit counting and rushed Timor shouting "You want to be a cow? I will whip you like a cow, you fucking Jew loving Communist." The SS officer pulled out an eight-foot long leather bull whip with a sharpened metal weight attached to the tip. Timor's blue eyes grew wide as the SS man took a few steps back and unleashed a full strength whiplash that struck Timor square in the face. He let out a painful howl and stumbled back, instinctively covering his wound with his hand.

The SS man wound up again and delivered another full strength whiplash to his head. The metal tip ripped a piece of his nose off, splattering blood and skin chunks on Vlad and Mikhail. Timor crumpled to his knees, his face deformed and covered in blood. The howls of agony could be heard by the other POWs a quarter mile away.

The gruesome spectacle continued as the SS man unloaded another full force blow. The metal tip of his whip landed on his right ear, tearing it in half. Blood poured onto his neck and Timor began to list over from his knees onto his side. As he tipped onto the dirt road, the SS man landed a direct hit to Timor's mouth. Four teeth flew out, and his lower lip was left dangling, barely attached to his face by a thin strip of bloody skin. It was the most gruesome act of violence Vlad, or any of the POWs had ever seen. The SS man appeared well practiced with the whip and seemed to take joy in the brutality.

Within sixty seconds, the SS officer whipped nearly all of the flesh off Timor's face. He lay on the road broken, covered in blood, disfigured and roiling in pain. The SS man drew his pistol and pointed the weapon down at Timor, shooting him in the chest at near point blank range. His body bounced up and landed back with a thud from the gunshot impact. The SS man spit on Timor, and savagely kicked his body repeatedly until his corpse lay on the side of the road. He holstered the sidearm and wiped the blood, skin, and hair from the whip. All while whistling a song composed by Richard Wagner.

Vlad shook with rage and began to step out of the ranks towards the SS man who just murdered his brother. Mikhail stopped him and whispered, "He will do the same to you, Vlad." If this had been two days ago, Vlad would have fought anyone throwing a punch at his brothers. Now he was forced to stand idly by and watch his brother whipped and shot to death. This showed what Nazi occupation had done to him in two days. It was the beginning of excruciating personal choices that would determine if he survived or perished.

The last two days were surreal. Vlad was hungry, thirsty, physically exhausted and mentally numb over Timor's death. The seventeen-year-old couldn't fathom the homicidal insanity awaiting the world and him.

Chapter 3
St. Louis Park, Minnesota
Present Day

A black government car drove slowly down the tree lined street of neatly kept, yet modest homes in St. Louis Park. A warm spring morning in early May brought the neighbors out, after a long Minnesota winter. They watched two men in suits park the car, and walk up to Vlad's front door. After no answer, they walked around back and found Vlad tending to his garden. Same as he had done for the past 70 years.

"Vladimir Chayka, I am Special Agent Whitman, and this is Special Agent Andreen of Immigration and Customs Enforcement. We have an arrest warrant for immigration fraud, and willful misrepresentation of your status upon entering the United States in 1945." 92-year-old Vlad slowly rose to his feet from a garden kneeling pad and turned around. His tuft of white hair blew in the spring wind, and the sun showed an attractive face for a man of his age. The agents read Vlad the Miranda Warning as he was handcuffed and led to their waiting car.

"I need to call my son," Vlad said in his thick Ukrainian accent.

The federal agents drove him to the Federal Court Building in Downtown Minneapolis. Vlad was escorted into an interview room on the fifth floor. Agent Whitman re-entered the room a few minutes later. "Mr. Chayka, your son returned the courtesy call you made from my desk. He is in court but on his way. He requested we wait to begin the interview until he arrives."

Twenty minutes later, Max Chayka parked in front of the Federal Court Building in a new S-Series 4-Matic Mercedes Benz, worth nearly the same as his dad's house. Max donned a suit tailored for him from Top Shelf Clothier in Minneapolis. It fit well on his six-foot-tall, lean, yet muscular frame. The suits were expensive, and so was Max's expert legal counsel.

Max enjoyed premier defense attorney status in Minneapolis, and became a well-known personality who gained wealth defending the upper crust in many high-profile cases. The 65-year-old was far from retiring, plus he looked 20 years younger due to regular workouts and a full head of dark wavy hair. Max was healthy, wealthy, single, and the women loved him. Max had a good life.

Max entered the interview room and immediately hugged his dad and kissed him on the cheek. "Please remove these handcuffs from my father" Max politely requested. "Dad, please let me do the talking." The special agents complied with the request, as did Vlad. "May I please read the complaint?" Vlad studied his son's face. He could tell by Max's eyes and facial expressions his many moods, as happens when a father raises a son by himself. There wasn't much to hide in the small home where Vlad raised Max into the man he was.

Max sat stunned as he finished reading the criminal complaint and set it on the table. "What the hell is this? You dragged a 92-year-old man down here for this crap?" Max defended lots of atrocious and deviant behavior from people. He was rarely shocked by the normally self-inflicted messes people got themselves into. But this was almost impossible to comprehend. Mainly because the charges were so incendiary, and directed against the man he most admired.

"I'm sorry son," Vlad said as his aged deep blue eyes filled up with tears. Max took a minute to recover, calm down and gather his thoughts.

The instinctual defense attorney finally kicked in as Max advised "Dad, don't say anything. I will post bail, call Judge Conley, and have you out of here in an hour."

Max led Vlad out of the Federal Court Building and into his waiting Mercedes an hour and fifteen minutes later. They drove in silence back to Vlad's house, but it wasn't the angry silent treatment that plagues many couples. Max was simply processing the complaint information and pondering his dad's defense. He also had to manage the barrage of questions flowing from the brain, but wisely stopping at the mouth.

Max's thought process was interrupted as they pulled into Vlad's driveway, crews from local TV stations were already camped in front. The news spread fast on social and traditional media. As Max helped Vlad out of the car, the reporters' questions started flying from the street. "Max, is your father a Nazi war criminal? Is your dad going to be stripped of his citizenship and deported? Are you going to defend your father?"

Max replied to the news media gathered "No comment right now guys." He was used to this. Many times while defending a high profile case, TV cameras and reporters routinely hounded him.

They walked up the front steps, and one question shouted by a local reporter got his attention. "How can you think of defending your dad of being a Nazi, when you are Jewish?" The usually unflappable Max Chayka turned and gave a hard glare to the reporter.

"That's out of line" he barked back. Max turned and helped Vlad through the door, both entered the house and disappeared from view.

Once inside, Vlad wearily looked at his son. "I'm suddenly exhausted," his accent sounding thicker than normal.

"Okay dad" Max replied with a deep breath. "Why don't you lay down and I will bring dinner over tonight. We can talk then." Vlad walked slowly upstairs. He insisted on the second-floor bedroom because stairs forced him to exercise. Max watched his dad navigate the last step and uncharacteristically waited for the camera crews to leave. After the small front yard was clear of media, he walked briskly to his car and started to drive.

The story was breaking on local news radio and starting to trend on his social media accounts. A fresh story and shocking news, perfect for the 24-hour news cycle America invented. An alleged Nazi war criminal living in a historically Jewish suburb of Minneapolis was big news. Vlad Chayka being Max Chayka's dad amplified the drama and intrigue by a staggering amount. CNN, FOX, and MSNBC would probably be discussing it within a few hours. They would find experts on the subject and locate people willing to speak publicly who knew Vlad or Max. It was a story easily sensationalized by the media and very consumable by the public.

As Max drove, he considered going to the office, the country club, his house in Minneapolis, or even his synagogue. None seemed appealing. When needing total solitude, he occasionally drove to the middle of Minneapolis and turned into Lakewood Cemetery. Strange as it may seem, it brought him peace of mind and a clear head to walk or drive the grounds of Lakewood.

Max always observed the headstones and thought of the lives they lived. He pondered what impact the dead had on the city and humanity during their lives. Max always thought about his mom, who had no grave to commemorate her death during World War II. What would she have been like? How would his life be different if she survived? Max had many unanswered questions, mainly because Vlad rarely spoke about her and life in general during that time. It haunted Max and was a nagging issue he never could shake. Max knew deep inside that not marrying was probably a result of lingering questions surrounding his mother. Despite the professional confidence and success, Max was fragile on the incompleteness of his ancestry.

Max knew a few things for sure, one was that his mom was Jewish and dad was Catholic. He also knew Vlad promised to raise Max Jewish, regardless of the horrific treatment of Jews in Europe at the time. A mixed marriage in Europe during the Second World War was a dangerous union. It was illegal and punishable by prison or even death in Nazi Germany and its occupied territories.

Max never really understood it, but it must have been quite a love to endure such a nasty environment. Max made a concrete and solemn decision during his Lakewood visit. To fully understand his mom, his dad, and most importantly himself, he needed the whole story. He needed the truth and the only one who could supply it was his dad.

Chapter 4

"Max Chayka," the lady at the counter shouted. Max got up from the bench where customers waited, walked to the cashier, and paid for the take out Chinese food. General Tso's chicken and beef with peppers were Vlad's favorite. Max got in his car and turned the radio to the top of the hour news. He sat in the parking space and listened to National Public Radio give the details of his dad's arrest.

This was a big story and not going away anytime soon, he thought to himself. Max fully expected a daily diet of innuendo, rumor and hearsay served up by the media. Frankly, there wasn't much he could do about it. Max had dinner to bring over and was running late. Max thought it funny his Ukrainian dad, who lived in the United Sates, loved Chinese food. A small world Max would say, and his dad would always disagree. "It is a big world son. So big it's almost two worlds, and I have lived in both."

Max never questioned what his dad meant. He accepted it at face value as Vlad's simplified explanation of the divide between Kiev and St. Louis Park. Max allowed the decade's long detente to go long enough with his dad. Time had come for truth.

A much calmer scene existed at Vlad's house compared to the morning. No reporters or camera crews this time, and the neighbors seemed to understand the need for privacy by waving hello from a distance. Max parked in the driveway, grabbed the bag of Chinese food and walked up to the door.

Vlad reclined in the back sunroom with a cocktail in hand. On the table serving as a bar sat a bottle of Johnnie Walker Black, drink glasses and a bucket of ice. Vlad smiled at Max. "Help yourself to a drink, son. I have mine already." Max was concerned about Vlad's mental state, and happy to find him both hungry and thirsty.

"Let me make you a plate dad. I got your usual favorites."

Max walked into the kitchen and glanced around. The number of meals laughs, and tears they shared in this modest space over the years was incalculable. Max never fully understood how easily different his fate could have been. Two worlds indeed.

Vlad accepted the plate from Max with a grateful thank you. Over the past ten or so years, Vlad tended to drink more than he ate, especially at dinner time. His appetite had diminished, plus the booze helped him sleep better. Vlad drained the last of his Johnnie Walker Black and did the usual wrist flip causing the ice cubes to clang on the side of his glass. "One more please."

"Ok dad, I'll pour you a half, but we need to talk for a while tonight. I can't have you falling asleep on me too soon."

Vlad and Max sat with food and drinks on the couch. They nonverbally acknowledged that much needed to unfold and buried memories unearthed. Max refused to play the role of tough attorney with Vlad, his dad was too kind and loving of a father for over 65 years. Max simply wanted to get his arms around the enormity of the accusations and let his dad begin the story on his accord. However, Max decided he would put steady and gentle pressure on Vlad to get to the truth.

Vlad took another long sip from his fresh cocktail and gently set the glass down. "Max, my boy, there is a part of my life that I have kept locked away. I wished to take it to my grave and only answer to the Almighty, but now must answer while I am still alive. Part of me is happy, and part of me is dreading this."

Max let the words rest a minute and then gently prodded Vlad. "Let's start with what part of you is happy."

Vlad locked eyes with Max. "I am glad you will understand your old man. More importantly, you may fully understand yourself. Learning about the first few years of your life should bring everything full circle. I don't have much to leave you when I die, but consider this your inheritance. The pain and embarrassment this may cause, we cannot control, and I am sorry. Please remember this, I love you and am most proud of you. A father could not have asked for a better son." Max fought back tears.

"I know you do Dad, and I love you too."

Vlad took the last bite of his dinner and set the plate down. "It was a beautiful spring in 1941, my three brothers and I lived in Kiev at the time. Dad made the successful transition from farming in the countryside to work as a civil servant in Kiev." Vlad described his young life for the first time to his son and got Max caught up to the point of Timor being whipped to death by the SS. Vlad wiped away his tears. "I never thought people could treat each other in such a manner. Evil took on a life form and gripped my hand tightly." With that simple opening, Vlad embarked on a journey that Max could never have imagined.

Chapter 5
Somewhere near the Polish border
June 1941

Vlad's column marched nonstop for three days and nights. Another fifteen thousand Soviet POWs were taken captive, resulting in a rapidly growing human catastrophe. Vlad could not see the beginning or end of the stretch of human misery moving through the countryside. Any POW who couldn't keep up or fell out of line was summarily executed. Vlad correctly figured they were heading east, in the direction of the pre-war Polish border. The weather remained stifling hot, and the dust kicked up from thousands marching was almost suffocating. Vlad, Stepan, and Mikhail managed to stay together and urged each other forward. None of them had ever understood real hunger or thirst, but did now.

The column suddenly halted around noon on day three. A German officer climbed atop his vehicle and observed the throngs of people held captive. His puffed out chest and arrogant sneer displayed utter contempt towards the Untermensch collected at his feet. The officer was in complete contrast to Vlad and the rest of the POWs. He was well fed, well dressed, shiny boots, fully armed, and overflowing with a massively inflated sense of racial greatness. The SS officer grabbed a bullhorn and spoke in accented Russian.

"We will give you 10 minutes to eat. You will be allowed no more than 30 feet on either side of the road to graze like the animals you are. If any escape attempt is made, you will be shot, and 100 more will be gunned down for your treachery. Now go and eat grass, insects and anything else you filthy scum can manage to find." The starving men moved to either side of the road and began devouring anything that was edible. Some even urinated into their hands and drank it to abate their thirst.

Vlad watched his brothers and fellow countrymen descended upon, and consume tall grass, shrubs, and bark from young trees. They ate crickets, worms, dandelions and anything else the mass of starving men could consume. The POWs were famished and exhausted, with many already psychologically broken. Vlad, Stepan, and Mikhail never saw anything like it. Less than a week ago these men were well fed, proud and confident. Now reduced to behaving like animals the Germans claimed them to be. It would be a homicidal self-fulfilling prophecy, based on race and pure hate repeated over the next four years. Ordered back into columns after ten minutes, the POWs continued to march.

The prisoners marched until dusk, guarded by well-armed Germans on foot, horseback and motorcycles. The Germans patrolled in front, in back and on the sides of the men. They divided the POWs into blocks of 300 each as they marched. This gave the Germans control while greatly outnumbered by their prisoners.

The ever growing prisoner of war column reached another massive open field surrounded by a hastily constructed barbed wire perimeter. This new area was ten times the size from the first night. Vlad estimated at least 30,000 men were crowded inside the barbed wire. It was dusty, hot, and it stank.

Hundreds of more German soldiers, tanks, and SS guarded the outside of this makeshift camp. Vlad, Mikhail, and Stepan entered the compound. The brothers held hands and quietly said the Hail Mary together at Mikhail's request. It was the first time Vlad prayed since the invasion and Timor's murder. He angrily reflected on that fact, which caused him to bitterly cry walking through the front gate. Vlad enjoyed conversations with God and reciting prayers memorized during his Catholic childhood. He prayed daily and took deep solace in his personal relationship with God. The fact he hadn't prayed until now was profoundly heartbreaking.

Again, there was no food, no water, no medical attention, and no bathroom facilities. Just an enormous open field packed with grown men starting to behave like animals. Vlad surveyed the area and saw people urinating on others, and pulling down their pants to defecate in the open. Many ate the little remaining grass and even dirt to assuage their hunger. The SS began playing a game where they threw a loaf of moldy bread over the wire and watched the POWs fight over it. People beat each other severely to eat, while the Germans laughed and took bets.

Stepan looked at Vlad and Mikhail saying wearily "I don't think I am going to survive this. I'm starving, my feet are killing me, and I can barely walk anymore. Look at these German soldiers. They are well fed and full of confidence. We are the exact opposite."

Mikhail replied to his youngest brother in a firm but sympathetic tone. "We will live through this brother, and you will see mom and dad again. But you need to dig deep from within and find strength. Most of these people have no one to rely on, but we are blessed to have each other. Plus we need to avenge Timor and kill some of these fascist bastards." The words seemed to calm Stepan for the time being.

Vlad couldn't stop thinking about his brother's murderer. The SS officer killed him so effortlessly and didn't seem to give it a second thought. Committing a violent act seemed as natural as breathing air. Vlad was ashamed he stood by and let it happen, but certain death waited had he tried to intervene. The choice resulted in a difficult tradeoff for Vlad to swallow, and there would be many more to come.

Suddenly, an SS officer with a bullhorn startled Vlad's thought process as he barked, "Any Jews need to come forward for special treatment." No one came forward. Even the least educated among the prisoners knew the Nazi's brutal attitudes regarding Jews. All were reluctant to comply with his request, as the POWs were unsure if it was a trap. Judging by the treatment meted so far, none were in any mood to cooperate with the Germans.

The SS officer waited for a few minutes and said sarcastically into his bullhorn "Anyone who gives me a Jew, will eat a nice dinner tonight." Every prisoner could smell meat and potatoes cooking outside the camp. It caused them to salivate and drove some to attempt a suicidal climb over the wire, only to be immediately shot by the Germans. Dead bodies were interwoven in the barbed wire like flies in a spider web.

The Germans understood the power of offering food to a starving person. Some men in the compound started pointing out people who had stereotypical Jewish features or betraying people they knew to be Jews. After a few minutes, Vlad watched fifty Jews forced to the front gate by their fellow POWs. The SS officer ordered it open, let the Jews out, and had them gather around ten-foot high wooden poles pounded into the ground. The wood poles had pulleys attached to the top, with twenty-foot lengths of rope laced through. "Stand with your hands behind your backs" he ordered. The Jewish POWs did as asked. A few SS men walked up and tied the prisoner's hands together behind their backs with sure knots. The rope rose from their wrists up to the pole, through the pulley, and down the other side almost reaching the ground.

The SS Officer sneered at the Jews "I want to hear you scream." The Jews were confused and stayed silent. The SS officer grew agitated "You goddamned Jews, I said scream." The group of bound Jews let out a nervous halfhearted scream, to the bewilderment of the now irate SS Officer.

He walked behind the first Jewish POW and nodded at the SS enlisted man holding the other end of the rope. The SS man pulled on his end of the rope which hoisted the prisoner's wrists behind the back, inflicting severe pain. The SS officer smiled and said, "Lift this bag of shit completely off the ground." The SS enlisted man did as ordered and pulled the rope until the Jewish victim's feet were a meter in the air. His entire body weight supported by cuffed wrists and hyperextended shoulders. The Jew let out a blood-curdling howl. "This is the scream I want to hear, you filthy pig." The SS Officer said with a smirk.

The screams were now real and rooted in agonizing pain most people will never experience. The cries coming from the Jewish victim were not loud enough to cover the sounds of his shoulders dislocating and tendons popping. Vlad heard of the torture method called the Strappado, but never witnessed it until now. The cries of agony caused Vlad to vomit up the grass eaten earlier on the side of the road.

"Hang up the rest of these vermin" the SS Officer ordered his men. After five minutes, all 50 Jews were hanging off pulleys the same way as the first. The screams, cries, and popping of shoulders were now louder than the din of 30,000 men inside the wire. It was the most awful thing Vlad and his brothers had ever seen or heard.

Upon finishing the 50th Jewish POW, the SS officer turned and spoke to the men inside the wire who handed over the Jews. "For those who helped me, here is your meal, enjoy." Three rotting dead dogs were thrown over the wire by snickering German soldiers to the awaiting men. Vlad watched as hundreds of delirious and starving men fought over three spoiled dead dogs. The animals were torn from limb to limb. Intestines were ripped out of their bellies, tongues were torn out, and eyeballs gouged from the heads.

Stepan started to rush in for anything to eat, but Mikhail stopped him. "Don't do it" he implored. "Either the meat or these men will kill you." Stepan gave a resigned look of hungry despair to his brother and turned away.

When the chaos ended, fifteen men lay on the ground beaten to death by fellow POWs fighting over rancid dog meat. The Germans roared with laughter on the other side of the wire. "Tomorrow it will be cats" one yelled.

"Brothers, we need to stick together," Mikhail said as he looked at Stepan. "We will only survive this madness if we remain united, and you all know that." They sat down and used each other's backs as support to rest. They were exhausted, starved and covered in filth. Stepan closed his eyes first and cried himself to sleep. Vlad and Mikhail stayed awake until sleep overtook them as well.

The next morning was full sun and already hot. Vlad and Mikhail awoke to moans from Jewish POWs still alive after being tortured the night before. Most were dead as their lifeless bodies were grotesquely propped up by outstretched shoulders, elongated by almost 6 inches. It sickened Vlad who had nothing to throw up, but it didn't stop the dry vomiting. Mikhail spoke first. "Where is Stepan?" Vlad stood up and gained his bearings as he did a quick survey of the surroundings trying to find his brother.

"I have no idea where the kid went" Vlad worriedly replied.

They both stood up on very sore feet and aching muscles. Vlad surveyed the open field as he wiped dust and filth away from his eyes. It was an ocean of human misery, with throngs of people who were filthy, sick, and wandering aimlessly. Trying to find Stepan among almost 30,000 people was not going to be easy. "Goddamn it, I told the kid to stick together," Mikhail said in a worried and angry voice. Vlad tried to guess where Stepan may have wandered off. They could only see immediate faces and tops of heads as both attempted to look out further.

Vlad gave a concerned look to Mikhail. "Let's split up and meet back here in about an hour. I will walk the perimeter clockwise, and you try to make it through the middle. Be careful, and I will see you back at this same spot. We need to find him."

Vlad started to walk around the field near the barbed wire, and he noticed conditions were deteriorating rapidly. What normally would be everyday petty issues were blowing up into violent life and death struggles. Vlad saw two men fight to the death over a pair of boots on a corpse lying in the urine-soaked mud. His pockets were emptied, clothes ripped off, and now his boots were being viciously fought over. Some POWs were fortunate enough to have food on them when captured and managed to smuggle it into camp.

Vlad saw an older POW take a half-eaten muffin out of his pocket and stuff it in his mouth. Others also witnessed it and jumped him, beating the older man senseless while smashing his jaw into pieces. He lay in the dirt unconscious while people picked pieces of soggy, half-chewed muffin out of his mouth with soiled fingers. The human behavior inside the wire had regressed back to the Stone Age in less than a week.

Vlad continued to walk the edge of the camp toward the front gate looking for Stepan. As he approached the gate, he spotted a large pile of corpses. Vlad rubbed his eyes and blinked in disbelief at the sight. The dead were piled almost twelve feet high and ten yards long. Vlad guessed at least 300 bodies were stacked in the morning sun. The Germans formed a small detail of prisoners to gather the dead each morning by the front gate and pile them up. Those that did the work were given a piece of bread to eat under guard, preventing any food riots from other POWs.

The dead were dragged by the POW work detail to a nearby grove of trees and dumped unceremoniously in a mass grave. The dead had expired from battle wounds, starvation, thirst, illness, beatings by fellow POWs, random gunshots from drunken guards, or simply lost the will to live. Vlad almost felt jealous, because their ordeal was over. No more humiliation, hunger, thirst, pain or physical abuse. This nightmare was not ending anytime soon, and the dead were in peace. Lucky bastards, he thought to himself as Vlad walked closer to the pile.

Vlad watched as the corpses were tossed onto carts like potato sacks by the selected POWs. The carts were simple flatbeds with two wheels and a long wooden neck that could be attached to a horse or tractor. Vlad had seen them used many times by farmers transporting hay. Under heavy German guard, the entrance opened, and the prisoner detail tried to pull the wooden cart to the awaiting mass grave. They had thrown too many corpses on the cart and could not move the load. One POW climbed on top and started tossing excess corpses onto the ground to lighten the weight. Vlad could hear the sickening thud as the dead hit the dirt and bounced off the ground. Their limbs and necks were like rubber, flailing about like rag dolls.

The POW corpse detail returned and started piling more bodies on the cart for a second trip when Vlad thought he spotted Stepan being loaded among the dead. Vlad walked briskly as possible through the crowd without drawing attention. He watched two POWs take each corpse, one grabbed wrists, and the other feet. They swung the body onto the cart, stacking them like firewood. Vlad found Stephan's head sticking out on the side under three corpses. His beautiful blue eyes were rolled back into his head, and his blonde wavy hair was a matted mess of dirt and blood. The left side of his face was bashed in by other prisoners or German guards for some unknown reason. Vlad gently touched his baby brothers beaten face, and felt cold rigor had set in.

He collapsed to his knees next to the cart and gazed up to heaven, "Where are you?" he angrily muttered out into the air. "Where are you, God? Where are you, Jesus? Blessed are the peacemakers? Blessed are the hungry? Blessed are the meek? Turn the other cheek? My family and fellow countrymen are being slaughtered and treated worse than animals! Lamb of God, what sins are you taking away from the world? And where is your mercy on us?"

Vlad continued his quiet rage. He didn't want to create a scene and draw attention to himself, but Stepan was the most innocent of the group. Stepan did nothing to deserve this, and now the second brother in a week was torn from him by the German occupiers. With tears streaming down his face and overflowing with emotional chaos, Vlad returned to the meeting place to find Mikhail. He was so overwhelmed with fury that he forgot about hunger for the first time since being captured. When Mikhail saw Vlad approaching, he knew the awful fate of Stepan.

They both stood silently and watched the cart full of corpses containing their youngest brother temporarily stop at the torture posts outside the wire. The dead Jews were cut down from the poles and tossed on top of the cart. A few were still alive, and the SS slit their throats with daggers. Like a team of oxen, the POWs pulled the cart uphill to the mass grave. As the oldest sibling with no parental support, Mikhail felt a fiduciary responsibility for his brother's well-being. The violent death of Timor and Stepan would present physical and mental ramifications which Mikhail would find difficult to overcome.

Chapter 6
Autumn 1941
Eastern Poland

Two months of misery had passed, and Vlad and Mikhail were still alive. They were forced marched to yet another prison camp inside Poland near a town named Chelm. Vlad was astounded to see over 200,000 defeated men in a massive open field. This camp was fenced in with barbed wire secured to ten-foot high wooden posts, with twenty-foot high wooden guard towers dispersed outside the perimeter.

Soldiers manned machine guns in the towers, patrolled the perimeter in armored half-tracks, and shot any man even feigning escape. The Germans again gave no shelter, toilet facilities or medical care to the prisoners. POWs dug holes in the ground with their bare hands to sleep, as the nights began to cool down.

Food was given to the prisoners. One bowl of watery soup made from grass and boiled horse bones, and one small piece of bread made from sawdust. Both Vlad and Mikhail lost over 35% of their body weight. They were on a cruel starvation diet designed on purpose. It was cheaper than using bullets, and starving POWs required much less manpower by the Germans.

Mikhail and Vlad heard rumors that over 5,000 prisoners were dying each day in these hell camps. From what Vlad and Mikhail had witnessed, the grisly death number was close to reality. The living conditions and daily routine in this camp were much like the others. Rampant lice and rats, the morning collection of the dead, one disgusting meal around noon, fights to the death continuously erupting among the POWs, dig a hole to sleep in, starve, and die.

Mikhail looked at Vlad "Dad made you read Leviathan, right?"

Vlad let out a knowing grin to his brother "Yes, Thomas Hobbes on the war of all against all, and the state of mankind 400 years ago. I remember it well, and this situation is exactly what he described."

Mikhail started the famous quote in the book and Vlad joined in "No knowledge of the face of the earth, no account of time, no arts, no letters, no society, and which is worst of all, continual fear and danger of violent death, and the life of man, solitary, poor, nasty, brutish, and short."

Gallows humor was altogether appropriate at this point, and the brothers knew as much. Many men had open sores infested with maggots, suffered from untreated battle wounds beginning to smell like spoiled cheese, and had rat bites on their faces. It was a disgusting cesspool of human misery and filth. The sad truth was Mikhail had contracted dysentery and could not stop excreting fecal matter. Feces, blood, and anal leakage streamed down his legs. Mikhail started to become emaciated, dehydrated, physically weak, and got worse by the day.

Thousands of sick people crammed into a space with bad food, dirty water, no medical care, no shelter and no toilet became a breeding ground for death and disease. The Germans wouldn't venture inside the wire due to fear of highly communicable diseases like Dysentery and Typhus. The POWs were dehumanized, which achieved the German objective. It is easier to mistreat, starve and murder sub-humans than regular people. It was part of the Nazi game plan that young Vlad would become complicit.

Mikhail spoke with Vlad in his weakened condition and said a profound thing "You know little brother, I feel lucky mom and dad insisted we were raised Catholic. That bastard Stalin left most of these people with no religious beliefs, and unable to draw spiritual strength. They are broken men. We are fortunate to have it, and for that, I will always be grateful."

Vlad had tears in his eyes as he observed Mikhail's sunken cheeks. "Mikhail, we were taught that faith, hope, and love were virtuous and timeless qualities. We are blessed to have grown up in a faith and family that fostered such beliefs. I have faith we will get through this alive, hope we will see mom and dad again, and most of all love for you."

Mikhail stared at the ground where he sat. "So God is here, in this place? You believe that?"

Vlad replied "Yes I do. He is here with us right now. I can't explain why Stepan and Timor are dead or explain any of this. But God has a plan. We need to trust in that." They both sat silently on the dirt that served as their home and rested against one another.

Vlad was in much better condition than Mikhail and most of his fellow prisoners. Vlad appeared filthy, malnourished, half starved, smelled awful, and had lice. But compared to many, he somehow avoided most of the nastiness and violence inside the wire. Vlad was physically, mentally, and spiritually intact.

Mikhail slipped further into despair as dysentery became worse day after day. Every time Mikhail ate his daily ration of horse bone soup and sawdust bread, it went straight through him and out his rear end. "I can't eat anymore," Mikhail said to Vlad in a voice weaker than normal a few days later. "My insides are seeping out, and I can feel myself slowly dying. What's become of our family and us?" Vlad wrapped his arms around his brother and hugged him. Vlad had tears in his eyes as Mikhail continued quietly crying and clinging to the hope this too would pass. He dreamt day and night the Red Army would charge to their rescue.

Vlad looked at Mikhail while observing his gaunt eyes and said with conviction "We will both survive this God-awful mess, you are my oldest brother and I love you. Plus, we need to avenge Stepan and Timor. These Nazi bastards need to pay for this."

Mikhail sighed "I am too weak to avenge anything right now."

That night, both of them crawled into the hole they dug and fell asleep. The stench coming from Mikhail's dysentery caused Vlad to vomit a few times. He was getting worse, which kept Vlad preoccupied with the fear of enduring this nightmare without any of his brothers. As the youngest, Vlad was used to being part of the group and found strength in numbers. Very few people messed with the Chayka brothers in Kiev because there were four of them, and retaliation would soon follow. He fell asleep preoccupied with his fear of being exposed and alone. It terrified Vlad, even more than his Nazi tormentors.

Chapter 7

Vlad and Mikhail awoke to shouts and commands in German the following morning, as a convoy of vehicles appeared from the west. In the lead were a few staff cars carrying officers wearing the telling black SS uniform. They were adorned with red swastika armbands, and skull with crossbones on their hats.

Behind the staff cars were 20 trucks used to carry troops, but none had the canvas cover. SS men armed with automatic weapons rode in the rear of each truck, and the transports were curiously empty besides the SS guards. Vlad witnessed the ruthless efficiency which the Germans operated since June, and these many trucks with so few men didn't seem right.

Vlad helped Mikhail to his feet. They both stood and watched as the SS staff cars drove to the main entrance. The regular German soldiers of the Wehrmacht were snapping to attention, scurrying about, and obeying their orders. It was obvious the recently arrived SS were of importance and meant business. It would be a momentous next hour for Vlad and Mikhail.

It was now mid-morning, and a cool October light rain chilled the underdressed prisoners. The SS officers took control of the situation from the regular Wehrmacht guards. One of the Panzer tanks moved from the side of the camp to the front gate and pointed its cannon directly into the throng of men inside the camp. A detail of 50 heavily armed SS men climbed onto the tank and stood with trigger fingers on their automatic weapons. The massive show of force worked. The POWs, believing an execution squad had arrived, reared back from the main gate. The SS officer in charge gave an order and the gates opened.

One of the SS officers grabbed a bullhorn and bellowed "Assemble in neatly formed rows, have an arm's length distance between you and the man on either your left or right. I want these rows 20 feet apart, if this is not done in the next five minutes, we will shoot any stragglers. Now move, schnell." The entire camp of nearly 200,000 men began to organize into rows. Many could barely walk or stand but were helped by their comrades. Vlad was impressed so many people in such horrible condition were able to assemble and get somewhat organized so quickly.

The fear of being gunned down was a powerful motivator, he thought to himself.

Mikhail was even weaker than yesterday. He moved gingerly and showed agonizing effects from dysentery, his ashen face and foul stench were dead giveaways. Vlad helped him walk making sure they were next to each other and in the same row. Mikhail had a hard time standing on his own, so Vlad put his arm around him and held his brother steady. The SS officers entered the camp, and a well-armed security detail walked closely behind them. They passed by most of the prisoners without saying a word, but would occasionally stop and ask a few questions of a POW.

Vlad and Mikhail were in the fifth row and could see what was happening in front of them. In each of the first four rows, a few POWs were asked to take five steps forward and stay there. Vlad observed the ones asked to step forward seemed to be healthier and in better condition than the rest. The SS officers and their security detail made it to Vlad and Mikhail's row and were moving quickly. "Let me go, Vlad," Mikhail said in a weak voice as the SS approached. "They gave orders to be arm's length apart, and we don't need any problems."

Vlad let go, and Mikhail was able to stand on his own. The SS Officers stopped in front of Vlad. The ranking officer turned right and approached him. "Name, age, and birthplace please," the officer asked in a fairly pleasant tone.

Vlad stood straight, stared the officer in the eye and replied "Vladimir Chayka, 17 years old, Kiev, Ukraine." The SS officer was impeccably dressed in polished riding boots. He was freshly showered, clean-shaven, tall, muscular and arrogant. The power divide between them was apparent to both.

The SS Officer continued "You look Aryan with your blue eyes and facial features. Is there any German blood in your family?"

Vlad cleared his throat and responded in a strong voice "My grandparents on my mother's side were half German, but I have lived in Ukraine my whole life, and consider myself full Ukrainian."

The SS man gave him a fleshy smile, stood for a few moments, and looked Vlad over. "Let me see your teeth, my proud Ukrainian." Vlad opened his mouth, showing a full set of near perfect teeth as they gleamed against his dirt-caked face. "Very well," said the SS man, "Take five steps forward, and stay there." The SS Officer walked three steps forward and spoke eyeball to eyeball with Vlad. "You are being selected for service in the Third Reich. You will leave here shortly with 500 other chosen POWs. You will be fed, housed, and receive medical treatment. Prepare to fall out."

The SS man started to walk away, "What about my brother?" Vlad asked while pointing to Mikhail.

"Your brother will be dead in a week, probably less," the SS man said as a matter of fact. He continued "Just like thousands more of the swine in here. Move out."

Vlad turned right, reached for Mikhail's hand and gave it a squeeze. "I love you brother," Vlad said with tears in his eyes.

Mikhail uttered the last words Vlad assumed he would ever hear from his oldest brother "Stay strong and survive for the family. I love you." Vlad turned away and walked with the SS security detail. He was marched to the front gate and joined 500 other POWs that had been selected.

"Form 10 columns of 50 men each" one of the SS men shouted. The selected POWs did their best counting off to get exactly 50 men per line, much to the amusement of the SS. After a few minutes, all were assembled as ordered. The group marched out of the camp and climbed into the back of the waiting trucks. The trucks had wooden benches on either side for the POWs and were now covered in canvas.

A few SS men were posted at the rear with automatic weapons. Cigarettes and matches were handed out to the prisoners. Vlad was not a smoker, but the first cigarette tasted great. It curbed his hunger and calmed the nerves. Vlad took a deep drag as the trucks started to move, it was the first time since June he wasn't forced to march. As the trucks departed, Vlad leaned forward and peered out the rear opening. The entire camp came into view, with his biggest fear realized. Vlad was alone in this world, and Mikhail didn't stand a chance without him.

Chapter 8
St. Louis Park, Minnesota.
Present Day

"Max, I'm tired and need to sleep," Vlad said, slowly rising from the couch with the help of a cane. He set the empty glass of scotch on the table and gently wiped tears from his eyes and continued "We have been talking for over two hours, and it's well past my bedtime. Discussing my brothers is difficult and something I have feared because it unearths emotions not present in my life for many years. Their unfulfilled lives and violent deaths were very hard to accept, especially by the awful choices I had to make. Not being able to defend them left a hole in me that I thought would eventually heal. It hasn't, even after seventy years."

Max got up from his chair and gave his dad a hug and kiss on the cheek. "I understand. I will work on your case tomorrow and bring dinner tomorrow night. You get some rest and don't answer questions if people from the media call or stop by. Just give them my name and number."

"My boy," said Vlad "tomorrow is promised to no one."

Max smiled and looked his father in the eyes. Max put his hands on Vlad's shoulders. "I love you, dad."

On his drive home, Max processed their conversation and tried to absorb the life thus unknown to him. Max never knew his father was a Soviet POW held by the Nazis and knew even less about his uncles. Vlad rarely spoke about his deep past and youth in the old country. The timeline always started when he and Max came to the United States after the war. Vlad was proud to be an American, proud to be Catholic, and most proud to have his Jewish son.

Max arrived back at his well-appointed Lake Harriet home about 11 pm. He plopped on the couch with a stiff drink, grabbed the remote and turned on the news. The top story was his dad, the accused Nazi, being represented by his Jewish son the attorney. He turned the TV off, sipped his cocktail and thought about life with his father. From Little League through Law School at the University of Minnesota, Vlad had dedicated his life to ensuring Max had the best friends, best education, and best life possible. He could not have asked for a more loving father and the gift of raising him Jewish was icing on the cake. Max loved being Jewish and owed it all to his dad.

An only child raised by a single father, Max shared a special and rare relationship with Vlad. Vlad worked full time over 50 years for a sheet metal fabricator, and was constantly there for his son. Between youth sports, school activities, girls, friends and Talmud Torah, Vlad always seemed present to listen and dispense wise advice. Vlad molded a great kid who became a great man.

Max took the last sip of his cocktail and checked the clock, which already read 1 a.m. Two hours had flown by, and Max decided to defend his dad, regardless of the outcome and possible damage to his career. Even though the charges pierced Max's soul, he knew of no other viable option for Vlad's legal defense. Max wanted to save the inevitable embarrassment resulting from attorneys refusing to take his dad's case.

He could think of no one who would want to defend a Nazi war criminal. Max correctly figured it wasn't worth the awkward appearance of asking others to do something he was unwilling to do. Max knew defending family in court was most rare, but he would take on the risk. "Lead from the front on this one," Max thought to himself. He rose from the leather sofa and went to bed. He too hadn't been this tired in a long time.

The next morning, Max paid a visit to his friend Dane Atkinson. Dane served as a Federal Prosecutor in Minneapolis and shared a deep friendship with Max spanning over 40 years. They joined the same fraternity as freshmen in college and hit it off immediately. Their friendship triumphed over the natural human trait of being semi-nomadic when it pertains to relationships. Max would constantly run into people he had known for years. Most were acquaintances, and after a few minutes of fun banter, both would be on their way.

A much smaller number of people Max considered actual friends. Of those, two or three people in his life rose to the friendship level of Dane Atkinson. Dane and Max shared a deep bond uncommon in the world. Complete trust and confidence, along with many fun times socially, was the cement that held them together.

They partied hard in and after college. Drinking to excess, smoking too much weed and chasing all sorts of women. They managed to change the nature of their friendship as life dictated, unlike most friendships that stagnate at a particular window in time. Dane was the one friend Max could turn for anything, both professionally and personally.

"I figured I would hear from you soon," Dane said half-kiddingly as Max entered his office. "But seriously, how are you and your dad holding up?"

Max looked at the floor and let out a deep breath, then redirected his eyes to Dane. "We are both doing okay. We talked last night for a few hours, and will again this evening. It's unbelievable what he's kept locked away. I had no clue. Just when a person thinks they know everything, you realize you don't know that much."

Dane smiled. "That's what led to my two divorces." They both laughed, Dane had an uncanny way to lighten a heavy situation, which helped greatly in front of juries.

They discussed the fact that Vlad was in his early 90's with health issues, and wouldn't do well in a drawn out trial. Deportation would most likely kill him. Max asked if there was any chance of delaying things long enough for his dad to spend the rest of his days in relative peace.

"Look, Max, you and I have been friends a long time, and I have always thought the world of your dad. No one knows better than you the wheels of justice turn slowly, and if you are asking me to stop the wheels, I can't. I am being watched on this one as much as you are, but I can slow them down a bit. This case will have to go to a Federal Grand Jury, then an indictment, evidentiary hearings and finally a trial. That could take easily up to a year, even longer with your expert delay tactics. Deportation would take another two years. If you lose, an appeal will add additional time. We will talk off the record, and out of this office, regarding motions you can file. There are legal maneuvers that will slow the case down by another six months. But in the end, my hands are tied as to the outcome."

Max and Dane spoke for another 15 minutes before the meeting concluded. "Let's meet at Nye's for a few drinks in the next week or two" Max suggested. Unlike many people they knew who hung up their cups, both of them still enjoyed having cocktails when time allowed.

"Perfect." Dane said, "I like the polka bar in the back. The place has been good to me over the years with a few women I wish I had never met, especially my first ex-wife."

Max laughed "I remember telling you that although she was hot, don't get on her bad side. Which of course you managed to do."

"It's one of my many talents," Dane chuckled. "Let me know when you want to connect, and I'll be there."

Max got up to leave, and the two powerhouses of Minneapolis prosecution and defense shook hands.

Dane looked Max in the eye "A Nazi death camp guard, your dad? Holy shit amigo, that's some crazy stuff. Never in a million years would I have thought that."

Max again looked uncharacteristically towards the floor "This is hard for me to wrap my head around, believe me. I will defend and delay to the best of my ability. It's the least I can do for him."

"Okay buddy, talk soon. Take care of your dad and give him my best. I love that guy, and so does everyone else."

Max left the Federal Building and headed to his office. A full caseload of well-paying clients needed his attention. They would help supplement his pro bono work for Vlad, which would consume many hours of his time.

Max decided to arrive at Vlad's house a little earlier. He wanted more time for them to talk. It was about 5:30 pm and a bit cooler as the sun started to cast shadows from trees in Vlad's front yard. Max had brought over some pasta dishes and bread from Broder's in Minneapolis. Both Vlad and Max loved their made-from-scratch dishes, some of the best Italian Max had ever eaten.

As Max walked in, Vlad had the local NBC newscast on TV. "Dad, it's not doing any good watching this stuff, let's turn it off so we can eat together in peace,"

Vlad gave Max an understanding look. "Nice choice for dinner son, I haven't had Broder's in a while, it's hard for me to get around since I don't drive much anymore." Max brought out a plate of food and a cocktail for Vlad and set it on the table next to his recliner.

"How was your day Max?" Vlad asked as he took a long sip of scotch. "Not bad, I did pay Dane Atkinson a visit at his office. He is willing to help with a few discrete delay tactics. But I am going to need to prepare a defense for you regardless."

"Max my boy" Vlad interrupted "I will be 92 years old in a month and have congestive heart failure. Hopefully, the good Lord will take me before it gets that far. I have tried to live a decent life, but often wonder what God will say to me when we finally meet. I have done some horrible things, son. But you must understand if I hadn't, we both wouldn't be here right now. My other choice was death, and I often regret not taking that option. You are the only reason I'm happy that I didn't.

"Dad, I am sure the Lord will forgive you for whatever you did as a teenager. Most people would envy your relationship with God. It's an admirable trait. I know you celebrate the Sacrament of Reconciliation a few times per year. All of my life it seems like you were going to confession." Max smiled as he finished reassuring his dad. Although Max was not Catholic, he certainly understood the church and truly believed that his dad believed. It's all that mattered.

Max started to redirect the conversation like his lawyer self. "Last night we left off when your brother Stepan died in the POW camp and you were selected by the SS. I am truly sorry for him, and for you having to leave Mikhail behind. They sounded like great guys, and it hurts me never to have known about them. Please know I don't fault you for not speaking of your brothers. One question that has been bothering me since our talk is why the Germans treated the Russians so horribly? I thought the Americans and British were treated relatively well for the most part by the same Wehrmacht."

Vlad started to explain the disparate treatment POWs from America received versus Soviet POWs. Hitler viewed the invasion of the Soviet Union much differently that the invasion of France or the war against the Americans. The invasion of the Soviet Union was code-named Operation Barbarossa, and it was a land grab for "Lebensraum" or living space for Aryan people in the Third Reich.

It was equally a complete war of racial attrition for the Nazis. Hitler viewed people living in the Soviet Union as Jewish-collaborating Communists, diametrically opposed to his racial policy. Two worlds were on a direct collision course. Hitler had no room for Communists, Jews, the mentally ill, people of Slavic descent or Gypsies in his thousand year Reich.

Vlad continued to explain this was a war of total annihilation, unlike anything the world had ever seen. Hitler cynically used the Soviet Union never ratifying the 1929 Geneva Convention regarding treatment of

POWs, as legal cover for his murderous plan. All German military members had total immunity for anything they did to the people of the Soviet Union. The more barbaric and cruel behavior directed at the vanquished, the better.

Vlad spoke about the Soviets being fair game for brutal treatment, especially Jews. That attitude and culture permeated the entire German war machine, from the top brass down to the infantryman. It made ordinary men commit abnormally violent acts upon people they never met. Unfortunately for Vlad and his brothers, they didn't realize the homicidal Nazi plan until it was too late.

The number of POWs the Germans took in the first few months of fighting was almost unimaginable. Vlad told Max between June 1941 and February 1942, over three million Soviet POWs were captured by Germany. A staggering two million would die during that same time. Life was considered cheap and snuffed out with less thought than sneezing. "Two worlds my boy," Vlad lamented.

"The United States lost almost 400,000 soldiers during four years of war in both Europe and the Pacific," Vlad said to Max. "We lost over two million in just seven months and 20 million during the entire war. It was living hell. The death and destruction were like nothing the world had ever seen."

Vlad let the mind-boggling numbers settle in Max's mind. It's hard for anyone to comprehend that didn't live through it, which Vlad fully understood. Vlad broke the silence and said "Pour me another scotch, my boy, and clear my plate. Then we will continue where I left off last night."

Max returned with another cocktail, placed it in his dad's wrinkled hands and asked "Dad, do you mind if I record this conversation?" As an excellent trial lawyer, Max rarely asked a question where he didn't already know the answer. He explained to Vlad "I just want it for myself, no one will hear it besides me. Your story is so intense and I don't want to miss anything."

Vlad replied as Max expected, "I don't mind son, and once I am gone, you have my permission to share it with whomever."

Max turned on the camera, making sure the sound and picture were good. In the living room where he grew up, Max was finally beginning to understand what his father endured. Max put his cocktail down. "Ready when you are."

Chapter 9
Eastern Poland
October 1941

The trucks drove the POWs on the main dirt road for about an hour. The rain had stopped. The weather was overcast with a chilly wind blowing, and it felt like late autumn had finally set in. As the trucks drove over potholes and the men bounced on wood benches, Vlad and the others wondered silently about their destination and fate.

The SS guards seated in the truck's rear complained about the stench coming from the POWs. "Give them all another cigarette. It will help and kill the smell in here" the ranking enlisted SS guard in Vlad's truck said.

The other guard passed around a fresh pack with matches and complained "If one of these filthy animals gives me lice, I will start shooting."

The ranking SS man gave him a hard stare. "No you won't, this project comes straight from the top. I heard Reichsfuhrer-SS Himmler, and General Heydrich have personally given orders for this. Plus we are here anyway."

The truck convoy came to a stop, and the SS men were first to jump out. With their cocked weapons pointed into the trucks at the prisoners, the order came. "Raus, schnell, out of the trucks now. Form 10 lines of 50 men. On the double, move!" The prisoners did as commanded and got into formation. In front of the gathered prisoners stood a group of imposing men, wearing their impeccably tailored SS uniforms. Black coats, black riding pants, red armbands with swastikas, black leather gloves, and tall black leather boots. The SS also wore the familiar black hats with the skull and crossbones on the front. The leader of the group started to speak.

"I am Sturmbannfuhrer Seitz, Commandant of Trawniki SS training camp, which is where you are." He let the words sink in as the prisoners tried to get their bearings. There were a number of brick buildings that took up the space of a city block, all surrounded by a 12-foot high barbed wire fence. Seitz continued "You have been selected for training to help protect the Third Reich and German people from our enemies.

There is one thing to remember at Trawniki, the orders given by the SS are to be followed as if they were given by God."

Seitz scowled at the group of POWs with disdain. "Any failure to obey orders will result in immediate execution. We won't even bother to return you to that cesspool in Chelm. Death on the spot for not following orders, I hope that is most clear." Seitz then spoke with the authoritative blandness of a technocrat. "You have received a second chance, a rebirth. My advice is to seize the opportunity, especially in light of where you came from. I understand it was most unpleasant. If this training and future duty does not suit you, your option is death."

Seitz turned to his right and nodded to an SS man who took a few steps forward. He took a spot standing between Seitz and the assembled POWs. "I now turn you over to Scharfuhrer Hecker, who will oversee training during your stay at Trawniki. He has my fullest confidence, and his word is law. Any problems with him will bring you in front of me. If that happens, you will pray for death. That is all. Heil Hitler."

Hecker clicked his heels, gave the Nazi salute to Commandant Seitz and said "Thank you for your confidence in me, Commandant, I will not let you down. Heil Hitler!"

Scharfuhrer Hecker silently stood and observed a half starved, filthy and smelly group of 500 men. He began to silently walk through the ranks, giving some a quick head to toe inspection. Hecker returned to the front of the group and addressed them "You will ask no questions at this point, I demand absolute silence. First, you will be processed, and then you will be fed and shown your quarters. Right face, march." The POWs turned right, marched through the open gate and into the unknown of Trawniki. Vlad's new life had begun.

The POWs marched to an open square in the middle of the grounds. The camp was an old sugar factory constructed with bricks and served its new purpose of an SS training center well. Hecker gave his first of many commands to the group. "Take off all clothes, shoes, and underwear. Put them in a pile to be burned." Vlad could hear quiet talk from some prisoners to his left as they undressed.

Hecker advanced on one of the two talking prisoners and delivered a painful rabbit punch to the kidney. The prisoner fell to his knees "You stupid dog." Hecker screamed. "I said silence. You talk when I say talk, eat when I say eat, shit when I say shit, and breathe when I say breathe.

On your feet and get undressed before I tear your goddamn head off, you miserable cockroach."

Vlad understood the cue and quickly took off his clothes, which before the war he wouldn't even use as rags. He checked out at his shivering fellow POWs. Ribs showed on every man from hunger. They were a sorry looking bunch, and Hecker let them know it. Vlad caught the eye of a familiar face among the men, he was embarrassed it happened when they were all naked, but he looked like Mikhail's friend Pavel from Kiev.

Hecker suddenly shouted, "You have just left a life of filth and chaos, and are entering one of cleanliness and order. Now move your asses." The men were led into a large heated tile shower room. Vlad instantly felt the warm rush of air against his naked body. One by one, each prisoner was sprayed by warm water from a fire hose. Vlad was given a bar of soap to wash his body while the hot water splashed over him. It lasted only 60 seconds, but the sensation of soap and warm water was better than sex. It was his first bath in almost four months. Vlad stepped to the next room and had two big scoops of delousing powder thrown on his head, face, and body. The powder burned his eyes and tasted awful, but the line moved fast, and he didn't dare protest.

Vlad was led in his bath towel to a bench where he sat down with 20 other POWs. They got their haircut and a warm towel on their face, followed by a close shave. Vlad had forgotten how precious the basics of normal living were, once taken away. Things like clean clothes, a shower, and a shave were worlds away compared to where he left just this morning. The new surroundings were a massive adjustment for any adult, more so for a 17-year-old.

The barbers were not SS. They wore striped pajamas, striped hats, and wooden clogs. The barbers had different patches on their uniform front jackets, consisting of various colors and geometric shapes. Vlad took notice but didn't understand what they meant. It was evident they were in servitude or prisoners of one form or another. He did recognize the ubiquitous Star of David. Many wore the badge.

Still in a bath towel and shower sandals after the barber, Vlad and his group were led into another room and given clothes. They were issued socks, boots, brown pants, underwear, brown shirts, and brown coats. The clothes were not new but in relatively decent shape. They were certainly not uniforms, but civilian clothes the Nazis tried to match as close as they could for 500 men. After receiving clothes, the men were moved along and issued shaving kits, a copy of Mein Kampf and a Russian to German dictionary.

Finally, Vlad and the others stepped up to a table and were each given a watch. The pile of watches behind the table surprised him. There were thousands of watches, and none were in new boxes which Vlad found strange. Where the Germans were getting all of these gently used items was beyond him. The watches, clothes and other items were distributed by people in the same striped pajamas with badges attached.

The entire group of men now stood outside in the same courtyard, cleaned and dressed. The whole operation took less than two hours for 500 men, and the bonfire made up of their POW clothes was smoldering. A pile of ashes was all that remained, and Vlad inexplicably couldn't take his eyes off the ash heap. Hecker interrupted Vlad's trance and shouted in his German-accented voice. "You will now be formed into five groups of 100. Each group of 100 will be designated as a company. These will be the men with whom you shall live and train. We have barracks and food waiting for you. You will now be remanded to the company instructors. You are dismissed." Vlad was assigned to Company A with Hecker as his instructor, and he was happy to see Pavel in Company A as well.

Vlad and company A marched across the courtyard and into a two-story gray brick building that once served as a warehouse for the sugar factory. The main level had a great room with wood floors and potbelly stoves. Long wooden eating tables were laid out in rows, and light fixtures hung from the ceiling. The inside walls were exposed brick, with six-pane framed windows regularly spaced throughout. The main floor would be used for eating, classroom and general socializing.

The SS retrofitted the upper level to contain toilets, showers, and sleeping quarters with bunks. It was spacious, warm and a world away from the POW camp in Chelm. "Dinner will consist of bread, cheese, sausage, and hot tea. Each man gets his ration" Hecker said in a lower and calmer voice than normal. "Lights out at 9 pm, and you are forbidden to leave the barracks under penalty of death. If any are stupid enough to leave, the SS will use you as target practice. You will be allowed a few days to eat, sleep and regain your strength. Use them wisely. You are now able to talk. That is all."

Chapter 10

Vlad sat down next to the familiar face at the long wooden dinner table. It was past dark, and the cold fall winds rattled the windows. The coal-fired stove kept it warm inside, and the electric lights overhead illuminated the space rather well.

Vlad took his ration of cheese and almost swallowed it whole. "Eat slow kid," the familiar face said kindly. "Your system needs to get used to real food again, build your strength up at a smart pace." He put his hand out "My name is Pavel, I know your brother Mikhail. We went to school together in Kiev, and all the ladies loved him. Where is he?"

Vlad looked down at his food, then back at Pavel with tears in his eyes and uttered "He is back at the prison camp in Chelm and not doing well. This cold wind tonight could kill him."

Pavel grabbed Vlad's hand "You are the youngest Chayka, it's Vlad, correct?" Vlad nodded in the affirmative. "Then listen to me, Vlad. There is nothing you can do except build your strength and live. It's okay to mourn your brother, but do it quickly and put it past you. I get the feeling we are going to need everything we have to survive this. Believe me. The Germans are not doing this out of kindness. They want something from us, and it's going to be a hard, long ride." Pavel let go of Vlad's hand. "Now eat your food slowly."

Vlad finished his sausage and drank his last bit of tea. The food settled well in his stomach. Although he carried an immense sense of guilt, the shower, shave, clothes, food, and warm barracks were a most welcome change from the hell at Chelm. He couldn't stop thinking of Mikhail facing a chilly night while sick and alone. Vlad once again faced gut-wrenching choices forced upon him by the Germans. He began to realize that his survival would likely come at the expense of others.

Pavel rose from the table, he was shorter than Vlad and had a solid build even after his ordeal at Chelm. His black hair and bushy eyebrows accented his square face. "Weren't you the wrestling champion back in Kiev?" Vlad asked.

"Absolutely" Pavel replied with a sigh. "It seems like a lifetime ago." Pavel motioned towards the stairs leading to the sleeping quarters on the second floor. "Let's get some sleep. We will share a bunk, you being younger and lighter, get the top. I sleep on the bottom."

Pavel and Vlad joined some of the other men heading upstairs to claim their bunks. They found one unoccupied in the corner of the room. The bunks had sheets, blankets, and pillows. Vlad had forgotten that people slept with sheets and blankets. How much the open air prison camps dehumanized him started to sink in. Vlad climbed into the top bunk and lay down. He stared at the ceiling and began to think about what a priest said at the beginning of every Mass.

He spoke very softly so no one else could hear him "In the name of the Father, and of the Son, and of the Holy Spirit, Amen. The grace of our Lord Jesus Christ, and the love of God, and the communion of the Holy Spirit be with you all." Tears welled up in his eyes, emotionally empty and alone he fell into a deep sleep.

The next few days were what Scharfuhrer Hecker promised, a decent meal three times a day and sleep. By the morning of day four, most of the men were feeling much better and starting to get restless. Hecker made his first appearance in the barracks since the first night.

"Out of the barracks and form five columns of 20 men, schnell!" Hecker barked. The morning mid-October sun did its best to warm things up, but Vlad could tell the sun was less powerful than even a few weeks ago. "Over the next 60 days, you will be taught to march and take orders in German. You will be issued a rifle that can hold ten rounds. The rifle will be yours to learn to disassemble, clean, repair and reassemble. You will be expected to become an acceptable representative of the SS. You will not, however, be SS. The SS are your Lords and Masters on whom you rely for all that is right in this world."

Hecker continued with a swagger in his voice. "You are privileged to be the first class at Trawniki. When you are finished with basic training, the title of Wachman shall be bestowed upon you. This is a camp the SS started for the sole purpose of training men to administer special treatment for the Jews. You will be instrumental in achieving the goal of the Fuhrer's wise policies."

The day consisted of marching drills. About half received military training with the Red Army, and soon they all marched like soldiers. The POWs were also rapidly learning German, Hecker made them memorize commonly used military words and phrases.

Lectures were at night after dinner, once their metal plates and cups were cleared from the tables. SS men gave demonstrations on how to clean and repair a rifle, read maps and use radios. They were shown how to shine boots, shine brass, iron clothes, and keep a clean barracks.

After dinner a few weeks into training, an unknown SS officer entered the barracks. Hecker shouted, "On your feet!" Vlad, Pavel, and the rest jumped to their feet.

"Heil Hitler," the SS officer said while giving the Nazi salute. The men remained standing but said nothing.

Hecker jumped in "When an SS Officer says Heil Hitler, you give the proper Nazi salute and say Heil Hitler back to him. Is that clear?"

"Yes Scharfuhrer Hecker" the men replied.

Hecker continued in a shrill voice "I will personally and gladly kick the living shit out of any man, and send him back to Chelm, who does not do it. Is that clear?"

The men replied even louder "Yes Scharfuhrer Hecker."

The SS officer again gave the Nazi salute, "Heil Hitler" he bellowed.

"Heil Hitler" the men replied thunderously. Both Vlad and Pavel gave each other a worried look as they outstretched their arms while shouting Heil Hitler. It was something Vlad couldn't have imagined at the beginning of summer, and Pavel was the same. It made Vlad almost sick to his stomach to even mutter the words and give the salute. But he knew the consequences if he did otherwise. Vlad's choice to survive would rear its ugly head many times.

The SS officer continued "Take a seat." Vlad, Pavel and the rest of the men sat down at the long wooden tables. "Scharfuhrer Hecker and Sturmbannfuhrer Seitz have told me you are all making excellent progress. Your German is coming along, and your target shooting has gotten much better. We did not rescue you from Chelm, and we are not investing resources so you can simply march, learn our language, and be proficient with a rifle. My name is Gruppenfuhrer Heine. I report directly to Reichsfuhrer-SS Heinrich Himmler in Berlin. He sent me here to observe and report back what is happening with the first class of recruits at Trawniki. The time has come to accelerate training and prepare you for duty."

Heine let the murmuring among the men abate. "Tonight we will discuss the racial policies of the Third Reich. We are an Aryan people, of pure blood and Nordic ancestry. We are the master race of Europe, and of the entire world. On the opposite end are the Jews, they are

Untermensch or subhuman. The Jew is worse than the rat-infested plague that ravaged our continent centuries ago, which they are likely responsible for causing. Jews cannot and will not be allowed to interfere with, or exploit, the fine Aryan people of Europe anymore. They are disease carrying vermin that must be dealt with in a harsh and brutal manner."

Heine sounded like a minister preaching about salvation. He was focused, intense, and he believed. "For the Jew and Aryan cannot live in the same world. We tried to get the Jews to emigrate, but no one would take them. Not Great Britain and not even the United States with its famous Statue of Liberty. This was proven when we sent our transatlantic liner named the St. Louis to Cuba. The ship was full of Jews. Cuba wisely refused entry. The United States refused entry, and Great Britain refused entry. These Hippocratic people showed their true colors. We had to take these filthy bags of shit back on European soil. The world hates the Jews, and we have to deal with that fact."

Heine took a pause. He commanded the room. All eyes were fixed on him, Vlad was not exactly sure where this was heading, but Pavel had a good idea. He leaned over to Vlad and whispered, "They are going to make us do their dirty work." Vlad gave him a curious glance. He didn't understand what Pavel meant.

Heine took a sip of water and continued. "With our grand territorial expansion into Poland, and your former hellhole country the Soviet Union, we need to create Lebensraum or living space for the Aryan people. Unfortunately, our Lebensraum is full of Jews. Millions and millions infest our land. We tried sterilizing them like dogs, but discovered it would take a few generations for them to die out. Which is far too long, we needed to act sooner. The decision has been made at the highest level to kill every Jewish man, woman, and child. Believe me when I say, we will exterminate the Jew scum. It will be hard work, as there are about nine million of these snakes slithering in our midst."

Heine observed the room for the men's reactions. All were earnestly listening. "The treatment you will dish out to the Jews will be severe, brutal and without remorse. Your experience in our POW camps was a walk in the park compared to what's in store for the sons of Abraham. The SS are in the process of building camps to turn millions of Jews into millions of corpses. You will assist with the complete annihilation of every Jewish rat in the Third Reich and beyond. It is a glorious page in history that will be talked about for 1,000 years. The SS will be the lightning, and you will be the thunder of this great storm."

Heine stood in front on the men, his chest puffed out and his fleshy lips wet with saliva. He looked like a person starved for a week, with a juicy steak sitting in front of him. If there had been a Jew in the room, Heine would have devoured the victim. The thought of finally putting a plan in action dealing a lethal blow to the Jews was his life's dream come true.

Heine took a minute as he needed to catch his breath. "Up to this point, Scharfuhrer Hecker has trained you exactly as ordered," Heine said looking at Hecker as if he were a proud father. The two knew each other since the euthanasia days, where they secretly helped murder thousands of mental patients in Germany. Hecker loved it when the mental patient was Jewish. He would practice his torture and maiming methods with zeal before killing them. Hecker's hatred of Jews and barbarism were pathological. He was legendary within SS circles. Hecker was handpicked for this position at the highest levels in Berlin.

"I want to reiterate one last time" Heine sternly warned "This is not normal guard duty. You are active and crucial components of the destruction of every Jew in the Reich. From old men to baby girls, a death sentence awaits. "If anyone cannot stomach what your SS Lords have in store, your fate shall be the same as the Jews."

Heine paused, and then his voice mellowed. "Now, every man in this room probably knows a Jew who they consider decent. You may be thinking that your butcher or doctor was Jewish and you liked him. You may be thinking we could spare that one person. Be cautious of such thoughts. The Jew has many tricks to seduce Aryans into believing these things. Don't be fooled, for our glorious Reich depends on the destruction of every single Jew. None can be allowed to live. Am I clear?"

"Yes, Gruppenfuhrer Heine."

"I will now release Scharfuhrer Hecker to harden and ready this group for duty that waits. His unmerciful and ruthless severity towards the Jews is a model for all. His orders are to be followed and carried out without hesitation and to the letter. Training starts tomorrow at six am. You are excused to your sleeping quarters."

Hecker jumped to his feet and shouted "Heil Hitler" with the Nazi salute.

The men in the room stood, raised their right arms and shouted in unison "Heil Hitler. "

Vlad and Pavel nonchalantly broke away from the group and walked outside where they could speak privately. Pavel lit a cigarette "You want one?"

"Please and thank you." Vlad replied and continued "I think I'm going to take up smoking, I will need it to calm myself. What is going on exactly? I don't understand what they want us to do."

Pavel gave Vlad a serious look with his deep brown eyes. "I'm not going to sugar coat it kid, but it seems the Germans want us to do some terrible things to the Jews. You need to prepare yourself for some awful times ahead. Some of these people might enjoy this, but not me, and I know not you."

Vlad paused and said in a nervous tone, "I don't quite understand how they plan on doing it. Nine million Jews is a lot of people, how could they possibly kill everyone? And why do they hate the Jews so much? This doesn't make any sense."

Pavel dropped his cigarette on the ground, extinguished it with the toe of his boot and whispered "None of this makes any sense. But this is the world in which we now live. If you want to survive, stay close to me and adapt as best you can."

The two walked back into the barracks, and the pre-lights-out chatter was heavier than normal amongst the men. Just as Pavel predicted, a group formed around one of the dining tables and excitedly talked about the prospect of killing Jews. A fellow recruit named Orlov was the most enthusiastic and vocal.

Chapter 11
St. Louis Park, Minnesota
Present Day

Max checked the video recorder to make sure it still had memory and looked at his dad. Max lived a comfortable life and tried to imagine himself in his dad's shoes at 17 years old. "Dad, at 17 years old, I played high school baseball, hung out with my buddies, and dated Katie Fischer. I feel guilty."

Vlad did his best to straighten his tired back. "Absolutely not. You were a great kid, the pride of my life. You have no idea the satisfaction and happiness your normal childhood brought me."

Max smiled at the reassurance. "Dad, this question may sound elementary coming from a well-educated attorney. But, do you have any idea why the Nazi's hated Jews so much? I mean, what was the root of the hate? After all, the Jewish population was relatively small and posed no clear or present danger to the Third Reich. They were not armed, although had they been, it may have been a different story."

Vlad gave a raised eyebrow look to Max. "Perhaps being armed may have helped somewhat, but ultimately it would not have changed anything. You need to understand Anti-Semitism was rampant in Europe for centuries, and many people already hated Jews for one reason or another. A predominant belief among many Christians was Blood Libel. Blood Libel was the belief that Jews would kidnap and bleed a Christian child to death, and then use the child's blood to make matzah during Passover. Whenever a child fell ill for no explained reason or simply disappeared, the Jews were blamed on many occasions. In addition to Blood Libel, many believed that Jews poisoned wells. If a well became contaminated, Jews were again to blame."

Max shook his head. "People actually believed that garbage? Were they all poor and uneducated? I mean who is gullible enough to have such beliefs?"

Vlad responded sharply "Lots of people, my boy. Yes, some were poor and uneducated, but many were not. Hate and fear cross all socioeconomic lines. There always was a small, but vocal and violent anti-Jewish group in every town. They would occasionally beat, and murder Jews during violent spasms called Pogroms. Nothing, in particular, would trigger a Pogrom. It just happened from time to time. Blood Libel and contaminated wells were triggers, but so were other unpredictable events. The majority of townspeople did not partake in anti-Jewish violence. However, they did not condemn the outrageous and homicidal actions of the few. Thus the few controlled the many on the treatment of the Jews."

Vlad wiped tears from his eyes. "I remember one occasion in Kiev when a group of Christians celebrated Christmas Eve by burning down the house of a prominent Jewish family. As the terrorized family fled the burning home, they were captured by the mob. The Jewish husband had to watch his wife gang raped by four married Christian men. She was always known for her beauty and charm. She never recovered emotionally from the incident. Her husband and two sons were brutally beaten with an iron pipe for trying to intervene and stop the attack. The crowd, along with the four rapists, walked back home singing Christmas carols to celebrate the Holiday with their families. No charges were filed, and things went back to normal. It was a strange and violent phenomenon indeed."

Max recoiled at the thought of such gratuitous violence. He pondered aloud "I can't imagine living in Saint Louis Park as a kid, and people actually burning down this home to celebrate Christmas."

Vlad nodded in agreement. "America is a nation of laws, thank God. You as a practicing attorney understand we are afforded equal treatment under the law, regardless of our station in life."

Max smiled, he occasionally felt guilt about defending unsavory people. Vlad had a way of making simple sense out of complicated issues and putting people at ease.

Max checked his watch. "Dad, it's late, and you should get some rest, but one more question. What did your father think of the people who participated in pogroms?"

Vlad replied quickly "My father always considered the pogrom perpetrators as simple minded, jealous, and prone to violence over intellect. He would always say 'beware of a little man with a little power,' and in truth, he couldn't stand them. My dad voiced his opinion many times to the family, but it stopped there. No one ever wanted to be accused of being a Jew-lover, which is horrible in today's context. That environment enabled SS recruitment of local populations to help wage war on the Jews. The Nazi's tapped into what already existed."

Max turned off the video recorder and gave his dad a hug goodnight. "Dad," Max said "I will call you tomorrow. Things should be hectic at the office, and I am not sure of my schedule. Please call me if you need anything, or if anyone comes knocking at the door. My secretary will send out a press release in the morning directing all media inquiries to me. Hopefully, you are left unbothered." Vlad gave Max a half smile and started up the stairs for a much-needed rest.

Chapter 12
Minneapolis, MN
Present Day

Max arrived at his 50th-floor office in the IDS tower in Downtown Minneapolis earlier than normal. The floor to ceiling windows gave sweeping views of the Mississippi River, Twins and Vikings stadiums and the western suburbs. The marble floors and mahogany walls gave an intimidating home field advantage against legal adversaries. The office deliberately oozed power and success.

Interview requests pouring in from around the world were overwhelming the three receptionists. The law office of Chayka, Kimo and Gust was always busy. With over 200 employees, including 40 attorneys, the office hummed with activity from Monday morning through Friday afternoon. The sudden avalanche of calls, emails and lobby visitors for Max bottlenecked the office. It became difficult to conduct routine legal business.

Calls were coming from the around the United States, Europe, Russia, Israel, Australia, and of course Ukraine. Every major news organization wanted Max for an interview. The Today Show, The BBC, Sky News, CNN, The New York Times, and even Al-Jazeera requested one on ones with Max. Local and regional media organizations camped outside the building, hoping to catch Max coming and going from the office.

Junior attorneys and paralegals with the firm were hounded by reporters looking for any information on the case. Max even got a call from a concerned neighbor saying that a stranger was going through his garbage and recycling bins. Max was used to media attention, but this level of spotlight was unprecedented.

Max left the office at 4 pm and attempted to avoid the media glare. He took the elevator down to 39, then switched to the next elevator bank, went down to 12, switched again, and came out three elevator banks away from where the crowd expected him. He rented a Honda Accord the previous day to stay incognito and met Dane Atkinson at Nye's Bar in Northeast Minneapolis a half hour later. With a piano bar in front, a restaurant in the middle and a polka bar in the back, it's a time capsule of ethnic neighborhoods that once made up Minneapolis. Well-worn carpet, red vinyl high back booths, and a wait staff of 25 years average tenure are hallmarks of the institution known as Nye's.

Max met Dane in the back, and couldn't help but notice a group of attractive female University of Minnesota undergraduates dancing to polka music. Max turned to Dane "Remember that age? You would always find an excuse not to call after spending the night. Her ears were too big, her laugh annoyed you, or she had a goofy middle name. Crazy what we took a pass on."

Dane laughed "It's a shame youth is wasted on the young. I wonder if guys their age realize wedding cake reduces a woman's sex drive by 90 percent. If only we knew, it might have saved me two very expensive divorces. Those divorce attorneys make a killing. My salary as a Federal Prosecutor is a drop in the bucket compared to what they make. Maybe I should change my area of practice and get rich, instead of doing the right thing and putting dangerous people away." Dane paused, "I'm sorry buddy, talking about myself again."

Max shot back with a smile "It's what you do. Plus your ego would never let you leave the prosecutor's office. You wouldn't be on TV or front page news as a lowly divorce attorney. You would miss it too much."

Dane laughed as he took a healthy gulp of his Manhattan. "Look who's talking, you are on the news way more than I am. I hear it's been pretty crazy around the office, anything I can do to help?"

The conversation shifted from friendly razzing to more substantive topics. Dane advised Max to hold a press conference soon, which would accomplish two things. First, it would consolidate all of the media requests into one event. Hopefully, this would give the people at Chayka, Kimo, and Gust the ability to get back to a regular work routine. Second, a press conference could help quell lingering questions and give Max the opportunity to strike a balanced narrative. He would control the message, at least for that point in time.

Max took Dane's advice to heart and agreed to consider a press conference in the near future, but only after Vlad finished divulging the whole incredible story. Max needed to understand the entirety of the situation before questions started flying at a press conference. Again, he wanted to have answers to questions before they were posed to him.

Dane then asked about Vlad. As a lifelong friend, Dane felt a special kinship and loyalty to Max's dad.

"Look, Max," Dane said sympathetically "I have inquired through different channels regarding your dad. As the Chief U.S Attorney for the District of Minnesota and your friend, I could recuse myself from the case. At this point, I will stay on it. I want to be in control, and the bosses in Washington D.C. have given me the green light to proceed. No conflict of interest in their opinion, and I agree. We both need to be careful and prudent meeting and communicating while this case is ongoing. Neither of us wants even a whiff of impropriety, but I can say with a fair amount of certainty that Vlad will not be deported due to his age and health. Prison is likely out of the question due to the same reasons if he is found guilty. I could see a suspended sentence or something of that nature given by the judge. My office will prosecute of course, but you have time to create a defense."

Max rose from the table after finishing his drink, walked around the table and gave Dane a hug. "Thanks buddy. I need to get over to my dad's house and continue where we left off last night."

Dane gave Max a hug back, "So where did you two leave off exactly?'

Max gave Dane a 'can you believe it' look, "He was recruited out of a Nazi POW camp and brought to Trawniki, Poland for training. It's an incredible story, and I look forward to hearing the rest of it. I would have a hard time believing the story if he were not my dad because it's almost too unreal to comprehend how this all went down. I know we all have heard the story, six million Jews killed and so on. But to have a living relative who participated is unbelievable. Plus, we always have heard from the survivors, but very rarely from those who perpetrated the Holocaust. Hell, maybe I will write a book on his life when this is all done. Just not sure if people would buy it or burn it."

Max arrived at Vlad's house with take-out from Kramarczuk's Deli, which is a few blocks north on East Hennepin Avenue from Nye's. He walked in the front door with a bag containing Ukrainian sausage, bread, cheese and chocolate dessert.

Vlad spied the Kramarczuk plastic bag in Max's hands and said excitedly "Kramarczuk's! You shouldn't have my boy. Let me guess, Kovbasa?" Max let out the telltale smile but didn't say anything. Vlad stayed seated in his recliner "Pour me a healthy drink and a small slice of sausage, please. I love Kovbasa, but not sure how much it likes me anymore. Scotch, thank God, still agrees with your old man."

Max brought out a plate of food and drink for Vlad. "Dad, I got plenty for you to eat. The rest is in the fridge and should last you a few days. I know how you love fried Kovbasa and eggs in the morning, Lord knows you ate your fair share as I was growing up in this house" Max said with a laugh.

Vlad smiled as he took a bite. "Well, I made sure you had Kishka to eat as well. Always wanted to ensure we followed the proper Jewish diet for you."

Max sat across from Vlad with a fresh drink and watched his dad eat dinner. Vlad was right. He made sure Max followed the no pork protocol and always had tasty food choices for him growing up. Max considered himself a reformed Jew as an adult, not overly observant or Kosher when it came to food, but mindful of choices at a restaurant or grocery shopping. One thing Max loved was bacon, a main dietary weakness he developed in college. No harm, no foul Max always thought when buying a pound of bacon for Sunday breakfast.

Vlad finished half his dinner when Max chimed in. "I saw Dane Atkinson after work. He sends his best. Dane is handling the case and thinks it will take time to make it through the courts. We have options to keep you in this house dad. I want you to understand that and not worry."

Vlad put down his fork and slid the plate away, but kept the scotch close at hand. "Thank you, son. I hate to put this in your hands or cause any problems for Dane. Just do your best to keep your old man here until the good Lord decides it's my time."

Max said gently "I don't think he will come calling anytime soon, you are in great shape and mentally sharp. Look at Sid Hartman, still doing his sports column and radio show at 96 years old. Anyway, I want to get back to where we left off last night. Let me set up the camera, and we can continue. Is that Okay?" Vlad gave a nod yes as Max opened up his black leather bag containing video and sound equipment.

"Dad, you were speaking about Trawniki last night. That must have been incredibly difficult. Being there without your brothers, while serving the very people who murdered them, how did you reconcile that?"

"Max," Vlad replied, "That is something no one can understand unless the person was there. I made the decision to save myself at a very steep price. It was selfish and haunts me to this day. As I said to you the other night, you are the one reason I am happy I made that choice. My friend Pavel was another reason I continued training. If not for Pavel, I could have quickly ended up back at Chelm or shot at Trawniki by the SS for not following their orders. The choices were horrible, but my faith and Pavel were my saving grace."

Chapter 13

Mid-November 1941
SS Training Camp Trawniki, Poland

Late fall had fully set in. The trees were bare of leaves and occasional snow flurries mixed with cold north winds. Scharfuhrer Hecker began to intensify training as Gruppenfuhrer Heine promised. The recruits mastered basic soldierly tasks, and Hecker was preparing them for more physical times ahead. Twice daily strength conditioning, five-mile daily runs, and boxing matches were hardening the recruits. Lectures with accompanying chalkboard instructions of rounding up civilians and controlling the condemned were occurring nightly by the SS.

Hecker started to form his opinions about the recruits. Three had washed out and were never heard from again. Everyone assumed they were shot or returned to Chelm. Groups started to form in the company based on ethnicity, common interests, educational backgrounds, and level of anti-Semitism. Most were smart enough not to complain about the duty, but some were more enthusiastic than the rest. Vlad and Pavel had the luxury of privately discussing their contempt of the SS, and their sinister mission in confidence. One person was rising through the ranks to earn the title of Scharfuhrer Hecker's teacher's pet.

Orlov was a tall, thin, bald, very pale Ukrainian and the most anti-Semitic Trawniki recruit in Vlad's Company. Now in his mid-30's, he spent six years in prison for murdering his girlfriend's uncle, because Orlov viewed him as a sexual threat and competitor. Orlov worked in a factory before the Nazi invasion and developed a reputation as strangely odd and a person to be avoided. His advances towards women were painfully awkward, and thus far in life formed no meaningful friendships. In truth, he privately habitually masturbated and tortured small animals. Fully sociopathic, sexually deviant, and profound desire to feel superior, Orlov was Scharfuhrer Hecker's favorite pupil.

Orlov found his true vocational calling under Hecker's perverse and violent tutelage at Trawniki. Once a societal castoff and conditioned to the rejection of being marginalized, he suddenly found a way to become a person of importance and worth. Even better for Orlov, that importance and self-worth would come at the cost of the Jews. People he despised and scapegoated for his lot in life. A lesson he learned from his abusive, non-educated, drunken Protestant father. He became a magnet for the impressionable and easily influenced Trawniki recruits, much to the delight of Scharfuhrer Hecker.

Orlov became, under Hecker's careful watch, the ringleader for the most uneducated, violent, and anti-Semitic of the company. He was the cruelest, most profane, and bestially inhumane recruit. Orlov survived Chelm and was chosen by the SS because his miserable childhood also was full of hunger, filth, humiliation, and beatings. He grew acclimated to it, and it served him well as a POW.

The boxing training took a disturbing turn for Vlad a few days later when local Jews were brought in as sparring partners for the recruits. Hecker summoned Orlov as the first to get in the ring with a frail Jewish man in his late 70's. The company watched a bearded and elderly Jewish man wearing traditional Jewish garb of a top hat, black coat and Tzitzit tassels hobble up the boxing ring stairs. The old man had difficulty climbing between the ropes, but used his cane as support and eventually made it into the ring.

Orlov danced and shadow boxed getting warmed up in his corner, as Hecker mockingly put boxing gloves on the old man's trembling hands. The elderly Jew stood bewildered at center ring, as Hecker departed and the company cheered Orlov wildly. Orlov flexed his muscles and mockingly attempted the Jewish wedding dance around the ring, while the recruits were whistling and clapping Hava Nagila. Hecker rang the ringside bell and Orlov shuffled behind the man, tore his pants off and delivered a strong kidney punch to his side. The old man dropped to his knees in pain as Orlov walked to the ropes and grabbed the man's cane.

Vlad and Pavel watched Orlov shove the cane into the rectum of the elderly Jew. The man screamed in agony as the other recruits cheered loudly, and Hecker smiled in amusement. Orlov pulled out the cane with bloody anal linings hanging off and raised it up for all to see. Blood covered the majority of the boxing ring floor, and the elderly Jewish man writhed in agony on his side.

Orlov started doing the wedding dance again when he slipped and fell, becoming covered in blood and feces from his victim. Orlov crawled over, took off his boxing gloves and proceeded to bash the man's skull bare-fisted with one hand while squeezing his windpipe with the other. After 20 head blows and cutting off his oxygen supply, the victim lay dead. Orlov kneeled above him covered in blood while raising his right hand in victory. Hecker rose to his feet, gave a whistle and clang the ring bell as the recruits chanted "Orlov, Orlov, Orlov!"

Hecker climbed into the ring and shouted to the recruits "I picked Orlov as first to fight due to his tenacious belief in the worthlessness of this human debris. They are lower than shit out of a dog's ass, and now it is open season on these vermin. The Jews have lost all legal protection and any moral ground to stand on. We will destroy the Jew the way Orlov destroyed this old man, except, it will be done in an orderly and efficient manner. You need to get ready and understand how your SS masters want this done, Heil Hitler."

Orlov finally stood with his bloody outstretched arm and yelled with the rest of the recruits "Heil Hitler."

Vlad had certainly seen violence since the Nazi invasion and began to worry about becoming desensitized to what he witnessed. The display Orlov performed was not a simple beating up of a Jew. It was humiliation, perversion, and torture all rolled into violence hard to explain. Instead of following SS orders to box him, Orlov took the initiative to make the treatment as cruel and unusual as he could. It was a phenomenon Vlad would witness from many men in his company.

Vlad and Pavel walked out of the brick building housing the boxing ring, and into the dirt courtyard. Vlad peered through the cold mist and saw the smokestack silhouette marking the border of the camp. Other gray brick buildings comprising the old sugar factory were also shrouded in fog, illuminated by inside lights radiating through the windows. From a distance, it could have been mistaken for a peaceful shtetl in rural Poland. Pavel lit a cigarette, passed it to Vlad, and lit another one for himself. The chilly and damp November breeze felt refreshing. It was like splashing cold water on his face, which Vlad needed. Vlad took a few deep breaths and started on his cigarette. "Pavel, do you believe that old Jewish man got what he deserved?"

Pavel gave Vlad a curious look and replied "Why would you ask such a thing after all of our talks? He got what these German monsters and SS psychopaths believe he deserved. But no, I don't believe the same thing, and you know that."

Vlad flicked his cigarette away and said "I am living in a world that is hard to recognize. I remember a bible reading from Mass that said 'and now these three remain: faith, hope, and love. But the greatest of these is love.' Now all that remains for me at Trawniki are violence, despair, and hate. The greatest of these is hate. It goes against everything I was raised to believe. Jesus was a Jew, his mom and dad were Jews, and the Apostles were Jews. It's a hate that I can't embrace and violence that I don't think I can commit. What will God say to me on judgment day about my treatment of His Chosen People?"

Pavel gave Vlad a hard look. "I'm sure that most of these SS maniacs are Lutheran, Catholic, or some Protestant, and none of them care about your religious sensitivity. Most Christians I know could care less about the Jews, and the Germans are exploiting that fact on a level the world won't believe. They pulled us out of that hellhole at Chelm to do some severe damage to these people. What exactly the SS have in mind for our duty, I don't know, and neither do you. They keep saying death for every Jew, but I just can't see that happening because of the sheer numbers involved. We have been for over eight weeks, and that's the first Jew we've seen murdered."

Pavel paused, took a deep breath in through his nose, exhaled through his mouth and continued. "Regardless, the SS said you certainly have a choice, either obey their insane demands or face certain death. I know your brothers would want you to survive this craziness, and carry on the Chayka name. Do it for them, and I will help you along the way. I have broad shoulders kid, climb on my back and let me carry you. Your death is not the answer. This screwed up world needs more people like Vlad Chayka. Not less."

Vlad gave Pavel a half smile. "Thank you," Vlad said quietly and continued in a hushed tone "You know something, Pavel. I've never been in a true fistfight. Shoving and shouting matches with other kids at school, and delivering body checks during hockey games, yes. But swinging and landing a punch on another person because I disagreed or didn't like them, never. I just was not a brawler, and always would talk or negotiate my way out of a potential confrontation. Not that I am afraid to fight, I just never understood how it solved any problems."

Pavel gave a light chuckle. "Chayka, most of these recruits are probably in the same boat as you. I'm a wrestling champion and all around brawler. I have been in bar fights, street fights and wrestling matches with some very tough opponents. I am blessed with a gift of sizing up the other guy rather quickly. I have studied our fellow recruits, and none of them could take me, especially that pussy Orlov."

Pavel took the last drag of his cigarette and tossed it on the ground. "Believe me, kid, these recruits in our company are no tougher than you. But many seem eager to punish feeble and defenseless Jews, which I think is an indicator of just how spineless they are. A person like Orlov beats an old Jew to death while sodomizing him, which shows exactly how weak he is. As for the SS, there are some tough people like Hecker. That guy is out of his mind and strong as a bull, he even scares me. The rest of the SS around here I could easily knock down, and they would have a hard time getting up."

Vlad and Pavel walked into the brick building that housed their company in time for dinner. The chatter among the recruits about Orlov's performance in the ring was nonstop. Vlad heard others excitedly wondering about their turn to 'box a Jew.' Many were openly bragging about knocking out a Jew with four punches, then another predicted three punches and still another claimed he could knock out a Jew with two punches. One of Orlov's followers stood on his chair and announced to all in the dining room that he could kill a Jew with one punch, and would take bets on that fact. Money started pouring onto the table with laughs and requests that Scharfuhrer Hecker hold the cash as the banker.

Pavel watched Vlad get up from the table and walk upstairs to the company sleeping quarters. He laid down and put a pillow over his ears attempting to muffle the commotion coming from below. Vlad started to softly cry as he thought about his parents, brothers and especially Mikhail who most likely perished back at Chelm. He looked so weak, sick and utterly helpless. A complete shell of the oldest brother Vlad had loved, respected and even at times feared. Vlad had abandoned him at the moment of greatest need and felt overcome with pangs of guilt. Stepan and Timor were both dead, and nothing more could be done for them, but to abandon a brother in need was entirely different. His choice to survive gave him overwhelming anxiety.

Vlad had not prayed in a few weeks and could not come up with anything meaningful to say to God. As sleep started to overtake him, the haunting words Vlad would hear at Mass kept cycling through his mind. "Whatever you do to the least of my brothers, that you do unto me."

Chapter 14
SS Camp Trawniki
December 23, 1941

After a particularly nice breakfast of all they could eat eggs and sausage, which raised Pavel's suspicions, Hecker summoned the men outside. "Fall in and get ready for a great day. This will be a day many of you will never forget for the rest of your lives" Hecker said with a smile on his face. The December cold winds and clouds had set in, and a foot of fresh snow blanketed the ground. The recruits did as ordered, organizing into their usual military formation while Vlad, Pavel, and the rest rubbed their hands and stomped their feet to keep warm.

Hecker waited a few minutes and then addressed the company. "I hope everyone has enjoyed the honeymoon here at Trawniki. You have been well treated, well fed, well clothed, trained in the use of a German rifle, trained to march like a German, learned enough German to follow orders and even allowed to beat up a few Jews. You are now ready for the next step in your training. By order of Gruppenfuhrer Heine and Reichsfuhrer-SS Himmler, you have all been promoted to the rank of Wachman. Also known as auxiliary guards in the SS. Congratulations."

Hecker continued like a commencement speaker. "You will proceed to receive the proper uniform and supplies. Your current clothes will be returned to the next group of Trawniki recruits who are arriving later today. We have brought in 100 Jews, one for each man in this company. The Jews will launder clothes, clean barracks, get bedding in proper order, and make the latrines spotless. You will be transported by truck to the town of Rabka, about 4 hours away to the south. Advanced training will take place at our special police school. It's the last part of training before you will physically help with the Fuhrer's brilliant Final Solution. I will be your drill sergeant during our two-month stay. Now fall out, you have exactly two hours."

The group filed into the same building as they did three months previously upon arriving at Trawniki. This time, they shed their clothes and received gray uniform pants, black leather boots, a gray tunic, a gray wool overcoat, black leather gloves, and gray triangle side hat. Everything was individually fitted for each Wachman. They were issued a dagger with a utility belt, a bolt action Mauser rifle, and a semi-automatic Luger sidearm with holster. The SS issued no ammunition, that would come soon enough.

Vlad stood next to Orlov after both received their Mauser rifles. "Hey Chayka," Orlov said as he pointed his rifle towards the wall while looking down the sight with one eye closed. "This is how you wink at a Jew." Orlov lowered his rifle, let out a menacing laugh, and walked away. Vlad turned pale and felt sick to his stomach.

Pavel watched Vlad's reaction to Orlov. "Look, kid, I hate to say this, but you need to harden your heart. Turn your heart, conscience, and soul into stone. People like Orlov and Hecker can smell any kindness and decency a mile away. They consider goodness the ultimate weakness. You are an honorable person who needs to find a way to get through this. Remember your brothers and the last POW camp you were at, stay mentally strong."

"Move your asses outside, on the double!" Hecker screamed into the building. The Wachmen scurried out the door in single file and saw several troop transport trucks with canvas covers waiting at the main gate. "Fall in to be counted." The men assumed the usual company formation and began to count off as it started snowing once again. Vlad always loved snow, and winter in general. Winter usually meant downhill skiing and ice hockey. He was gifted at both, but hockey remained his favorite. Vlad was a strong skater with a nasty slap shot, and many Ukrainian women loved guys who played the sport. "Not this year" Vlad muttered to himself.

Hecker stood in front of Company A and stared at his men, giving them a proud look. He began to walk up and down each row, handing out one bullet to each man. "Wachmen, you have one final act of duty before we leave Trawniki for Rabka. These Jews who have cleaned the barracks and laundered the bedding over the past few hours have done a great job. Everything is truly spotless. They worked hard and would make an excellent crew at a fine hotel somewhere. As a reward, they have the honor of being shot, one at a time, by the first class of newly promoted Wachmen. You will not hesitate. I will be watching each of you closely. Lock and load."

Each Wachman loaded the one bullet they received into the chamber and locked the bolt action. The Jews were led out into the freezing courtyard wearing only underwear. They were barefoot and shivered from cold and fear. Most were men from a neighboring village aged 20 to 50.

Vlad pictured the victims in his mind. Not long ago they were probably living somewhat normal lives as tailors, blacksmiths, musicians, and doctors. They likely held positions of trust and respect and lived among their fellow villagers for generations with few problems. Interfaith marriages were not uncommon either.

After the Nazi invasion of Poland, their emboldened fellow villagers turned on them. Vlad knew from SS lectures that these people lost total control of their lives. They had no protection from the law, the church or the community at large. The Jews were summarily stripped of homes, possessions, businesses and any way to make a living. There was no recourse for the transgression of simply being Jewish. For the SS that meant one thing, death. Vlad and his fellow Wachmen were now fully engaged.

"I understand this may be the first time many of you have killed someone. However, these are not people. They are dogs that need to be put down. Keep that top of mind as we do the Reich and the rest of the world a favor." Hecker said with an excited voice. "One Wachman at a time, and shoot the rotten Jew in the chest or head. The Reich does not waste ammunition on Jewish arms or legs, and do not miss." Pavel stood in the front row of the formation. "We will start with you," Hecker said as he pointed to Pavel.

An SS man led a male about 25 years old to the center of the courtyard. The man shivered uncontrollably, and his teeth were chattering so loud that all in the company could hear. Pavel took ten steps forward, which placed him 50 feet from the victim. Pavel could see fear emanating from the man's eyes, which was not something new to him with his history of fistfights and wrestling matches. Pavel had seen fear from an overmatched opponent, but this look was entirely foreign to him. The Jewish victim gave Pavel a look that comes when somebody is about to take his entire past, present, future and make him nothing but a memory. There would be no funeral for this man. Just a small box emblazoned with a swastika, full of his ashes, delivered to his widow and young son.

"Fire at will" Hecker commanded in an excited voice. Hecker had been waiting for this moment since the ragged recruits arrived from

Chelm back in September. Hecker felt truly invested with this group of men and was bullish on their future ability to achieve murder on a scale that would make history. It all started here, in the Trawniki courtyard, with each Wachman personally murdering a Jew. It was the unbroken continuum of real life dehumanization, pure evil, and desensitization to murder. Pavel raised the rifle to his shoulder, took aim at the trembling man, and squeezed the trigger. It was a direct hit to the center of his upper chest and knocked the Jew off his feet. The impact of the round blew a fist sized exit wound in his back, with a bloody and pulsating half lung protruding out. The man gasped for air and withered on the frozen ground for a short time before succumbing. The entire company stood silent, and the remaining group of 99 Jews recoiled in terror.

"Excellent. Well done!" Hecker said loudly and proudly to Pavel. "Next man get ready to wipe a human reject off the face of the Fuhrer's Earth. Move it. We don't have all day." Another terrorized, freezing, and underwear-clad man was brought up by two SS enlisted men. He was made to stand next to his murdered friend and wait for a bullet from a newly promoted Wachman. Thirty seconds later he lay violently dead.

The company of 100 Wachmen had shot about 50 Jews when Orlov stepped forward. All had mortally wounded or killed their victims with a single shot. None had missed to this point. Orlov was facing an older Jewish man in his sixties who was tall, balding, overweight and overwhelmed with anxiety at his imminent death. The man shivered in fear and soiled his underwear. Feces ran down his legs and steamed in the cold.

Orlov raised the rifle to his shoulder and took aim. He hesitated and suddenly lowered the weapon. He gave Hecker and the rest of the company a menacing smile and rushed the terrified man. Orlov spun his rifle around, so the wooden stock faced his victim, and violently thrust the rifle butt into the man's large stomach. The Jewish victim instinctively doubled over in pain. Orlov then removed his Luger sidearm and pistol-whipped the man in the face and head seven times. After holstering the Luger, Orlov scooped up the rifle with his blood-stained hands and smashed the man's head until his brains oozed onto the blood-soaked frozen dirt of the courtyard.

Orlov executed a perfect military about face, marched to Hecker and unloaded his weapon. Orlov obediently bowed his head, "Your bullet returned Scharfuhrer Hecker."

Hecker beamed with pride and deliberately exclaimed loud enough for all to hear. "Orlov, you are a credit to this company and the Reich. A fine example of what a true Wachman is made of. You are my star pupil and first in line for a promotion when that time comes. It's a damn shame you are not German. Blessed are the spillers of Jewish blood, for the Fuhrer's reward will be great!"

A few more Wachmen shot Jews after Orlov without incident. Some aimed for the head, but more went for the chest area because nobody wanted to miss. By the time Vlad's turn came, over 70 murdered people were piled up in the courtyard. The ground steamed with warm blood, warm flesh and warm brains scattered about. The young man presented to be shot by Vlad appeared to be about 19 or 20 years old, right about Vlad's age.

Vlad noticed the Jewish kid was not shivering and almost staring him down. He was barefoot in a pool of blood and only in underwear. He stood amongst 70 of his murdered friends and family showing no fear. "Fire at will Chayka" Hecker barked. "Kill this Jewish piece of shit. Look at him giving you attitude. Who does he think he is? Don't you want just to tear him apart? Now shoot him."

Vlad raised his rifle. His hands were shaking, and eyes welled with tears. Suddenly the Jewish man yelled out "Hear O Israel. The Lord our God, the Lord is one. Avenge these murderers. They kill for no reason, may God's wrath befall these filthy beasts!"

"Kill him Chayka" Hecker screamed.

Vlad squeezed the trigger, the rifle recoiled upward, and the bullet sailed harmlessly over the man's head.

"Are you fucking kidding me? You missed!" Hecker said in an agitated and shrill voice. "Take this round Orlov gave me and do your goddamn job. If you miss again, it's back to Chelm for your sorry ass. Now kill this arrogant Jew pig."

Vlad loaded Orlov's round into his rifle and raised it at the Jewish kid whose eyes were on fire. He started to silently recite the Hail Mary. Vlad waited until "Holy Mary, Mother of God, pray for us sinners." He then gently squeezed the trigger sending the round at 1,000 feet per second. It struck his victim in the mouth, sending teeth out the back of his head. The Jew was knocked off his feet by the impact and dropped to the ground with a thud.

It was the most surreal moment of Vlad's young life, and he most definitely had many since June. His mental and physical numbness was interrupted by Hecker. "Nice shot Chayka, so much for that Jew boy's dental work."

Many in the company started laughing at Hecker's joke, with Orlov laughing the hardest. Vlad turned and joined the other Wachmen who had already performed their grisly task. Pavel gave Vlad a silent empathetic nod of the head. He returned the gesture, looked down in shame and fought back vomiting and tears.

The final men in the company finished off the remaining Jews. When it was all over, 100 murdered men lay on the frozen ground tangled together. More local Jews were on the way to clean up the hellacious mess. Their fate was probably going to be the same.

The men were then ordered to the waiting trucks by Hecker. "Twenty men per truck. You also have two armed SS men riding with each transport. Remember your places. You are just Wachmen. We SS are your masters, never forget that. You have been issued firearms, but no ammunition besides the one bullet you expended today. In Chayka's case two bullets, because apparently, he can't hit the broadside of a barn with a shoe. Your SS escorts have fully loaded automatic weapons at the ready, in case any of you decide to jump out and go sightseeing during our trip to Rabka. Keep in mind it would be the last thing you do on this Earth. Now mount up and move out. Heil Hitler."

"Heil Hitler" the company responded to Hecker.

Chapter 15
Rabka, Poland

The truck convoy arrived in Rabka at dinnertime. The snow continued to fall, and with just a few days before Christmas, the sleepy spa town of 7,000 residents looked like a postcard. The building where Vlad and the Wachmen would be staying was a stunning four-story former secondary girl's school. The school sat on a hill overlooking the picturesque Raba River that flowed through town. The well-maintained building was a source of pride for the girls and families who attended from Rabka and the surrounding area. The SS picked a beautiful setting for this most unique of schools.

Vlad and the rest of the company got out of the trucks and stretched their legs. Vlad looked up and noticed a giant black flag with a swastika in the middle. It flew from the top of the building and was illuminated by floodlights. Vlad had seen many Nazi flags, but they were always red, with a white circle, and a swastika in the middle. This particular flag looked menacing, even with the pleasant snowfall. Everyone who saw the flag felt an evil energy emanating from the school and understood the SS occupiers meant business. To further make their point, the SS put up large black letters on the top floor of the building reading "School of the Commander-in-Chief of the Security Police and Security Services." Rabka was a school for torture and mass murder, the first of its kind on the planet.

Vlad couldn't stop thinking about the young man he shot earlier in the day. What a robust and fearless life he snuffed out. The victim was braver than Vlad felt he could ever be under such harrowing conditions. Vlad kept mostly quiet on the truck ride from Trawniki to Rabka, and recited the Catholic Profession of Faith silently at least 100 times. The part he kept coming back to over and over again was "He will come again in glory to judge the living and the dead, and his kingdom will have no end. I believe in the Holy Spirit, the Lord, the giver of life." Vlad said the prayer every Sunday at Mass. He committed it to memory as a kid, and it now haunted him.

As a taker of innocent life, he became the antithesis to the prayer. Vlad also believed he would be subject to a final judgment for crimes against God's chosen people. Vlad could feel himself in the beginning stages of entering the abyss mentally and spiritually. If it all stopped now, he felt recovery wouldn't be a problem. If the violent craziness continued at an accelerated pace, Vlad wasn't sure how much longer he could hold on.

The company walked up the brick steps, through the doors and entered a well-appointed dining hall. Chandeliers hung from the timber-beamed ceiling. Long mahogany dining tables were set up with plentiful food, beer, vodka, schnapps, and desserts. Vlad noticed the gleaming oak floors and beautiful tile work adorning the walls. The Commandant of the school stood in front, elevated on a podium with a microphone in hand. The company gathered in a reception area near the back and set their gear down in neat rows. Vlad, Pavel, and the others quieted down as the Commandant began to speak.

"My name is Josef Krueger, Commandant of Rabka Police School. I am aware of your hard work and good fortune to have graduated from Trawniki basic training. You will spend the next twelve weeks at this institution, mastering the skills necessary for duty that awaits. This is a place of profound higher learning. It's a fascinating and exciting time in the history of the Third Reich and the world. We will accomplish things considered improbable just a few short years ago. We are launching Operation Reinhard, which I will brief you on now. You newly commissioned Wachmen will be crucial components of this vital operation."

Krueger continued, and the men listened intently. "Operation Reinhard, simply put, is the total elimination of about two million Jews. These Jews are living in the General Government of what used to be Poland, and now is part of the greater Reich. We will not only take their lives, but we will also take their houses, their apartments, their businesses, their cash, their stocks, their bonds, their cars, their boats, their gold, their watches, their diamonds, their artwork, their shoes, their clothes and their wine collections. This will be the biggest robbery of wealth since the Americans stole almost four million square miles of land rich in natural resources from the natives. We will take their flat granite gravestones to pave pathways and build sheds for livestock. We will even use their hair for U-boat insulation. This will be your honor and sacred duty. As Reichsfuhrer-SS Heinrich Himmler told me, it's a glorious page in history that will never be written."

Krueger paused then continued "I know you are hungry and tomorrow is Christmas Eve, we will celebrate and enjoy. Then it's back to work on December 26th, as we have lots to do. I will now lead us in prayer. Please bow your heads." The dining hall grew silent. Even the kitchen staff and servers, some of whom were Jewish prisoners, stopped what they were doing and stood still.

Krueger bowed his head and said solemnly "My Fuhrer, thank you for this food we are about to eat. We are grateful this food is being used to nourish your faithful servants, instead of feeding the Jewish parasites that plague your ever-expanding domain. Thank you, Fuhrer, for the opportunity to kill Jews and rid Europe of these vermin and enemies of The Thousand Year Reich. To be alive during this time is a symbol of The Fuhrer's love for us. We promise absolute allegiance until death. Heil Hitler."

Everyone replied "Heil Hitler."

Vlad and company sat at tables of ten with plenty to eat and drink for everyone. The room was warmly heated and well lit. A Christmas tree stood decorated in the corner with swastikas, SS lightning bolts, and Death's Head insignia. Instead of garland, the SS draped strings of dried Jew's ears around the tree. At the top of the tree where a star is typically perched, sat a sizeable framed photograph of Adolf Hitler.

After dinner, Krueger again mounted the podium. He tapped the microphone to get everyone's attention. The room quieted down, although not the pure silence during his prayer. He leaned into the microphone and spoke. "I hope everyone got enough to eat and drink. Your rooms are prepared on the third level. It will be four per room and baths are located on either end of the floor. I am sure you will find the accommodations most suitable during your stay. Tomorrow is Christmas Eve, and it will be a light work day except for some reindeer games in the morning. You will find out tomorrow what those games are, but I feel you will enjoy them greatly."

The men in Vlad's company all clapped and cheered. Hecker stood, excitedly raised his right arm doing the Nazi salute and shouted "Sieg Heil."

The rest of the men jumped to their feet and thundered a return "Heil Hitler."

Commandant Krueger stood at the podium, his face beaming with pride. He let the room quiet down and proceeded to speak. "I have been told by Scharfuhrer Hecker that none of you have had a woman in quite some time. Is that correct?" The men in Vlad's company all moaned and groaned in agreement.

Krueger continued "We have a treat before retiring to your sleeping quarters. Everyone here has the opportunity to have sex with a young woman tonight." The men all howled in approval. Even Vlad clapped and cheered.

"There is one little detail, however," Krueger continued. "We have found the prettiest Jewess in the area. She is 16 years old with a well-developed body, long legs, and great backside. She is a known virgin and very religious. We kidnapped her at gunpoint from her family yesterday for this special occasion. Her idiot father tried stopping us, so we slit his throat, and he bled like a Jewish pig."

Commandant Krueger kept speaking "I have a jar of 100 army issue condoms here in front, and require that you use them. The spread of venereal disease is a problem, so we must take precautions. Every man in the company who desires will come forward, drop his uniform pants, put on a condom and jackhammer this pretty Jew. Please know you are not required, but all are most welcome to use her. I would love to rape her, especially with that body. But as an officer in the SS, I must abide by and enforce the Fuhrer's wise racial purity laws which forbid sexual contact between Aryans and Jews. You, however, being Russian and Ukrainian can do so without penalty."

The men stood and cheered while the naked 16-year-old beautiful girl was wheeled out in a barber's chair. The girl's hands and ankles were handcuffed to the sturdy metal chair frame, and her legs spread apart by leather straps. She trembled in fear. Krueger grabbed a bottle of vodka and knelt down, did the sign of the cross over the bottle and said to the crowd, "I hereby bless this vodka. Let's now get some holy spirits in this sweet little Jewess." He poured almost a third of it down her throat. She tried to fight back by spitting it out, but he plugged her nose which forced the girl to gasp for air and swallow. "Some liquid courage for the Jew whore," Krueger shouted to the men as he continued to mock her. The men in Vlad's Company roared in approval.

Krueger stepped onto the podium and spoke into the microphone on more time. "Based on Scharfuhrer Hecker's recommendation, Wachman Orlov goes last."

Many in the company started laughing and chanting "sloppy seconds." Orlov turned beet red with embarrassment.

"This is an honor for Orlov. All of you who wish to penetrate her can do so, yes." Krueger continued "However, Wachman Orlov has the distinction of finishing. He has the honor of choking this Jewess to death while he penetrates her in the ass, and Orlov does not have to use a condom. The rest of you penetrate her vagina and keep your hands off her. I want you to use the armrests on either side of the chair as leverage. The only laying of hands on this girl will be Orlov."

Orlov stood and shouted, "Start raping her, I don't have all night!"

Both Pavel and Vlad were surprised at the number of men lining up to take part. Krueger was right. Most of them had not had a woman in many months, and this helpless girl was going to suffer the pent up sexual energy of over 80 strong young men. As they took their turns, the Wachmen assaulted her mercilessly while the rest cheered on their comrades through hoots, hollers, and chants. The remaining 20 or so Wachmen who did not partake were simply unable to perform in front of such a large crowd. Vlad and Pavel were the only ones who stood back due to moral outrage.

Orlov's turn finally arrived. He lowered his pants, ready to penetrate the abused and half-conscious girl in the rectum. But he became quickly irritated that she was slipping in and out of consciousness. Orlov wanted her fully aware of her current misery, and the final few minutes of her life. Vlad watched as Orlov urinated on her face, and slapped the girl repeatedly to revive her. It worked. She regained consciousness.

The girl screamed in pain as he thrust in and out of her backside. The crowd went wild as he put his hands on her throat and began squeezing her windpipe. As Orlov approached climax, he kept one hand tightly clenched on her throat and started closed fist smashing the girl in the face with the other hand. The girl turned blue from lack of oxygen and red from blood pouring out of her nose and mouth. Orlov's leg muscles tightened as he ejaculated while smashing his fist against her left ear and screaming "Heil Hitler."

When finished, Orlov stood up out of breath, covered in blood and zipped up his pants. The girl lay dead with her unrecognizable face and broken body still strapped to the chair. The room erupted in wild chants, high fives, and general pandemonium. Both Hecker and Commandant Krueger were fist pumping into the air while giving shouts of approval. It was the saddest and most disturbing thing Vlad had ever seen in his life.

Vlad walked to the table containing the bottles of alcohol, downed two big shots of whiskey, and went upstairs to his room shaken and exhausted. He lay down and tried to pray, but couldn't. He began to question for the first time if God even existed. These were his supposed Chosen People, where did God fit in this awful mess and why wasn't he helping them? Vlad knew Rabka was going to be worse than Trawniki and worried about the unknown horrors that lay ahead. For the first time in his life, Vlad longed for the past and feared the future.

He recalled in a depressed state more words from the priest at the beginning of Mass. "May Almighty God have mercy on us, forgive us our sins, and bring us to everlasting life." As Vlad started to pass out, he figured Christianity was either a fairy tale, or he entered some evil netherworld. A place where life was cheap and the Holy Trinity had abandoned. The entire third floor remained remarkably quiet. The men were drunk, tired, and transferred their energy into the dead Jewish girl downstairs. Most slept well that first night in Rabka.

Chapter 16
December 24th, 1941

After Vlad, Pavel and the rest of the company ate a breakfast of eggs and sausages in the dining hall, they were ordered by Hecker to the courtyard in the back of the building. Beyond the courtyard was a large field once used for soccer matches, and beyond the field was a heavily wooded forest. The weather remained windy, cold, and overcast. Their rifles were neatly assembled in pyramid formations of ten each, with the rifle butts on the ground and barrels pointed into the air. Vlad noticed the rifles were equipped with magazines. They were locked and loaded.

Scharfuhrer Hecker walked in front of the men and spoke. "Wachmen, I hope you all enjoyed yourselves last night. The Commandant promised two easy days with some reindeer games, and he truly is a man of his word. He wants the company to have some fun while learning a valuable lesson in marksmanship. He is most aware your last day of Trawniki consisted of every graduate shooting a Jew. It's easy to shoot somebody, especially an adult standing still and less than 50 feet away. I want to give our Commandant the best Christmas gift ever, and that is 100 fewer Jews on the planet. He will be pleased with such a gift, and will be happy that you also received challenging target practice."

Hecker paused and continued "As I just said, it's easy to shoot a big, still target. However, it's harder to hit a small moving target, and that's what we shall do this morning. After target practice, all Wachmen will have free time to eat, drink and lounge until the 26th. Just think how far many of you have come since last summer at Chelm. You have much to be thankful for and have the Fuhrer to thank for it. Don't forget that, ever. Each man grab your rifle, they are loaded with seven rounds of ammunition. Hopefully, that's all you need for this exercise, now form ten lines of ten men. On the double!"

Vlad and the rest of the men did as instructed. Ten groups of ten Wachmen were formed, with the first group shouldering their rifles. At that moment, three covered transport trucks pulled up to the side of the soccer field. Hecker barked out, "The first group of ten ready your rifles, pick your target and fire on my command." The rear gates of the first transport truck opened, and SS men began tossing out ten terrified Jewish children ages four to eight years old onto the ground.

"Run children. It will keep you warm, schnell" the SS yelled from inside the trucks.

As the ten children began to run around the field, Hecker gave the command "Commence firing." The first ten Wachmen discharged their rifles in rapid succession, and the children were no match for the high-powered weapons. Every child was shredded being hit once, twice, four or even five times by the Wachmen.

The children in the trucks began to scream at the horror they were witnessing and pressed away from the tailgate towards the driver's end of the truck. The SS inside ordered the driver to slowly drive around the soccer field as they grabbed the next ten children and threw them out of the moving vehicle. "Commence firing" Hecker commanded the next group of ten Wachmen. They opened fire on the running children, cutting them to pieces. Heads, arms, and legs were blown off by the incoming rifle shots. Some were still alive crying out in pain as they lay wounded on the ground.

Vlad couldn't believe the barbaric evil unfolding in front of him. He experienced the sensation of floating above his body and watching the horror outside himself. His senses became overloaded. Sounds of screaming children and gunshots, sights of innocent children shredded apart, and the smell of gunpowder added to the surreal atmosphere. His sane mind attempted to process the insane.

Vlad was in the third group. He stepped up and fired on command. He shot one five-year-old child in the chest and another eight-year-old in the leg. Vlad fired his seven rounds faster than anyone else in his group, and Hecker saw he hit at least two children. When Vlad's group of ten Wachmen fired all of their ammunition, an additional ten children lay either dead or mortally wounded on the field.

Hecker called out from the side where he observed. "Well done, Chayka. I was watching and hoping you didn't pull the same antics with that arrogant, loudmouth Jew you missed at Trawniki. You never hesitated, and actually hit two of the Jewish runts. Nice shooting." Orlov gave Vlad a jealous glare, but Vlad was unaware of it all.

Vlad thought he heard Hecker say something, but his mind wasn't processing the words. He blankly stared at Hecker and joined the others who had finished their shooting. Vlad watched the remaining seven groups do their grisly work. When the last group finished, the screaming of the children stopped. That's when Vlad started to regain his senses. Only the soft moans, whimpers, and cries of the wounded remained. The truck began to drive around the field running over the children who were severely wounded but still alive. The entire company heard the bones cracking under the wheels, and saw the transport truck lift up every time it ran over a child as if it were going over a speed bump.

After the transport trucks had exited, the soccer field grew silent. The men stood and stared at the carnage. Even Orlov was speechless. Just the sound of the cold wind remained, as the gunfire scared away any birds. Hecker interrupted the quiet "Very nice shooting all of you. I am most proud and will report our action as a Christmas gift to the Commandant. You are all excused until 6 am on the 26th for classroom instruction. As a reminder, all are forbidden to leave the school grounds under penalty of death, but everything you need is right here. That is all. Fallout."

The men walked back into the building, and Vlad heard quiet chatter among them. Pavel grabbed Vlad's arm and said, "Let's grab a drink." They walked into the dining hall where a long table against the wall held of vodka, beer, whiskey, and schnapps. Plenty to drink for everyone, which became a recurring theme as the SS understood this work required large amounts of alcohol for the men. Pavel poured two stiff vodkas and handed one to Vlad whose hands were shaking. Vlad downed the drink in three gulps. "Easy kid, I understand the need to have a few, but pace yourself. You don't want to drink this hard, this young, and this early." Pavel poured another for Vlad and continued speaking in a soft tone, as he pointed to an empty table away from the rest of the company. "Now sip this one and let's sit over there where we can talk a while."

Pavel and Vlad walked to the back corner of the dining hall and sat down at the empty table. Vlad's hands were still trembling as he took another long sip. He looked at Pavel despondently. "I can't do this. I am not a killer of anybody, especially kids. These bastards made me kill a guy about my age back at Trawniki, now I just shot and killed two kids. This is not who I am. I am going to find Hecker and tell him I'm out."

Vlad started to get up as Pavel reached across the table and firmly grabbed Vlad's arm, spilling the vodka drink in the process. The other men checked out the commotion and went back to their binge drinking. Vlad wasn't the only one who needed to get drunk.

Pavel spoke in a quiet but agitated voice "Sit down, shut up, and listen to me, Chayka. I understand this is total insanity, and not what you envisioned for Christmas. But it's either you or them. You die, or these Jews die. The choice is simple as that. This is a horrible situation. This is criminal insanity at its worst, and these bastards are making us their executioners. If you speak with Hecker, you will be shot, and somebody else will gladly take your place out of Chelm or Trawniki. Is that what you want?"

Pavel let go of Vlad's arm and let the words sink in. Vlad picked up his glass of vodka and downed it in three big gulps. "Never in a million years could I have guessed this would be my Christmas in 1941. All of my brothers are dead, and I'm murdering children for the Nazis. How much deeper into the abyss are we going to go? I believe I have descended into hell. Am I the only one who feels like this? Orlov and his disciples seem to be enjoying every minute of this madness. This is some parallel world. Who let these animals in charge and take over all of Europe? And what about these Jews?"

"What about them?" Pavel asked.

"Jesus was Jewish" Vlad lamented through tear filled eyes. "Ziv the barber we all went to in Kiev was Jewish, and everyone loved him. Some of my favorite teachers were Jews. Why on Earth are the Nazi's out to destroy these people and how can one people hate another with such searing fury? We are murdering kids, for Christ's sake."

"I don't know kid, and honestly I don't give a damn," Pavel whispered as he took a long sip from his vodka. "It's a hate people have going back centuries. I haven't known that many Jews to have an opinion one way or another. But I did like Ziv, the barber, he was a good man. The Germans are simply exploiting old prejudices and taking them to insane homicidal levels. I don't understand it myself, but I am going to survive this war, and so are you. I know this is horrible, but we are going to do what we have to do."

Vlad drank his vodka while choking back tears and said "What happens when I die, meet God and have to answer for this? How am I going to explain shooting two kids today and the other one at Trawniki? How am I going to tell God that I murdered his chosen people to save myself?"

Pavel thought a minute. "I'm not a priest kid and don't have the answers you seek. In my opinion, there is no God. How can there be a God with this homicidal craziness happening? If there is a God and you meet him upon your death, ask him where the fuck he was in this stinking mess? Ask him why you were forced to make such horrendous choices? The fact is God is nowhere to be found around here. God may as well be dead in my life, and in the lives of any Jews the SS come across. It's open season on these people, and God is not going to help them, help me, or help you. The entire concept of God is a damn joke."

Vlad poured another vodka for Pavel and himself and lit a cigarette. Vlad took a slow deep drag and let out a long exhale as if he were trying to cast off the evil mayhem that overtook them both. Vlad once again drank his in three quick gulps, set the glass down and stood up from the table. He stumbled slightly but regained his footing. "I am going to bed." Vlad walked across the room and up the stairs to go pass out. He slept for the next day.

Chapter 17
Rabka Police School

Both Scharfuhrer Hecker and Commandant Krueger were standing at the front of the classroom. Vlad and his company took their seats at 6:30 a.m. on a cold and snowy December 26th. The classroom was large and well heated with chairs and desks for all. Pens and writing tablets were provided for each Wachman to take notes. This place could easily be mistaken for a typical lecture hall, but the courses taught were a first in the history of the human race.

Krueger started "Men of Trawniki, I want to thank you for the fine Christmas gift. There are now 100 less Jewish piglets who will not grow up to foul and sully the Reich or its Master Race. Beautifully done."

Hecker snapped to attention, raised his right outstretched arm and yelled out, "Heil Hitler."

The men all rose up from their chairs, returned the salute and bellowed, "Heil Hitler."

Krueger gave Hecker an approving nod and continued "As you saw the other day, shooting 100 people takes time, energy, ammunition, and is grossly inefficient. We have devised a new and better way to rid the Third Reich of this human garbage. Let me be clear, and let there be no misunderstanding on this issue. The death warrant for every man, woman, and child who is Jewish has been signed by the Fuhrer himself. We have been charged with a task that has never been tried in the history of humanity, eliminating a race of nine million people."

Krueger let the number sink in for a minute and continued "Nine million is a hard number to comprehend for most people, so let me break it down for you. Just a few short months ago, Scharfuhrer Hecker and 50 other men were in a special group that I commanded named Einsatzgruppen C. Einsatzgruppen C entered Kiev in late September. We gathered every Jew and made them march to a huge ravine called Babi Yar, located just outside of the city. Once at Babi Yar, my group forced the Jews to undress, walked them in groups of ten and shot each one. The next group walked up, and we shot them just the same. The dead Jews fell on top of each other. Quite honestly, it resulted in general chaos. Not chaos in the sense that the Jews were uncooperative, these conniving rats lined up to be slaughtered. They deserved to die, and we were overjoyed to wipe out every Yid in Kiev. We shot over 33,000 Jews in two days. I am proud to report that Kiev is now Judenrein, or free of Jews.

Krueger gave Hecker a smile and watched the Ukrainian Wachmen look at each other in disbelief. Some were from Kiev and played at Babi Yar as kids. "The chaos was in the process, very messy and unorganized. The Jews valuables were mostly lost or stolen by the locals. It wasn't the organized German way we conduct our business. Reichsfuhrer-SS Himmler decided to complete this mission in a smarter way."

"However," Krueger continued in a professorial tone "33,000 Jews is just point zero three percent of 9 million. We did not even wipe out one-half of one percent of European Jews. 33,000 dead Jews may sound like many, but it's barely a dent in the massive goals of the Final Solution. It also took too long and was too costly in ammunition and manpower. Some of the men in my Einsatzgruppen began to complain of the physical and mental exhaustion that came with shooting so many people at close range. I hold no ill will towards my men. They did a difficult job in difficult conditions."

Krueger gave Hecker a nod of his head, then redirected back to the class. "Scharfuhrer Hecker was exemplary during the aktion at Babi Yar. He was one of my best men. He showed no mercy when Jewish mothers begged for their lives and the lives of their children. Many of the children were at a very tender age. Most men would have succumbed to such heart-wrenching scenes, but Scharfuhrer Hecker was my most lethal and barbaric weapon. He not only viewed it as his duty, he thoroughly enjoyed the work. Ankle deep in blood. He made the Jews climb on top of their murdered friends and families, and then shot them all. He did this repeatedly for two days straight. I believe Scharfuhrer Hecker personally killed over 5,000 Jews."

Krueger paused and took a sip of water. Vlad and the rest of the class were listening in disbelief to such a story. "I witnessed him saving ammunition by lining up three or four children and killing them all with one shot through the heart. He even picked up a boy about two years of age, held him upside down by the ankles, and tore him in half. The boys' naked and terrorized mother unwisely tried intervening. Hecker gnawed a huge chunk of flesh out of her left breast, spit it in her mouth and smashed in her face with a rifle butt. It almost gives me an erection just thinking about it. He is a hero to the German people and a legend in the SS. Hecker is a man of steel and total ruthlessness. He is a fine example for all of you to follow."

"Thank you, Commandant Krueger," Hecker said proudly. "It was indeed an honor to serve with you, and I look forward to our next step in making The Reich and the world Judenrein."

Krueger continued in a more excited voice "We have devised a plan that will greatly accelerate and streamline the process in which we organize, plunder, and exterminate these vermin. We have constructed a special camp in the woods outside Belzec. It will serve as an industrial-grade center designed for the sole purpose of the orderly killing of Jews. What Henry Ford did for automobile production, Belzec will accomplish for Aktion Reinhard. We will incorporate the same process for assembly line murder of every Jew in the General Government. That is what you will be learning how to do here at Rabka before duty at Belzec. Our syllabus consists of orderly and quick elimination of the Jews, organizing their valuables and personal items for shipment to the Reich, and disposing of the corpses."

Krueger gave an evil grin and said "Don't worry, it will also be fun. We will teach Jew torture, strangulation, burning, whipping, hanging, skull splitting, one shot kills to the back of the neck, and a few other games. But for the most part, this is crowd control and total deception up to the last minute so we can kill as calmly as possible. We believe a way has been found using gas chambers to wipe out entire trainloads of Yids in just a few hours. It is a very exciting time to be alive, gentlemen. I want you to study hard, pay attention, and learn. By the end of February, you will be experts and full participants in Aktion Reinhard and the Final Solution to the Jewish Question. You are expected at Belzec by mid-March, and killing operations on a mass scale will begin shortly thereafter. Heil Hitler"

Chapter 18

St. Louis Park, MN
Present Day

Max walked into Bunny's Bar for happy hour after listening to, and recording, Vlad's story the night before. A spring cold front with rain was passing through, and Max liked the darker ambiance of Bunny's when the weather turned inclement. Dane took his seat at the end of the bar, where only friends of the owner or the well-connected sat. It is a quirky and unwritten Bunny's policy never to occupy that particular area unless one belonged.

Max sat down next to Dane, and the bartender with the dubious nickname 'Crazy' immediately approached. Crazy and other bartenders at Bunny's would typically wait on those in the designated area first, much to the chagrin of other customers waiting for service. "Coors light and a shot of Cuervo please" Max requested.

"Starting off with a shot? That long of a day or what?" Dane asked half-jokingly.

"The law firm had a solid day, except for the avalanche of interview requests, which I am getting used to. It was a long one with my dad last night, and I haven't had a drink since we ended our conversation. We decided to take this evening off and give each other some breathing room. It's an intense story, and hard for him to relive that chapter of his life. Quite honestly, it's hard for me to listen to. But, what he's telling me is so morbidly fascinating, that I almost can't get enough. It's a strange phenomenon."

Crazy, the bartender, set down the beer and shot in front of Max, with no training wheels for the tequila. Max always declined salt or lime and preferred to shoot it straight. He drank the shot in front of Dane, quickly followed by a long sip of beer to cover the aftertaste. Max glanced around the room and felt no stares from fellow patrons. He knew Bunny's was safe territory from being approached and asked about the exploding news story. Even Crazy had the sense to leave Max alone, except refilling his beer and shot glass.

Dane sat patiently waiting for Max to speak first. Dane figured Max would drive the narrative. He would simply listen and dispense advice where appropriate. "I like your advice about the press conference, but we are still not there yet. My dad has gotten to the point of the story where he attended an SS operated school in Poland. The school existed for the purpose of training him and others to kill Jews."

Dane gave Max a quizzical look and said "They had schools for killing Jews? I have never heard of such a thing. Maybe I was too hungover and missed that lecture in Professor Mulholland's world history class at the university."

Max gave a laugh, "Buddy, you missed many lectures due to the three wise men of Jimmy, Johnny, and Jack. I still can't believe you managed to graduate with a 4.0 GPA. But no, good old Professor Mulholland did not discuss this place. It was located in a town called Rabka. I have never heard of it until last night. Crazy stuff he went through there, he told me they shot kids for target practice."

Dane's eyes widened. "Holy shit."

Max gazed down at the bar. "Exactly."

"I hate to ask," Dane said breaking the promise he made to himself not to drive the conversation. "But then it's true? He did serve in Nazi death camps?"

Vlad took his second shot of tequila, set down the glass, and picked up his Coors Light. "I'm not sure yet because we haven't gotten that far, but it's looking that way. The twist is he was forced to do it. It most definitely sounds like coercion, not collusion."

Dane pondered the legal aspects about the new revelations. "Knowing your dad for all these years, I believe that. But regarding everyone else who is following this story, including my bosses in Washington, proving that fact will be almost impossible I am afraid."

"I know, but maybe something will surface during our future conversations, or somebody will emerge from the woodwork. Given the worldwide media attention, it's not impossible for a person to corroborate my dad's version of events." Max said speaking like a defense attorney.

Dane finished his Manhattan and signaled 'one more' to Crazy, then spoke "I need to schedule a preliminary hearing to determine probable cause against your dad. Fortunately for you, I pushed it until mid-July. You and Vlad have almost two months to get through his story and make sense of what happened. But I am here to tell you, the excuse of 'I was following orders' has not held up in court. From the Nazi's to Mai

Lai, to Iraq, I have never seen a successful defense based on that argument."

Max nodded in agreement with Dane "From all of my years as a defense attorney, duress has worked as an argument for some things like being coerced into signing a contract. But never for murder." Dane and Max chatted some more, finished their drinks, gave each other a brotherly hug and left Bunny's at the same time in separate cars.

Max was hungry and decided to stop at Lunds grocery store, in an eclectic and rambunctious part of Minneapolis known as Uptown. Max always liked Uptown with its interesting stores, cafes, and bars. He and Dane were roommates for many years in the area, after graduation from the University of Minnesota Law School. They enjoyed a fun lifestyle of two young and unattached attorneys. Max often reminisced about those magical and carefree years that blew by way too fast.

Max waited at the deli counter to order his favorites, Thai peanut pasta, and chocolate dessert when a gentle hand touched his shoulder. Max turned and saw his former girlfriend of two years standing next to him. She was alone and looking good. "Susan, how are you?" Max asked in a surprised voice. "You look great."

Susan stood confidently with her blue eyes locked on Max, "I am well. I went out with some friends from work for happy hour and thought I would pick up some dinner on my way home. It seems every time I turn on the television or open a paper, there's a story about your dad. I hope both of you are doing okay."

Max flashed his legendary smile "It's been a rough few weeks, but we are doing well. It's been tough on dad, but he will get through it. By the way, I was at Bunny's with Dane Atkinson. He will love it when I tell him we saw each other. He always thought the world of you, and still does." They laughed, shared some more small talk and walked out together towards their cars.

Susan was the first to ask "Anybody special in your life right now, Max?"

Max smiled again, "No, how about you?"

Susan gave max a seductive look "Nothing committed. Are you going to your dad's or your place?"

Max eyed her back, both did happy hour, and this was a serendipitous moment that he decided not to let pass. "I'm on my way home and have a nice bottle of wine, why don't you come over with your food and we can have dinner together."

Susan gave Max a sexy nod of her head and flipped her hair "Still the huge house on Lake Harriet?"

Max nodded and smiled. "See you there." Max and Susan got into their cars and drove out of the parking lot, Max laughed and said to himself "It's going to be a good night," and indeed it was.

The next day at work was busy, and the law office of Chayka, Kimo and Gust hummed with activity. Max sat in his spacious office downloading Vlad's video onto his computer and Google Docs. He wanted a backup just in case somebody tried to launch a cyber-attack on the company's internal computer system. With worldwide media attention, Max was certain there would be groups opposed to him representing his dad and may try to get revenge somehow. He alerted the law firm's IT people to redouble their security measures and hired a retired FBI agent to help with physical security of the office and employees. Max left nothing to chance.

Max and Vlad agreed to get together again that evening and continue their talk. Max left the office at 5:30 pm with his video equipment, and was eager to learn more about his dad's early life. Vlad said not to worry about dinner, but bring a bottle of scotch instead. Max worried his dad might be drinking too much, but at his age and what he had been through, Max decided to give him a break and pick one up on the way. He walked in as Vlad's grandfather clock chimed to six o'clock. The news was on, and Vlad sat on the sofa with his cocktail glass almost empty. "Dad, I told you to quit watching this stuff, it's not doing either of us any favors."

"I can't believe the things they are saying about me, not one of these damn reporters has the story even half right. I am ready to call up one of these jerks, and give them a piece of my mind" Vlad said in a tone that Max didn't hear very often. His Ukrainian accent grew more pronounced when driven to anger or annoyance.

"Look, Dad," Max said in a calm voice. "I understand reporters getting it wrong and spreading false information. Believe me. It happens all the time. But I don't watch them do it, and I don't dwell on it to the point of anger. Does you and nobody any good. When the time is right, I may hold a press conference and set these guys straight. In the meantime, please turn off the TV when they start talking about you."

Vlad had a sheepish frown. "I'm sorry son, didn't mean to sound off and I appreciate what you are doing. I won't turn on the news until it's time for sports and weather. It's all I care about these days."

"Sounds good dad, I just want you to take it easy on yourself," Max said as he brought Vlad a fresh scotch on the rocks and set up his video equipment. "Did you eat the rest of that Kovbasa for dinner or do you want me to make you something?"

Vlad took a long sip of his drink. "I finished the sausage last night and made myself a grilled cheese a while ago. It's all I really need at my age, and would rather drink my dinner anyway."

Max gave his dad a wary smile. "I am happy you are eating, just go easy on the sauce. Okay?"

Max set up the recording equipment and sat down in the living room across from Vlad. "Dad, I have been pondering how we present your defense in court and to the public. Dane Atkinson correctly said the argument of simply following orders would not work. They would laugh us out of court, so we need to come up with a plausible explanation."

Vlad interrupted "Max, my boy, there is no plausible explanation. As a matter of fact, unless somebody was there, it's impossible to explain. How do you explain unhinged hate, robbery, torture and mass murder? How do you explain shooting those kids as a Christmas present for my Commandant? There is no good explanation. I did horrible things to save myself. Tell that to the judge."

"Okay dad, I understand. Or at least I am beginning to understand, and you opening up to me is a gift which I greatly appreciate." Max said as he calmed down his dad. "The more you tell me about that time, the more I can help. When the time is right, I also need to understand my mom. I have been thinking about her non-stop since we started having these talks."

Vlad gave his son a loving look. "Don't worry, Max. We will get there together. I am ready to start where we left off."

Max turned on the power to the recording equipment. "Ready when you are dad." Vlad set down his drink, took a deep breath and momentarily closed his eyes. He began to speak.

Chapter 19
Mid-February 1942
SS Police School. Rabka, Poland

It was a cold Tuesday morning at Rabka, and Vlad could hear the wind-blown sleet tapping against his dormitory window. The wake-up alarm bells were ringing an hour earlier than normal, and Vlad sensed something out of the ordinary was brewing. He looked out and saw three newly constructed wooden structures on the soccer field. The Wachmen were told to dress warmly for outdoor exercises at yesterday's final afternoon class. Vlad grabbed his overcoat and headed down to breakfast.

During the past seven weeks, Vlad and the company received indoor classroom lectures and demonstrations detailing how the industrial-grade homicide and larceny would be carried out.

These were important topics for murder and robbery on an unprecedented scale, but with few hands-on activities. The lack of real world violence helped sooth Vlad's psyche, and his despair had somewhat abated. But he still feared the future, which he grew weary of doing.

Today had a different feel. There was more commotion than usual both inside the building and outside around the soccer field. Vlad, Pavel and the rest of the company gathered in the main dining hall at seven a.m. dressed in their winter gear as instructed. Hecker stood at the podium with a microphone and began to speak as the company seated themselves. "This company has made fine progress in all areas of instruction. The Commandant and I are pleased. Today we will be doing a live exercise simulating a real world scenario at Belzec. As you have been taught, Jews will arrive at Belzec in trainloads of up to 50 cattle cars. Each cattle car will hold at least 100 Jews. That's 5,000 or more to be processed on a daily basis. Your exercise today will consist of both observing and participating in this procedure from beginning to end."

Hecker took a sip from his coffee cup and continued. "Of course, we cannot simulate the exact conditions at Belzec, but this should give you a reasonable idea of what is expected. A high-ranking SS officer will be selecting a few Jews from the group who are fit for work here at Rabka. The rest will all die. At Belzec we will use gas chambers and shooting pits, today will be somewhat different. Now fall out to the assembly area outside for further instruction."

Vlad and the company assembled in the courtyard. All could see three newly constructed sheds with waist high coiled barbed wire surrounding the soccer field. Behind the enclosed soccer field, Vlad saw mounds of dirt indicating a mass grave in the woods. Each Wachman had his loaded rifle, loaded sidearm, and bull whip.

Orlov spoke first. "Scharfuhrer Hecker, do we get to kill a Jew today? I am having a hard time eating because my hunger to kill Jews is stronger than my hunger for food. I am becoming malnourished both in body and spirit, please sir."

Hecker gave a proud smile to Orlov and replied in a loud voice to the entire group, "Would 500 Jews suffice? We have rounded up families from area villages. The SS wisely focused on kidnapping younger families with multiple children. We are going to simulate processing five cattle cars of Jews. We don't have a train, but these vermin will be unloaded from the trucks all at once. The Commandant, Rabka SS staff, and I will supervise and give direction. We want you to observe, participate as ordered, learn, and become hardened. The scenes would be heartbreaking for the weak of character, but not for the strong willed Wachman. You need to ignore the pleas of parents begging for their children's lives and do your job without pity. For this is what you will be doing within just six weeks. If any of you don't like what you see, do us all a favor and join the Jews in their fate this morning. Kids have their playgrounds, and this one is mine. Your SS masters make the rules and not you, don't fuck with my playground."

The company of Trawniki Wachmen divided up to perform different tasks. Many armed Wachman were stationed at the unloading area. Intimidation would quell any ideas of resistance by the doomed. It was essential to separate the men from the women in a quick and efficient manner. One Wachman stood with a rifle every 25 feet where the Jews would disembark. It served as a wall of violence ready to be unleashed if they did not comply with SS demands.

Other Wachman were posted at the valuables depository, also simply known as 'the cashier.' Jews would be forced to surrender all gold, diamonds, watches, money, and other precious items under pain of death. The searches by the SS and Trawniki Men, especially of Jewish women, would become legendary in their savagery. More Trawniki Men were posted in the barber building, where the hair of Jewish women would be shaved and shipped back to the Reich in bales to be used for submarine insulation and the making of slippers. After the Jews were separated, had deposited their valuables and had their heads shaved, they were to be herded into the corridor and driven into the gas chamber building. The corridor, or the tube, is where Vlad, Pavel, and Orlov were ordered to stand post.

Suddenly a mass of transport trucks pulled up and unloaded 500 Jews in the designated area. Families naturally clung together, and husbands tried to shield their wives from the lustful leers of the Wachmen. The SS were shouting and screaming orders at the Jews. Leashed and muzzled German Shepherds barked, snarled and lunged at the frightened people. The Wachmen observed how the SS cracked whips above the Jews heads while ordering women to the left and men to the right. The sound of the whiplash served as a menacing motivator for Jewish men to let go of their families and form the columns the SS wanted.

Vlad, Pavel, and Orlov watched from the tube as the Jewish men and women were separated in the unloading area. Their fellow Trawniki Men helped forcefully pull apart families and friends, to achieve the desires of their SS masters as quickly as possible. Some Jews resisted, and the Wachmen were encouraged by the SS to use rifle butt blows to get them in line. Most of the Wachmen happily obliged. After watching the SS example, they also became more aggressive with the Jews. Vlad watched Orlov smile and laugh as the pushing, shoving, bullying and shouting intensified while the Wachmen took cues from the SS.

Orlov turned to Vlad and Pavel and said in a high-pitched and excited voice as he rubbed his crotch area "This is the most beautiful sight I have ever seen in my life. Finally, these fucking Jews are getting what they deserve. Do you think Hecker would mind if I pulled out the best young girl and raped her?"

Pavel glowered at Orlov. "Shut the fuck up, you idiot." Orlov docilely complied.

Once the Jews were separated and lines formed, Commandant Krueger stepped up to a microphone and spoke "Jews, I am Commandant Krueger, and you are at Rabka transit camp. You will be soon transported east for work. All are needed to help on farms to grow food for the German Army. The work will be hard, but you will be well fed, housed, and treated fairly."

Many of the Jews clapped and shouted out "Thank you, Commandant."

Krueger continued in a calm but authoritative tone "Typhus epidemics are spreading in the area, and we need your cooperation. You will have your clothes disinfected and take a warm disinfecting shower. After which your clothes will be returned to you. Be sure to tie your shoes together and keep your clothes neatly folded. All valuables will be turned in to the cashier, you will get a receipt, and they will be returned after your shower. Also, for the sake of hygiene, all women will have their heads shaved. Don't worry. It will grow back. We have lots to get done in a short period, as your comfortable passenger train leaves for the east in exactly one hour. I will now turn you over to my caring staff for processing. Scharfuhrer Hecker, please proceed."

Hecker called out "Jewish Men please move to the middle of the courtyard and undress. Then proceed to the cashier and deposit your valuables. Jewish women, please undress your children first and yourselves next, then move on to the barber for your haircut. It's cold, and the faster you move, the quicker you get a warm shower. We have to do this quickly. Your comfortable transport train waits to bring you all to your new homes."

Orlov looked at Pavel and Vlad and wondered aloud. "Why are they so polite to them? We know and believe they are subhuman scum and deserve to die. I don't get it."

Vlad, Pavel, and Orlov watched in silent amazement as the Jews undressed, leaving their shoes tied together and clothes neatly piled as asked. The crying of the children and mothers weeping overpowered the sounds of barking dogs and SS commands. They proceeded to the unheated cashier shack, naked and freezing, with valuables in hand and were issued receipts. The SS closely supervised the Wachmen and secured the small piles of diamonds, gold, silver, cash, and watches.

As the Jewish men exited the depository, they were driven to the tube while the women were escorted to the barber. Everything went according to plan. The SS were teaching the Wachmen to be fast and keep the Jews from resisting. A state of bewilderment and confusion, but not panic, is what the SS wanted from the condemned. Jewish men and boys over 14 years old bottlenecked at the entrance of the tube. Vlad and Pavel stood speechless next to the doors of the wooden structure and stared at the spectacle of 250 naked and freezing men eager to get inside.

Suddenly Commandant Krueger spoke up loudly from the rear of the group. "Jews, move quickly, the water is getting cold." The naked men were pushed through the tube by the SS and towards Vlad, Pavel, and Orlov. As the Jews approached the open doors to the building, they began to recoil and step back. The men realized they were being driven through the shack, and into the rear of a moving van. At that moment the bullwhips were brought out, and the SS began landing lashes on the bare backs of the freezing men. "Use your whips and rifle butts to drive these pigs inside," Hecker shouted tensely to Vlad, Pavel, and Orlov. Hecker wanted to impress the Commandant and have this crucial part of the process go flawlessly.

Hecker, Commandant Krueger, and other SS used their whips in an overhand fashion. They struck them in the head, shoulders and upper back. To escape the blows, the Jews ran into the wooden shed and out the opposite side onto a ramp. The ramp led up to the moving truck with its rear doors open. The inside cargo area was lined with aluminum sheeting, with an open air grate in the middle of the floor. As the Jewish men were crammed into the truck, it became overcrowded and more could not fit in.

Hecker screamed at Vlad, Pavel, and Orlov. "Do your goddamned job and make all of them fit into the back of this truck, or I will throw you in as well. Now get off your asses and make it happen." All three stood frozen to this point, overwhelmed by the events and unsure what exactly to do. Orlov acted first and took a position directly behind the Jews who would not fit in, and began lashing out wildly with his whip.

He cursed and screamed at the Jews in a possessed like manner "You filthy animals, get in this truck or I will tear every piece of diseased Jewish skin off your bodies." Orlov surprised Pavel, Vlad and even Hecker who all took a few steps back to ensure they would not be struck by the uncontrolled outburst of anger that overtook Orlov and his whip. Orlov managed to drive every Jewish man into the back of the moving truck. At that moment, two SS men slammed the back doors shut. The fate of the Jewish men and older children was sealed.

They watched the SS driver get out of the front, and remove the customized, flexible exhaust hose from the muffler. The driver attached the hose onto the grate, diverting the exhaust into the cargo area holding the Jews. The SS driver fired up the engine and revved it. He gave a thumbs up to the Commandant, while Orlov tried to overcome an awkward bout of nervous laughter.

The Jewish men pounded on the sheet metal lining the inside walls. Vlad could hear the screams and cries of the condemned. They were sounds that Vlad, Pavel, and even Orlov didn't know humans could make. Guttural and primitive howls released by the subcortex part of the brain, hidden away since caveman days. Other Jews were beginning to say the Kaddish, the Jewish prayer for the dead. Vlad recognized the prayer from Jewish funeral processions back in Kiev during his childhood. The truck drove off, not to return for 30 minutes as the carbon monoxide did its deadly job.

Another gas van waited off to the side and backed into position, ready to receive the women and children who just finished their haircuts. Vlad, Pavel, Orlov, and Hecker walked through the shed and took their post again at the end of the tube.

Hecker broke the silence as they waited "Orlov that was fine work. We need to be as efficient as possible and stuff as much Jewish shit as we can into the gas vans. Same goes for the gas chambers at Belzec. We don't want to leave any room. It's amazing how many Jews we can fit when using whips, bayonets, and rifle butts. When the women and children come through the tube, be just as ruthless. Don't be affected by the fact they are women and kids. All Jews must die. That is the will of the Fuhrer, and we are carrying out his divine wishes. Jesus had his Apostles. The Fuhrer has us."

The doors to barber shed burst open. 250 women and children ran out and were driven to the tube's entrance. Vlad could tell the women sensed their impending fate more than the men did. They heard the violent commotion and cries of the men just a few minutes earlier. There was nothing to muffle out the sound at Rabka, which would be corrected as the SS took detailed notes of processes and procedures. Music would be played over loudspeakers at Belzec to drown out the screams. The women panicked and resisted walking through the tube and into the shed.

Hecker again shouted out. "Jewesses and children, the water is getting cold. Hurry to the warm disinfecting showers."

The naked and shaved women started crying and moaning while shielding their children. Their intuition was spot on. As they were driven through the tube, some lost control of their bodily functions and defecated onto the frozen ground.

One woman whose eyes were on fire broke through the moans and started screaming at Vlad. "You are murderers of innocent women and children. God will have his vengeance upon you."

The line into the shed stopped as Vlad stood frozen with a whip in hand. Hecker calmly walked up to the woman, drew his pistol, and shot her in the head. Her eight-year-old boy dropped to his knees sobbing next to his mother's body. Orlov raised his rifle and shot him through the chest, spewing blood on the bodies of the remaining naked women.

The Commandant barked out "Drive these vermin into the shed and transport truck, show absolutely no mercy and your reward will be great."

Pavel and Vlad raised their whips and began cracking at head level. They had practiced for months and became proficient at the art. Vlad tried to aim high but accidentally struck a beautiful teenage Jewish girl in the face. Blood spattered back at him from the gaping wound on her left cheek, which immediately caused him to vomit. The wounds on the girl terrorized the women, who helped keep the children in line moving. As the women and children crushed into the back of the second gas van, there were about 50 people who could not fit, most of whom were young mothers with children.

Orlov again took the initiative and began wildly flailing his whip, driving the screaming children into the cold van. An SS officer started picking up the small children and shoved them in-between the space of women's heads and the ceiling of the moving van. Orlov drove in the rest of the bloodied and naked women with his whip and screams of "Jew whores, I command you like Moses to squeeze in. Make room or I will rip your kids apart."

Once the van was full, the doors were hermetically sealed shut and the exhaust pipe attached to the floor grate. The driver did not wait this time. He drove off immediately as the screams of the children were hard to listen to for all.

The van drove away, and Hecker walked up to Vlad. "Chayka, nice shot to that Jew's disgusting face, but what the hell is with you throwing up? Does this work not agree with you?"

Pavel stepped in and spoke right away, "Scharfuhrer Hecker, the shit from the Jews smells awful, as many soiled themselves on their way to the trucks. I almost vomited. Wachman Chayka is most fit for duty."

Hecker gave Vlad a nod and said with a smile "Their shit does stink. It must be all that matzah. You now see why the Fuhrer wisely enacted racial purity laws. No SS man would ever stick his dick in that nasty filth."

Hecker was interrupted as the first gas van carrying the men returned. Vlad noticed the quiet coming from the back of the truck. Commandant Krueger ordered in a gleeful tone, "Trawniki Wachmen, follow me to the forest behind Scharfuhrer Hecker's playground."

Vlad and the company walked through an opening in the coiled barbed wire encircling the soccer field. They continued to the woods where a mass grave had been excavated the day before. The men stood in silent macabre curiosity as the van backed up to the edge of the pit. The driver got as close as possible without the entire truck going in the wide hole in the ground and turned off the engine. Two SS men opened the rear doors. Vlad, Pavel, and Orlov stared unbelievably at the gruesome sight inside. 250 naked men stood upright with arms and legs intertwined with each other. All were dead. Their skin had a bluish tint, urine and feces covered the sheet metal floor.

Vlad was surprised they didn't all tumble out of the door. The Jews became one compressed mass of death that needed to be separated individually. As the rear of the van aired out, Hecker commanded "All of you Wachmen get these Jews out of the van and into the grave. For them to all fit, you must stack them correctly. Just think of a can of sardines, neatly stacked row by row and head to foot. Do the same with these corpses."

Vlad did as ordered, and the intensity of the manual labor surprised him. Each body took two men to carry, and the job of correct grave stacking took considerable manpower. To get 250 dead bodies out of the van and into the grave as ordered took the entire company an hour. After the first van had left, the second backed up to the half-filled grave in the same manner. The doors opened, and this time small children tumbled onto the ground. Many of the Wachmen vomited at the terrifying spectacle.

Hecker demanded, "Set the little runts aside until we put their dead whore mothers in. Then toss the small ones on top. If this grave is properly filled, the last of the bodies should be about two feet above ground level. We will then cover up this filth with a mound of dirt. After a few days, they will settle, and the dirt mound should not be noticeable after a few weeks."

When the Wachmen finished, all were sweating in the cold and out of breath. Hecker surveyed the crime scene proudly "Reconvene at 8 a.m. tomorrow in the classroom for debriefing and process improvement discussion. Come prepared with your ideas on today's action. Plenty of alcoholic refreshments are available in the dining hall. The Commandant and I are proud of each and every one of you. This is hard but most necessary work. That is all, dismissed."

Pavel and Vlad walked silently back to the main building through the snow. They entered the dining hall, and Vlad grabbed a bottle of vodka. He drank a third of it under a minute and walked upstairs. He fell into his bed crying softly so others would not hear him.

Vlad lay on his back intoxicated, while staring at the ceiling and began to recite the Penitential Act he said at Mass on Sundays. "I confess to almighty God, and you my brothers and sisters, that I have greatly sinned, in my thoughts and my words, in what I have done and what I have failed to do. Therefore I ask the Blessed Virgin Mary, and you my brothers and sisters, to pray for me to the Lord our God."

Any angels, saints or even the Virgin Mary interceding in this hell seemed like a distant dream. His mental despair and anguish were returning with a vengeance, and the chasm between Vlad and God grew rapidly. Reconciliation would be a long way off.

Chapter 20
Minneapolis, MN
Present Day

Max met with local columnist Carl Jeffries at Bunny's Bar for lunch. Carl Jeffries was the preeminent columnist for the leading newspaper in town and scooped more stories than the rest of the newsroom combined. Max and Carl were friends for over 30 years and had built a solid working relationship. Carl got the inside story on many high profile criminal cases, and Max gained access to information only Carl knew from his many trusted sources.

Barbara waited on customers at Bunny's for over 30 years and knew all of the regulars by name. She set down two bottles of beer, burgers, and orders of fries on the well-worn table for Max and Carl. "I've been following the news about your dad and must say that I find the whole thing hard to believe. I just feel awful for everybody." Barbara then grabbed Max's hand. "It's been awhile since Vlad has been in here, can I make a burger to go and you get it to him? They are great reheated."

Max squeezed her hand before letting go, "That's an excellent idea. Please have it ready to go in an hour, and I will bring it to him tonight with love from you."

Barbara turned away, Max and Carl took a bite of their burgers. Carl gave Max a grin "God I love these things, I swear it will be the death of me someday."

Max smiled replying "It would be a hell of a way to go, my friend."

Carl took a sip of beer. "You have no idea how many reporters have contacted me trying to get bits of information about you and your dad. They all believe I have inside information based on our friendship and assume I would be willing to share. TMZ even offered me $25,000 for anything they could use."

Max gave Carl a surprised look and said "25 grand? That's all?" They both laughed. Max then asked, "If you had the whole story, what would you do?"

Carl leaned back and took another sip of beer. "I'm not going to lie to you, Max. It would probably be the biggest story of my career. I consider this conversation off the record and confidential. Any article I write on this would most likely be a series, encompassing three or four Sunday papers. I would also do for you what I have never done for anybody. Allow you preview the series before it goes to print. I would also agree to limited editing and content suggestions, but overall it's my call, and you need to trust me on that. I have met your dad a number of times, but don't know him that well. I would be able to bring a perspective that you, with all due respect, cannot provide."

Max picked up his burger, set it back on his plate and said to Carl "I am considering a press conference once my dad finishes telling me his entire story. I have been recording him recounting the time spent in forced service to the SS. I think we are about half way there, but not sure. So far, it's been an incredible journey listening to his story. It's amazing how the old man's memory remains so vivid. For a guy in his early 90's, he is sharp as a tack. Anyway, what are your thoughts about me holding a press conference, versus you doing a series of articles about his life?"

Carl thought a minute. "You need to make the decision that works best for you and Vlad, but one consideration is controlling the message. At a press conference, the questions will not be given to you on a sheet of paper in advance. You have no control over what's being asked, and the questions will be leading. Reporters may be out for blood, and if they smell it during a press conference, the sharks will come out for the kill. The story is fascinating enough. Then throw gas on the fire with you being a prominent person who is Jewish, his kid, and his defense attorney. That fact brings this to a level I have never seen before. Personally, I would take the offer to help shape the story in a way that tells the truth of course, but in a fashion limiting embarrassment to you or your dad."

Max nodded in agreement. Even though Carl's advice could be construed as a bit self-serving, Max knew he was right. A press conference could spiral out of control fast, even for an experienced and media-savvy person like Max. Max believed his personal reputation was secondary to preserving Vlad's legacy. Nothing else mattered.

"Okay, here is the plan," Max said to Carl as they finished their burger and beers. "I will scrub the idea of a press conference, with you writing a series of articles. I will take you up on advance reading and content advice. Plan on me turning over the pertinent video to you in the next few weeks when we finish up. But..."

Carl gave Max a quizzical expression, "But what?"

Maxed diverted his eyes down at the table, and then back at Carl. "We have not reached the point in the story about my mom. My dad told me she died during the war. Her life has always been a confounding mystery to me. It's something I have naively taken at face value. For being a tough cross-examiner, I never pressed the subject. It probably sounds strange to hear, but there has been a quiet detente between my dad and me on that subject. Apparently, Vlad promised my mom before she died that he would raise me Jewish. At least that's the romanticized version of events. It's a great narrative of love and devotion, but it's not the truth. Don't get me wrong, Carl. My Dad has been a loving, full supporter of my Jewish life. But it obviously doesn't add up, and the news will be a very personal revelation to me. I am not quite sure it should be on the front page of the Sunday paper."

Carl gave Max an empathetic smile. "Don't worry. Your mom has nothing to do with this story. It's about Vlad and to a lesser extent you. If your mom comes into play as a larger part of the narrative, and you decide it will help explain your dad's actions during the war, then it's something we can approach together. One more thing, the opportunity I offered of limited editing and content control must remain strictly between us. If any of my bosses or co-workers got wind of you collaborating on a series about Vlad, it would be my reputation and job. At this point in our careers, it's a headache that neither of us wants or needs."

Barbara brought over Vlad's burger wrapped in foil and innocently asked "Max, did your dad work in those awful death camps and help kill all of those poor people?"

Max looked surprised, but not angry. He knew Barbara asked out of concern and kindness. She had known Max as a customer since his days at the University of Minnesota when he and Dane Atkinson would bring their dates to Bunny's for dinner before fraternity formals. When the other guys went to fancy and expensive restaurants with their ladies, Dane and Max went here. At first, they got laughed at their by fellow fraternity brothers. By their senior year in college, Bunny's became the cool and hip place to bring a girl. Barbara waited on them ever since.

Max replied quietly to Barbara "He may have been involved, but was forced to do so or face certain death himself. It's something he has kept hidden away for many years, and I am only learning about it now."

Barbara gave a smile and said "Believe me, boys. I have tried to hide the past as well. But throwing away the pint of ice cream I ate from the night before doesn't mean I won't gain the weight." They all laughed, and Max gave Carl a knowing look acknowledging the simple homespun wisdom that Barbara would give her legions of customers.

They paid the tab and stepped outside into the early afternoon sun, the spring rains finally moved out, and both commented how green everything was getting. After some brief small talk, Carl said to Max, "Do not email anything. Text me on my cell. We will connect again in a few weeks to plan our landmark piece."

Max spent the rest of his day tending to clients who paid the bills, much to the happiness of the partners at the law firm of Chayka, Kimo, and Gust. All of Max's clients had the means to pay his sizeable hourly rate and were due equal protection under the law. The drug dealing kid with wealthy parents, and the local NFL great who once again beat up his girlfriend, all seemed petty in their legal needs compared to his dad. Max always tried to stay clear of judging the moral turpitude of his clients, but he knew the full character of Vlad. Focusing on much else this afternoon was proving futile. Realizing as much, Max left the office early to bring Vlad his burger and continue their talk.

"Dad, Barbara at Bunny's sends this burger with love," Max said as he walked into Vlad's house.

Vlad gave Max a surprised look from the sofa. "I haven't had a Bunny's burger since last year, please heat it up in the microwave and pour your dad a scotch. I miss places like Bunny's and seeing old friends like Barbara. My driving is so limited these days. Maybe I shouldn't complain. Many people my age don't drive at all. Hell, most people my age are six feet under."

Max walked from the kitchen to the living room with a plate of food, and a glass of scotch for Vlad. Max had heated up the burger and put some Old Dutch potato chips on the side. Vlad loved scooping up any mess left on the plate with an Old Dutch. It was not the proper table manners Vlad regularly preached to Max during his younger years, but it remained one of Vlad's simple pleasures in life. When Max would question Vlad on the etiquette using a chip to scoop up leftover Sloppy Joe's during his childhood, Vlad would smile and say half-kiddingly "Do as I say, not as I do."

Vlad drank his scotch and ate his burger. They spoke about Max's meeting earlier in the day with Carl Jeffries. Vlad seemed comfortable with the idea of an article series, which likely would be picked up by other media outlets throughout the world. Vlad approved the idea of Carl Jeffries writing the piece. Carl had always been kind to Max. Vlad trusted Carl's judgment and fairness in what could be a permanent record of his character. Vlad understood that reputation was beyond his control, but character firmly within his grasp. Vlad also understood his time with the SS made up part of his moral fabric, but not all of it. He certainly grasped the notion the rest of world simply viewed him as a Nazi.

Vlad finished dinner with a second scotch in hand and relaxed. Max began to guide the conversation back to Rabka and his state of mind after murdering 500 people in gas vans. Max turned on the video equipment and could see the recollection of that time come to the forefront of Vlad's memory bank. Vlad started where he left off and began speaking in general terms about the state of the world when he turned 18 years old.

"I believe that time was the most violent and tumultuous in the history of the world. Never before, and hopefully never again, will humanity experience such a war. Never again can state sanctioned wholesale murder against a single people occur. When you think about it, the war raged from Europe to Asia and everywhere in between. The year 1942 was probably the most homicidal year mankind has ever seen. Unless nuclear war breaks out, it could remain that way for centuries."

Vlad halted, cleared his throat as he became emotional and continued. "I have been thinking about Pavel quite often since my arrest, and all of this came to light. My sincere belief is the Holy Spirit sent Pavel to me. Without him, I wouldn't have survived. You cannot begin to understand how broken and damaged I became. After murdering 500 people in gas vans, many of whom were young families, I languished in a deep state of despair. I truly thought things couldn't get any worse. How could they? How could things get any worse after driving 500 people to their deaths? The girl I whipped the face, the women and children we crammed into gas vans, and screams of the victims were enough to drive a sane person crazy. The lack of sleep from constant nightmares and my crumbling belief in God sent me to the breaking point. I would have either drunk myself to death or committed suicide with my Luger. I was a dead man, if not for Pavel."

Vlad took a long sip from his scotch and said, "If Pavel had not been there to be my emotional savior, I wouldn't have survived to raise you into the man you are. You know that poem about footprints in the sand? When a person questions God's existence during hard times. That truly refers to Pavel. He carried me. People forget God works through others on our behalf. Many look for divine intervention and are disappointed. God parting the Red Sea for Moses and Jesus healing the leper don't happen very often. The simple act of being present for another person during times of trouble is the divine work of the Holy Spirit. Too many people today abandon those at their low point, look at me for example. Thank God I have people like you, Dane, and Carl in my life. Otherwise, I would be fed to the wolves and most people would be happy about it."

Chapter 21
March 7th, 1942
SS Police School Rabka, Poland

The entire company assembled in the main dining area after breakfast. Each Wachman had his pack of personal items, with weapons and extra gear, neatly arranged in the back area along the walls. The March sun warmed things up and started melting the substantial snowpack. Vlad could see water dripping off the roof and passing by the windows. Training had concluded. Time for destruction on a scale Vlad and the rest of the Wachmen could not imagine rapidly approached. The selection at Chelm, basic training at Trawniki, and the school of murder at Rabka led to this graduation day. The death camp at Belzec was open and ready for transports, it just needed staff.

Five platoons would be formed out of Vlad's company, each consisting of 20 men and a platoon leader. Vlad and Pavel were both assigned to First Platoon, much to the relief of Vlad. He was happy to attempt to endure this nightmare with his most solid friend. Pavel reminded Vlad of Jesus's best friend, Peter. Jesus said to Peter "On this rock, I will build my church." Vlad could have said about Pavel "On this rock, I will survive." Vlad confided in Pavel that he would have contemplated suicide, had they been placed in different units. The names and promotions of Wachmen to become Platoon Leaders had not yet been released.

Commandant Krueger took his usual place at the podium with Scharfuhrer Hecker at this right-hand side. "Wachmen of Trawniki, I want to congratulate you all on the fine progress made here at Rabka Police School. This first class has been judged a resounding success by Reichsfuhrer-SS Himmler in Berlin. Our first camp for the relocation of the Jews located in Belzec is ready. This camp is our laboratory on perfecting the processing of Jews for Aktion Reinhard and the Final Solution. I now need to speak about a few items of great importance. Afterward, we shall conclude your commencement with the secrecy oath. You will then immediately leave this building and take the train to Belzec, where operations will commence within a few days. Are you ready?"

The men replied, "Yes, Commandant."

"Many people in the highest positions of power both here and in Berlin will be watching this operation carefully. How you conduct yourselves will be very important. All of you will be exposed to temptation, the cash and valuables these vermin will bring with them to Belzec will be most significant. Theft of any sort is strictly forbidden. This is the rightful property of The Third Reich, and stealing from The Reich will result in severe punishment. Punishment will consist of 20 lashes to the back meted out by the SS, to ultimately being thrown in the gas chambers with the Jews for repeat offenders. Remember, we choose our words carefully. Jews are being relocated for work in the east, not deported. We are also processing Jews, not murdering them. For murder is applicable only to humans, not lice infested garbage. One cannot murder a rat."

Krueger let the light laughter from some of the Wachmen subside and continued. "Please know that we are all decent men in this room. We are carrying out a necessary and sacred task that requires hardness and brutality. Many men in the SS have families. They hug their wives and tuck their children into bed when on leave and return home. I want you to be able to do the same when this most important job is completed. You can be hard and good. We are doing the world a favor and carrying out the divine wishes of our Fuhrer. Keep this in mind as you go about your jobs."

Krueger paused and lifted up a wine bottle used as a prop. "I also want to touch on the point of drinking. We want to limit drinking while on duty. Off duty platoons will have liberty to visit town, drink alcohol, and consort with local girls. Keep in mind you will need to uphold the secrecy oath that will be taken shortly, do not reveal to anyone what is happening at Belzec. Don't write about our actions in any letters, or speak about it lying in bed drunk with a Polish prostitute. Violation of the secrecy oath will result in a death sentence. You have been warned. As you all know, five platoons of 20 Wachmen have been formed. Platoons will rotate duty on a daily basis with 24 hours on duty and 24 hours off. Four platoons will be on duty at once, while one platoon is completely on leave. Start times will be staggered to ensure enough coverage for processing Jewish transports, and leave enough free time for you."

Krueger gave Scharfuhrer Hecker a nod as he backed away from the podium. Hecker stepped up to the microphone "Thank you, Commandant Krueger," Hecker said looking at Krueger as if he were his father. "Let's all give The Commandant a big round of applause for his hospitality and guidance." The room erupted in applause. Hecker continued after the applause died down. "Please know the way to promotion for you is both orderly processing of Jews, while also showing sheer brutality and vile contempt for this pig vomit. We cannot forget how conniving and underhanded these people are. The more harshly you deal with them, without interrupting the smooth process of extermination, the more promotable you will become. Without further delay, the following men are promoted to Oberwachmen or Platoon Leaders. Wachman Orlov will command First Platoon."

Vlad didn't hear the rest of the announced Platoon Leaders. Of all the Trawniki Wachmen, Vlad would be commanded by criminally insane and obsessively violent Orlov. Orlov still held a jealous grudge against Vlad for shooting the two Jewish kids at Christmas, and Hecker praising him for doing so. Orlov also suspected Vlad as a 'Jew-lover,' and instigated a whispering campaign against him at Rabka for weeks. Pavel and Vlad gave each other a worried look, then shrugged their shoulders as if to say 'the devil you know is better than the devil you don't.' If it not Orlov, Vlad guessed it would be another uneducated psychopath leading the platoon.

The Commandant stepped back up to the microphone. "Before you are dismissed, all must raise your right hand and repeat after me." Everyone raised their hands and listened for the oath. "I promise never to speak or write about my life at Rabka, Trawniki or any other duty that involves Aktion Reinhard. If I am caught violating this oath, the penalty shall be my death." The men all repeated the oath, Vlad and Pavel included.

Krueger concluded "That is all, please organize by platoon and assemble outside for transport to the train station. Comfortable passenger cars are waiting to take you all to Belzec. I also want to take this final opportunity to thank Scharfuhrer Hecker for taking you from nothings, and molding you into the men that you are. He has requested, and I have approved, his continuation with you as company Scharfuhrer.

I commend him, and will always be here to take his call if needed. That is all. You are dismissed and Heil Hitler."

The men all stood and shouted back to the Commandant "Heil Hitler."

Chapter 22
Early April 1942
Belzec Death Camp

Vlad and the Wachmen had been on duty for about a month at Belzec. They already murdered over 40,000 Jews from the Lvov Ghetto in Poland. But operations were not going as planned. Mountains of clothes, shoes, and luggage lay strewn about the camp. Piles of naked and bloated corpses lay out in the open. The undersized gas chambers proved wholly inadequate to accommodate the crush of Jews needing to be killed. Vlad later learned that future industrial death factories of places like Auschwitz studied the trials and errors of Belzec.

Most of the Wachmen, Vlad included, were in a perpetual state of drunkenness to cope with the barbaric insanity. The small detachment of SS tried their best to keep discipline. The organized and efficient German way of conducting business became overwhelmed by the daily task of robbing, murdering and disposing of thousands of people. The first attempt of mechanized murder in the history of the world had flaws, and they had much to learn.

The Wachmen had the task of shooting Jewish men, women, and children in the neck when the gas chambers were at capacity. The engine supplying carbon monoxide to the small gas chambers regularly broke down and was in need of major repairs. After the Jews had been either gassed or shot, the Wachmen dragged the corpses to shallow burial pits they manually dug by shovel. The grueling work slowed down the entire death production process considerably.

Rampant theft inside the camp created problems. Cash, diamonds, and gold to be deposited in the Reichsbank disappeared at an alarming rate. Many Wachmen used jewels to pay local women for a night of drunken sex. Rumors spread quickly in the surrounding area of what happened to the Jews. The locals saw trainloads of Jews arriving, and empty boxcars leaving. Wachmen paid their bar tabs in gold dental fillings, and most Poles drew their conclusions.

The morale among the Wachmen and SS sank to new lows. The only people enjoying the chaos were Orlov and the camp Commandant. Orlov developed the deranged habit of being unable to eat breakfast until strangling a Jewish child with his bare hands. It disturbed everybody. Even the SS viewed the practice unfavorably. The Commandant also became unhinged and lost control of camp operations. Psychotically obsessed with urinating or defecating into the mouths of Jewish teenage boys, he kept a small stable of boys near his residence for this purpose. He refused to use a regular toilet, and roamed the unloading ramp looking for Jewish boys with 'potty mouths.' This grew to be his main concern instead of murdering Jews efficiently, and the camp turned into a disorganized mess because of it.

Orlov became an expert at driving Jews into the gas chambers through the tube, using particularly sadistic and cruel methods. Vlad and Pavel were normally stationed with Orlov and witnessed him perfecting his brutal techniques. The Jews knew imminent death awaited, especially the women. Their intuition of impending doom was something Orlov sensed at Rabka and did his best to cruelly expose at Belzec. Deception ceased at the end of the tube. All that mattered to the SS at that point was driving them into the gas chambers, closing the doors, and starting up the engine piping in carbon monoxide.

One activity Orlov enjoyed greatly was picking out large breasted Jewish females and using a sharpened cavalry sword to slice off one or both breasts. He gleefully picked up the dismembered, mutilated breast and threw it in the faces of the remaining Jewish women. He would scream at the top of his voice "I will do this to all of you if this line does not speed up, all of you ugly hook-nosed Shylocks must fit inside. Now get in and take your goddamned shower." This caused such a panic among Jewish women that they willingly stuffed themselves into the gas chamber. It was perverse, disgusting, messy and yet another source of nightmares for Vlad.

On a sunny mid-April morning Vlad, Pavel and First Platoon ate a breakfast of eggs, cheese, bread and sausage in the camp mess hall. A transport of 3,000 Jews was due to arrive shortly, and the men had a long day of murderous, physical work ahead of them. Orlov sat at the end of a table closest to the door drinking black coffee. He had not yet strangled a child and couldn't eat. Orlov overslept after drinking an entire bottle of fine cognac he stole the night before. Any remaining kids from the previous day's transport had already been gassed by drunken Wachmen, causing a sullen and jealous Orlov to miss the opportunity to kill and eat.

Suddenly Orlov jumped off his bench seat and screamed, "What the fuck is this on my boots, and oh my God the smell!" Orlov looked down on the ground towards the door, covering his nose and mouth with a napkin as he began to vomit. The pungent smell overtook the mess hall, and most of the men followed Orlov by vomiting where they sat. Vlad never smelled anything so disgusting. A confusing combination of death and hell, the foulest stench any human being could imagine. The Wachmen and SS hurried outside to find the source, leaving their vomit strewn breakfasts half eaten.

The very first mass grave was the problem. 5,000 bodies putrefied and bloated at a faster rate than expected, causing the grave to heave open. Spring rains mixed with the putrefaction, resulting in overflowing bile spilling into the camp. Even an experienced and hardened killer like Scharfuhrer Hecker vomited upon inspection and stench of the grave. Hecker and Orlov became even more upset because this would cause delays in the killing.

The overflowing grave meant this transport of Jews would have to wait. The hapless Commandant told Vlad and the men he was worried other mass graves would heave open as well, and became reluctant to continue operations. Word quickly reached Reichsfuhrer-SS Himmler in Berlin, who dispatched Rabka Commandant Krueger to investigate. Delays in the destruction of Jews were unacceptable to the top Nazi officials. Any breakdown in the process would need to be addressed and corrected immediately.

Orlov pouted, and Hecker paced around the camp as the train waited outside the main gate. Commandant Krueger would be arriving from Rabka in a few hours, and for the first time since opening for business, Belzec stood still. The Commandant of Belzec nervously surveyed the disorganized chaos as he stood and stared blankly at the mess. His nerves suddenly kicked in, and he excused himself to go diarrhea in the mouth of a 12-year-old Jewish boy he kept near his quarters. An SS enlisted man slit the boy's throat soon after.

Vlad and Pavel sat away from the mess hall near the bear pit. Hecker somehow procured a European Brown Bear who easily weighed 600 pounds. He forced local masons to construct a pen that would contain the wild animal. The walls were tall enough to hold the bear in, but with good vantage points for all SS and Wachmen to view the happenings inside.

For entertainment, Orlov or Hecker would grab a Jewish father with a child off a transport and detain them. After their family and the others in the transport had been gassed or shot, Hecker would throw the remaining two into the bear pit. All camp staff stayed entertained watching the hungry bear maul the condemned. Orlov loved putting the terrified small child in first, so the bear could have an appetizer. He forced the father to watch the hungry bear tear apart the helpless youngster. Orlov occasionally chose between strangling a child or feeding the bear. He joked it depended on what was being served for breakfast.

The SS teased the animal on purpose, to ensure a constant agitated and ready to attack state. It was how the SS and Wachmen unwound from the daily stress. They placed bets on how long Jews would last against the animal, got drunk and socialized. The bear pit also was popular for scavenger birds picking at the dead. Wachmen used the birds for target practice as well, not even a bird entered Belzec and left alive.

They sat next to the bear pit waiting for Krueger to arrive from Rabka, and Vlad spoke to Pavel with sunken eyes. "My dad made me read Dante's Inferno, have you ever read it?" Pavel shook his head no, and Vlad continued "The book was written in the 14th century, and in the book Dante described entering the gates of Hell. Above the gates, an inscription read, 'Abandon all hope, ye who enter here.' That is true for not only Jews we murder, but for myself as well. I can't do this anymore, look around at this madness and look at me. I get stumbling drunk to sleep, and have nightmares that I remember when I wake up. I vomit nearly every day, then drink again until I blackout. I feel like I am going insane."

Pavel gave Vlad a look of strength but said nothing. Vlad continued in a resigned hollow voice, "How many people do you think we have helped kill during our first month in this place?

Pavel furrowed his bushy eyebrows "A lot kid, I am not sure. Rumor is the SS are intensifying Aktion Reinhard, and are looking to eliminate all Jews in Poland and Russia within a year. We will probably have hundreds of thousands of Jews pass through this hell. Listen to these people begging to get off that train sitting over there. They have no clue what awaits them. Either exhaust from that piece of shit engine or a bullet. Those are the lucky ones. Some could wind up in the Commandant's stable as his personal toilet, or in Orlov's hands as he strangles yet another kid so he can eat breakfast."

Pavel paused to light a cigarette and continued "The real unfortunates will face this goddamned bear. How could anyone imagine such a fate? It's hard to comprehend this is happening in 1942. But you must hang on, Chayka, because good always triumphs over evil. It's just a matter of time. Plus, think about your parents and Mikhail. He may still be alive. I also heard that the United States has entered the war against Germany and Japan. Who knows, it could help put an end to this madness."

Vlad then started to cry. "I'm telling you now Pavel. We are all going to pay for this crime. Either in this life or the next, there will be a reckoning. If Germany loses this war, we will be held to account by our countrymen and the rest of the world as collaborators and murderers. We will be shown no mercy by God or man."

Vlad continued to wipe away tears as he spoke. "What about the Christian faithful? Why are they silent? Germany is mostly Lutheran and Catholic. Where is the leadership from both faiths condemning this barbarism?"

Pavel shrugged his shoulders. "They most likely don't know about this place kid. No one would believe it anyway. Such a refined people like the Germans. The world would only say it's a fantastic lie. We have both seen some priests packed in with the Jews. Some must be speaking out."

Vlad peered into the bear pit where scavenger birds picked at the bloody skull of a child. "Maybe so, but surely the world knows how Germany is treating its Jews. That's no secret. From the Nuremberg Laws to Kristallnacht, people know."

Three SS staff cars, accompanied by two motorcycles with mounted machine guns interrupted their conversation and pulled up to the main gate. Commandant Krueger came from Rabka to relieve the current commander of his duties and restore order to Belzec. Krueger was under intense pressure from Berlin to start processing trainloads of Jews immediately. The new Commandant was all business as he exited the staff car, and began thundering orders amid the chaos. All Wachmen and SS responded immediately to Krueger. A new era for Belzec began.

Chapter 23
Belzec Death Camp
June 15. 1942

The warm summer sun shone brightly on the Belzec grounds, and Commandant Krueger stood in front of the men assembled to hear him speak. It was late afternoon, and the heat of a record warm summer affected the Wachmen, the dead, and the condemned. The heat impacted the Jews especially hard, as they endured stifling and appalling conditions in the overcrowded boxcars. Vlad watched Krueger institute massive reforms over the past two months. Krueger devised new processes and procedures that greatly increased the murdering capacity of Belzec. He procured a steam shovel to dig massive, deep graves that could easily fit three houses. In a very shrewd move, Krueger created Sonderkommandos. Teams of Jews selected from transports to carry out many of Belzec's morbid daily operations.

Sonderkommando Jews helped with orderly disembarking of trains, sorting and bundling all clothing, cutting women's hair, removing corpses from the gas chambers, pulling gold teeth from the dead, and dragged the bodies to mass graves. Sonderkommando Jews were allowed to live for a few months before being worked to death or shot. The SS replaced them with a new batch selected from the transports. Krueger devised a revolutionary concept that streamlined operations at Belzec.

Krueger selected Jewish stonemasons to construct new gas chambers that could fit over a thousand of their people at a time. He replaced the old motor with a modern, powerful Russian tank engine. It was ten times more lethal. The carbon monoxide filled the gas chambers quickly, resulting in more people killed in less time. The Jewish stonemasons became the first ones gassed in the virgin gas chambers. Vlad, Pavel, and Orlov drove them in using particular harshness because the victims knew their fate.

Commandant Krueger waited for the assembled men to quiet down and finally started to speak in a confident and almost boastful tone. "I am very pleased with the progress made at Belzec over the past two months. Since my arrival, we have been able to process over 80,000 Jews in a clean and efficient manner. On duty drunkenness has abated. Jewish personal belongings are being repurposed for the German people. Jewish gold, diamonds, and money are rightly deposited into the Reichsbank. Berlin is most happy, and they are applying my innovations to other camps assisting with Aktion Reinhard. We are contributing beyond measure to the Final Solution, and every man here should be most proud. I certainly know that I am."

Krueger paused as hot winds blew and kicked up dust in the camp. He continued after the wind gust passed. "As you know, we built new gas chambers to handle the volume expected here. The Jewish work brigades, or Sonderkommandos, are eager to do our bidding and ensure smooth operations. These Untermensch enjoy participating in the robbery and destruction of their people. They are even ripping gold out of the mouths of their dead after the gas chamber. That fact alone reinforces the Fuhrer's wise policy. We estimate over 600,000 to be exterminated here within a year. That's 50,000 Jews per month to be processed."

Vlad joined the rest in affirming his ability to carry out the Commandant's orders. Pavel was concerned for Vlad's health, both physical and mental. Vlad easily downed a liter of whiskey or vodka per day. What he drank depended on what the Jews brought with them on the train. Pavel noticed Vlad losing his inhibitions to violence. His inner kindness diminished, and Vlad became unusually rough with his whip and pistol to Jews in the tube.

Krueger continued speaking, interrupting Pavel's thoughts about Vlad. "We have the biggest transport yet to be processed at Belzec. It is scheduled to arrive within an hour. We have 80 cattle cars full of Jews in route to our humble camp. That's 8,000 Jews we need to destroy in the name of my friend Reinhard Heydrich, who was recently assassinated by a Jewish partisan. We shall kill, without pity or mercy, all of them.

Krueger finished by commanding, "I am asking we work through the night and have every Jew on this transport dead by sunrise. I have taught you all how to do this in an orderly and efficient manner. I have taught you to keep them calm and deceived until the last minute. I have taught you how to do this correctly, and none of you have deviated from my reforms. However, with this particular transport of Jews, I command you to treat them with unflinching violence and total depravity."

Commandant Krueger let the loud applause and whistling from the men subside before he continued. "Scharfuhrer Hecker has a new hound named Barry. Barry has been trained to rip the cocks and balls off Jewish men and boys. Let's put Barry to the test. I want whips cracking and faces bashed in. I want you to unleash my personal fury and rage of Heydrich's death on these people. This is for tonight only. This is for Reinhard Heydrich."

The Wachmen roared with approval. Vlad cheered along with the rest, as Pavel quietly observed the madness around him. Drunk once again, Vlad began to blame the Jews themselves for his current lot in life. How could they let this happen to themselves? Why did they show up day after day, month after month, to be slaughtered like sheep? He became partially unhinged and felt the fastest way to exit the hell of Belzec was to kill as many Jews as possible.

His rationale made little sense, but nothing made sense at Belzec. Pavel rightly understood and gave Vlad some mental breathing room. He regularly watched Vlad's back and made sure he didn't go over the deep end. Pavel indeed carried Vlad at this point. Footprints in the sand, but Vlad had no idea.

"I have one final and important personal command." Krueger bellowed as the approaching train whistle shrieked in the distance. "I want a nice June wedding tomorrow. Pick out the prettiest Jew female and most handsome Jew male. Find the finest clothes being sorted by the Sonderkommando and most beautiful diamond ring stored at the cashier office. Tell them it's on my orders. I will officiate the wedding of these two Jews. We will all celebrate, drink and dance in honor of this mid-summer nuptial. It will be a fun party after this immediate hard work we have in front of us. Now bring on death and destruction of this human debris." The Wachmen all clapped, whistled and shouted vulgar obscenities about the Jews. A day and night of hell followed.

As the first section of ten cars rolled into camp, the SS and Wachmen on the unloading ramp paced back and forth. They constantly checked their weapons, cracked whips in the air and swung clubs in their hands. Many adjusted their leather gloves for a perfect fit, and others stood still clenching their jaws. The tension and pent up violence to be unleashed was palatable. The Jewish sonderkommandos throughout the camp stood at the ready. They knew any missteps meant instant death.

The cattle car doors opened, and the screaming started immediately. Orlov wandered from his post in the tube to greet the first transport. His title as Oberwachman gave him more freedom to roam the camp, which he often used to instill constant fear in the sonderkommandos. The Jews nicknamed him 'Der Hammer' after the blunt tool. Orlov menacingly jumped into the first car packed with thirsty, frightened and bewildered people.

"You goddamned filthy animals get off my train and take a shower," Orlov screamed as if demonically possessed. The Jews stood frozen in fear and didn't move, which agitated Orlov even more as he continued to scream in a high-pitched voice. "I said move your disease ridden asses, or I will shoot you like the dogs you are." He began wildly swinging his whip, as fast and hard as he could. People in the cattle car became panicked and trampled each other trying to get out. Orlov and his whip did serious damage. Jews dove out the train door twisting ankles and breaking wrists from the fall to the ramp below.

Orlov saw a beautiful young mother protecting her two-year-old child in the corner of the cattle car. Her husband defiantly stood in front on them both. Orlov screamed with hateful contempt "You rotten, stupid son of a bitch. Who in God's name do you think you are? You stand in front of as if you were an equal?" He put down the whip and pulled out a dagger. Orlov walked up to the husband and stood eye to eye with him. He took the tip of the dagger and started to carve a swastika into the husband's forehead. The man flinched at the pain. "Stand still" Orlov screamed just inches away from his ear and continued to carve the swastika. Blood poured from his forehead, down his face, and onto Orlov's hand. Orlov finished the swastika, wiped his bloodied hand on the husband's shirt and stepped back a few feet.

Orlov looked at the terrified young wife "I will carve a bigger one into the little pig you have in your arms unless you let me screw you right here and now."

The husband yelled "No" and stepped towards Orlov, who drew his Luger and shot the man in the throat at point blank range. The husband was thrown against the sidewall of the cattle car by the impact and fell to the floor dead in a pool of blood

Orlov picked up his dagger off the floor and leered at the woman. "Lift up your dress and get on all fours, or I start carving up your kid." The young mother set her son down and did as ordered. Orlov dropped his pants and attempted penetration, but her vagina was dry from dehydration and fear. He walked over to her dead husband, dipped his right hand into the pool of blood and rubbed it on his penis for lubrication. He mounted her and the violation was done with ease. The child sat quietly and watched.

When Orlov finished, he pulled up his pants, picked the child off the floor by his throat and strangled him. The child turned blue flailing his arms and legs, while the mother begged for his life. Orlov squeezed so hard, both of them heard the neck bones crack as the child went limp. Orlov tossed him on the floor like a dirty rag. He grabbed the woman's arm, who was paralyzed with fear and said in a calm voice "Don't worry about your dead family, you are getting married tomorrow. Come with me."

Vlad saw Orlov gently help the woman out of the box car and onto the unloading ramp. He held her hand and politely guided the woman through the violent chaos on the ramp. She stumbled around in a daze as Wachmen whipped people she knew from her hometown. Vlad could see Wachmen grab small children by the feet and smash their heads into the sides of the cattle cars. Snarling dogs, cries, screams and moans permeated the air throughout the camp.

The SS separated the men and women after the Wachmen had tired of their reindeer games with the first batch of Jews. They needed to conserve energy for the remaining 7,500 or so victims who waited in their locked cattle cars outside the camp. They too could hear everything.

At the cashier where Jews were searched and handed over valuables, Orlov found Hecker zipping up his pants. His fists were covered in blood. Hecker made sport of knocking the front teeth out of any women who resisted being raped. "Scharfuhrer Hecker," Orlov said proudly holding the woman's hand. "May I present the bride to the Commandant?"

Hecker checked out the dazed young mother. "Nice work Orlov. Yes, she should do just fine. Bring her to the Commandant's Quarters. He requests she is given food, wine, and a warm bath. His staff is waiting to pamper and ready her for the big day tomorrow. Hurry, because we need you at the tube."

Even the Commandant helped bring up the rear of each naked group headed to the gas chambers on this night. They were driven in by Vlad, Pavel, Orlov and a new source of terror, Barry, the dog. The German

Shepard named Barry had been trained by Hecker to attack and tear off the genitals of naked Jewish men and boys. A barbaric and grotesque skill the dog was taught over the last few months at Belzec. SS dog handlers would take Jewish males of all ages, from children to old men, off the train and bring them to Barry's kennel.

Hecker tied the men and boys to a post, hands cuffed above their heads and pants pulled down. The SS would point to the genitals and command "Barry, schwanz." They would beat and starve the dog until he learned his new grisly trick. If Barry showed any affection or hesitation towards his victims, the SS would beat him without mercy. The cries and screams coming from the dog kennel became intolerable for Vlad to hear. The children victim's screams of terror and agony drove him to drink even more.

They were harder for Vlad to hear than cries of children saying, "But mommy, I have been good." As engine exhaust entered the gas chambers.

The final group of Jews to be gassed were all males. Vlad selected one strong and handsome Jew in his late teens. He would serve as the groom in the Commandant's twisted wedding ceremony. Vlad whispered to him, "This will allow you to live another day. It's all I can do for you, and I'm sorry." It was the first time in a month Vlad was not in a total drunken stupor, he began to exit his emotional and spiritual fog.

Vlad watched as Commandant Krueger unleashed Barry in the tube, the dog tore off the genitals of a 70-year-old naked grandfather. His adult son instinctively attempted to fight the dog but was savagely beaten in the face with a club containing nails and razor blades affixed to the end. A makeshift device Orlov created in his drunken spare time. The adult son was shoved into the gas chamber, his face thoroughly mangled. The grandfather bled profusely and staggered in behind him. Orlov locked the door, and the Russian tank engine did its deadly job.

Hecker ordered the prisoners to clean up the tube. The Sonderkommando nicknamed it the 'Himmelstrasse,' or 'road to heaven.' The ground in the tube was full of excrement and blood. Blood came from Orlov slicing off breasts or using his medieval club. Barry, the dog, tearing off genitals contributed to the mess. Excrement was the common physical reaction of people who realized imminent death waited, a phenomenon Vlad had seen many times by now. The 8,000 Jews were all dead except the bride and groom. The sun began to rise in the east, and the Jewish cooks had breakfast ready for the hungry men.

The wedding started at noon that same day. Heat gripped the camp, and most were drunk as no more transports were due. The Commandant wanted a party, and all seemed happy to comply. Vlad and Pavel shared a bottle of expensive whiskey. Fine wine and alcohol always overflowed in the camp from Jews arriving on transports. The Commandant normally looked the other way at liquor theft, he didn't mind men pilfering. Hecker called the men to order as the Commandant took his place in the courtyard. Krueger stood in full SS dress uniform, carrying a copy of Mein Kampf emblazoned with a black swastika on the cover.

Vlad stood next to Pavel and watched the man and woman emerge from the Commandant's house. He was dressed in a tailored suit, and she in a white flowing dress. Her hair was beautifully done, and the diamond ring reflected the hot sun most brilliantly. They walked hand in hand on a dirt path surrounded by whistling and clapping SS and Wachmen. The couple stood in front of the Commandant and crowd silently. Their poise amid the chaos and stress struck Vlad as extraordinary.

"Dearly beloved," Commandant Krueger said in a sarcastic tone. "We are witnessing two Jews in love, and literally hand-picked for each other." The words elicited drunken laughs, jeers, and snickering from the men. Krueger continued looking at the man "Do you take this Jew cunt to be your wife, for as long as you both shall live?" The SS and Wachmen roared with laughter. Only semi- intoxicated, the liquor didn't dull Vlad's guilt. The humiliation of these two innocent and beautiful people brought him to a desperate mental state.

"Yes." Said the man.

Krueger turned to the woman. "Do you take this foul circumcision to be your husband, as long as you both shall live?"

"Yes" replied the woman, staring at the ground in shame and embarrassment. In the past 24 hours, she endured her husband's murder, child strangled and herself raped. All three acts committed by Orlov, who drunkenly hurled insults and profanities at the couple.

Krueger then announced to all assembled, "By the power vested in me, I pronounce you man and wife. You may now rape the bride."

The SS and Wachmen started cheering and chanting "Off with the dress. Off with the dress." The couple stood frozen as the SS and Wachmen continued their chant. Vlad and Pavel could feel the tension rising. They understood this would not end well for the two young people in extreme danger.

Suddenly Orlov jumped out of the crowd and screamed in slurred speech. "The Commandant said rape your whore bride. Now! On the ground, right here! Give us a goddamned show."

Orlov violently tore off her dress, while another Wachman unzipped his pants and urinated on it. She stood naked alone in front of 150 drunken, screaming men. Vlad stood awestruck by her beauty and poise. The bride had long flowing black hair, deep brown eyes, perfect skin and a youthful body. "Do it now, or I will have every man ravage her in front of you." Orlov slurred menacingly in the man's ear. The man did as ordered. He undressed and laid the woman down in the dirt. The guards went wild, screaming profanities while pumping their fists in the air.

The man tried, but could not get hard in the stressful and insane environment. He stood above the naked woman, looking defeated and ashamed.

"Barry, schwanz," Hecker commanded as he unleashed the dog. Barry lunged at the man and clenched his genitals in his teeth. With a violent head shake, the dog tore off his scrotum. Blood poured out, and the man howled in pain as he dropped to his knees. Hecker picked up an axe and split his head in half as if splitting a log.

The woman lay naked in the dirt covered in the man's blood from his destroyed scrotum and gaping head wound.

"Chayka," Hecker said calmly but out of breath. "Take this whore to the pit and shoot her."

Vlad motioned for the woman to get up, which she did. They walked through the camp to the fifth mass grave dug by the steam shovel. The first four graves had reached capacity and were concealed with dirt. Grass and weeds already took root over them. The woman walked to the edge of the grave which could easily fit three or four houses. She looked down inside and saw a pile of 15,000 dead people intertwined on top of each other. Vlad had seen it many times. Thousands of naked corpses thrown away like garbage. For the uninitiated, the unreal sight normally overwhelmed people to the point of vomiting, fainting, or total loss of emotional control.

The naked woman turned and stared at Vlad. She readied for death unafraid. Vlad stood stunned at her bravery and composure. Vlad experienced a moment of spiritual lucidity and rapidly realized he stood fully clothed, armed and afraid. Facing him stood a naked and innocent young woman, raped and terrorized. She remained confident and silent. They locked eyes and Vlad blinked. He realized the enormity of the situation and couldn't shoot her.

"Stand aside kid. I'm going to save your ass again." Pavel said as he walked up behind Vlad. Pavel raised his rifle and shot her in the chest. The impact knocked the woman off her feet and into the pit. Vlad vomited, and said in a bleak manner, "He suffered under Pontius Pilate, was crucified, died and was buried. He descended into hell."

Pavel gave Vlad a look as if to say 'what are you talking about?'

"Part of the Apostles Creed. I too have descended into hell, and don't care if I live or die anymore." Vlad vomited again into the mass grave, stumbled back to his bunk and passed out. The nightmares would start right away.

Chapter 24
Mid-October 1942
Belzec Death Camp

Vlad was unimpressed when Reichsfuhrer-SS Heinrich Himmler stepped out of his staff car at Belzec on a cool, sunny, fall afternoon. Himmler looked more unattractive and diminutive than Vlad expected. As the second most powerful man in the Third Reich, and enforcer of the Final Solution, Vlad anticipated a Teutonic Knight. Instead, a mousy looking former chicken farmer led the feared and mighty SS with total impunity.

The power Heinrich Himmler wielded impressed Vlad and the entire world. People like Orlov, Scharfuhrer Hecker, and Commandant Krueger were puppets of the Reichsfuhrer-SS. Hundreds of millions of lives remained in the balance under his perverse and direct control.

It was a paramount event to have the Reichsfuhrer-SS in the remote woods of Eastern Poland. Commandant Krueger greeted Himmler in full dress uniform, with a crisp Nazi salute and Heil Hitler. Himmler returned the salute and shook Krueger's hand. They immediately walked into the Commandant's house and didn't emerge for 90 minutes.

After the meeting, Himmler toured the camp and spoke briefly with SS staff and Wachmen. The staff stood in formation for inspection by the Reichsfuhrer-SS. Vlad, Pavel, and Orlov snapped to attention as Himmler approached their platoon. They stood tall, stared straight ahead, and didn't move when Himmler slowly walked in front of them.

Orlov couldn't help himself. He believed the rank of Oberwachman came with special status, and with an outstretched arm screamed "Heil Hitler" directly in Himmler's face. Himmler gave him a curious look, raised his hand in a half salute, and kept walking. Both Hecker and the Commandant scowled at Orlov. The unwritten protocol was never to speak to the Reichsfuhrer -SS unless spoken to. Orlov committed a major faux pas, but nothing fatal.

Himmler proceeded to observe a routine gassing operation of 1,000 Jews and view a mass grave. By now, over 600,000 Jews lay dead in 12 mass graves. Himmler seemed emotionally disturbed and physically ill after witnessing the carnage. He excused himself and nervously smoked a cigarette. Vlad assumed his first up close experience in a death camp was more gruesome than issuing orders from a desk in Berlin. Himmler had seen enough. Vlad watched him speak with the Commandant for another ten minutes, then leave Belzec with his entourage. The entire visit lasted under three hours.

Commandant Krueger assembled the men that evening and spoke. "Reichsfuhrer-SS Himmler is pleased with our progress. Belzec has served the Reich in many important ways, primarily as a proving ground for best practices to destroy the Jewish race. There are newer, bigger, and better places suited to finishing the job we have started. New and efficient ways of gassing Jews have been put into practice, using Zyklon B instead of carbon monoxide. A new camp located near Auschwitz can easily gas and cremate 20,000 Jews per day. You can all take pride in being key contributors to this magnificent achievement."

Krueger paused and got emotional at the thought of his beloved camp shutting down. He recovered and continued. "The Reichsfuhrer has ordered us to open the graves and burn every Jew we have killed. There are over 600,000 corpses to roast. We must leave no evidence of our glorious work here at Belzec. A bone crushing machine is on its way to dispose of every last trace. These Jews will all disappear in plumes of smoke. They never existed, and this never happened. We were never here."

Commandant Krueger took a moment to soak in the finality of the situation. "The Jewish Sonderkommando will, of course, do the work. We will continue to receive transports, but at a much lower volume. Most Jews will be diverted to our new facility at Auschwitz. Try not to torture, maim or kill too many Sonderkommandos. This will be hard and dirty work. We need them for the next few months during this important job. No trace shall remain, and we can deny to the world this ever happened. Some in Berlin believe future generations will not appreciate what we have accomplished. Therefore, we erase everything."

Krueger finished his speech by saying. "If these Sonderkommandos get out of line or slow work down, give a few lashes with a whip. Maybe chop off a finger. That should get the rest moving again. Unless you want to dig up and burn over a half million dead Jews, keep them alive and somewhat fed. We shall commence outdoor cooking tomorrow. Get ready for a massive Jew barbecue. It's going to be a beautiful sight. That is all. Dismissed."

Chapter 25
Late March 1943
Belzec, Poland

First Platoon was the last group of Wachmen at Belzec, along with Scharfuhrer Hecker and a handful of SS officers. Belzec was officially decommissioned, and no transports had arrived in months. The only task remaining was guarding the Sonderkommando, who were forced to cover up by flame this most historic crime. Vlad, Pavel, and Orlov supervised the Jews performing the grisly task of digging up and burning over 600,000 of their fellow people.

The bodies were in various stages of decomposition, yet many in the Sonderkommando recognized friends and family among the corpses they exhumed. One Jewish man pulled his five-year-old daughter out of a mass grave to be burned. He mentally snapped and rushed Orlov, who happily drew his Luger and shot him dead. Besides that one incident, the Wachmen obeyed the Commandant's orders of decent treatment until the last body was burned.

The burning of over a half million corpses did not go well at first. Never in the history of the world were so many bodies in need of disposal, in such a short period. The SS tried pouring 200 gallons of diesel oil into the first mass grave and set it ablaze. The fuel burned, but the corpses did not catch fire as hoped. Vlad watched as the SS tried large quantities of dynamite which also failed to ignite the bodies. The explosions created a disgusting mess, strewing rotting human flesh throughout the camp. Decomposing body parts hanging from tree limbs, barracks and gas chamber roofs from the blast added to the hell on earth environment. It took weeks of trial and error, but the SS finally succeeded. Once again, other death camps would learn lessons from the death laboratory known as Belzec.

Commandant Krueger imported specialists in the macabre business of burning Jews. Vlad observed the specialists adopt the basic concept of a backyard grill, and perversely engineer a massive grill for copious amounts of human corpses. Two parallel railroad tracks set on concrete pillars four feet off the ground, with smaller gauge railroad tracks set perpendicular forming a massive grill grate. The engineers piled corpses high on the grate, with kerosene soaked logs set ablaze underneath. It worked, and the engineers constructed four additional massive grills for the project.

The Sonderkommando were under SS orders never to let the fire burn out. They were arranged in three shifts of eight hours each for round the clock work. The job of exhumation, dragging bodies to the grills and arranging them correctly for the best burn rate continued unabated. Vlad witnessed many instances of decomposing limbs and heads falling off corpses being dragged from grave to grill.

The Sonderkommando learned to put women on the bottom, their body fat dripped into the flames and served as a fuel source to ignite the bodies above. Vlad witnessed the gruesome sight of a pregnant woman's belly bursting open and the dead unborn spilling into the flames. Children were always thrown on top, with men usually in the middle. The Jews learned never to touch their faces while working, due to the foulness of the diseased and decomposing bodies. One Sonderkommando rubbed his eyes during a shift of pulling corpses and soon went blind from bacterial infection. The SS threw him alive into the fire as a warning to the rest.

Thick and acrid smoke billowed from Belzec, which drew complaints from people 60 miles away. Children could not play outside, and a greasy film from human fat coated everything from roads to windows. The sun was blocked out on a regular basis, and people noticed that birds disappeared from the area. Vlad and the Wachmen covered freshwater wells to prevent contamination from fallout, and traffic accidents increased due to slick roads. Sure footed animals like horses slipped and fell on slimy cobblestone streets, breaking their legs which resulting in being shot. Death hung like a cloud, no one in the area could deny what was happening. Many locals spoke among themselves about opportunities to ransack the camp, once the Germans finished burning their Jews.

Vlad was drunk most of the time, and Pavel made sure he didn't run into problems with Orlov or Hecker. When Vlad did manage to sleep, the nightmares were uncontrollable. Faces and cries of the murdered played in his mind like a movie. Vlad sat on a wooden bench outside during a sleepless night, sipping vodka and watching the grills in action. The flames seemed alive as they licked into the night sky, consuming the dead. Vlad always liked Psalms from the Bible and began to recite one of them. "Even though I walk through the valley of the shadow of death, I fear no evil, for you are with me. Your rod and your staff, they comfort me."

Unknown to Vlad, Pavel stood directly behind him and heard the Psalm. He startled Vlad by saying, "That's one I have actually heard, kid. This place is the valley of death. No one would believe if they didn't see it with their own eyes. These depraved German dogs are counting on exactly that, by digging up and torching every last person killed here. I am concerned what they are going to do with us when this is all over."

Vlad continued to stare at the flames and replied in drunken monotone. "I don't care what they do with us, Pavel. I am at the end of my rope and can't hang on for much longer. That psalm says I shall fear no evil, for the Lord is with me. Bullshit if he is. Where the hell is God? His rod and staff comfort me? Bullshit if they do. What a bunch of total lies. Going to Mass and actually believing in the Trinity. Where are the Father, Son, and Holy Spirit? I wonder if we are actually dead and in hell right now, but we just don't realize it. In my opinion, fuck God."

Pavel grabbed Vlad's right earlobe and twisted it as hard as he could. Vlad instinctively stood up and knocked Pavel's hand away from his ear. "What the hell are you doing?"

Pavel stepped back. "See, you are alive! Our work here is almost finished. Hopefully, life will improve wherever they are going to take us next. Stop drinking yourself to oblivion and start living. You hear me, kid? I swear to God, I will kick your ass into next week if you don't start coming back from wherever the hell you've been. Now hit the sack. You are on duty in five hours, and I haven't seen you sleep in three days." Vlad did as Pavel demanded and passed out in his bunk. So utterly exhausted, the nightmares could not supersede his body's need for sleep.

After the last bodies were burned and ashes buried, the SS made the Jews plant grass, trees, and shrubs over the grounds of Belzec. The rail line leading into the camp was ripped up, the structures dismantled, and everything else hauled away. The fences were taken down, and Belzec ceased to exist. The Jewish Sonderkommandos that dug up and cremated the bodies were transported to Treblinka earlier in the afternoon. Knowing their fate, all jumped out of the cattle cars upon arrival and ran wildly throughout the camp. Vlad heard the SS and Wachmen picked them off with rifles for the remainder of the day. Only the

Commandant's house stood at Belzec, which is where Vlad and First Platoon spent their last night.

First Platoon was well on their way to finishing off the remaining vodka as they lounged inside the Commandants former residence. Most of the men downed a half-liter each, including Vlad and Pavel. With the exception of Orlov, they were grateful to be done with Belzec. Pavel gave Vlad a reassuring look as if to say 'Glad you're coming back because things may improve.' The Wachmen ate the rest of the sausage, bread, and chocolate. Nothing remained. The ashes and ground up bones were spread on nearby roads and cobblestone streets, as an anti-slip measure from the burned corpse's greasy residue.

Suddenly Hecker barged inside the house with a piece of paper in his hand and shouted incredulously. "France? First Platoon is being reassigned to France? Why not the Bahamas for Christ's sake. Whose dick did you suck to get assigned to France? Unbelievable! You lucky bastards ship out tomorrow morning and have your written orders. I am due at Buchenwald in two days and will be spending the final night in Poland with my favorite local prostitute. I shall miss her more than you Ukrainian dogs, whom I rescued and created from nothing. Remember your secrecy oath and the penalty that comes for violating it. The oath applies until the day you die. Heil Hitler" Hecker walked out the door, Vlad would never see him again.

For the first time in two years, Vlad actually felt light may be at the end of a very long tunnel. He wondered if the Holy Spirit finally intervened on his behalf. Vlad understood they were not in the clear, as no one knew the next assignment. But France sounded much better than Belzec, Poland. In actuality, anywhere did.

Orlov addressed First Platoon "Be at the station by 7 am. Don't be late and miss the train, or there will be hell to pay. I am visiting my favorite local girl for the last time. She wants one more diamond before I leave. This Polish whore has a diamond for every time we had sex, and her husband doesn't care. I even get drunk with him after I screw his hot wife. They have gotten rich off me."

Vlad frowned at Orlov as he walked out the door and said sarcastically. "You mean they've gotten rich off murdered Jews and the diamonds you stole from the cashier, not you."

Orlov stopped, turned around and asked "Are there many Jews in France? God, I miss the thrill of the kill and strangling a little piglet every morning. Plus I need to stash away some retirement loot."

Vlad quickly replied, "I hope not."

Orlov looked surprised "Why the hell would you say that? Tired of killing Jews Chayka?"

Vlad replied in a weary tone, "I actually am sick of killing Jews. I prefer a change of scenery."

Orlov sneered and said spitefully "You fucking pussy Chayka, you were tired of killing Jews after that first one you missed at Trawniki. You weak Jew lover."

Vlad stood up, walked over to Orlov and smashed him in the face with his fist. Orlov flew against the wall but regained his footing. "You rotten Jew lover Chayka, you are a dead man. I am going to kill you!"

"Nobody is going to kill anybody goddamn it," Pavel demanded as he stepped in between the two men. "Go get laid, Orlov." Pavel continued "And you kid, go sleep it off. That was a foolish thing you just did."

The next morning First Platoon awoke to sounds of shovels and pickaxes clanging outside. "What the hell is that," Vlad asked Pavel with a bad hangover. They opened the front door and couldn't believe what they saw. Hundreds of Polish locals descended upon the camp and dug up the grounds looking for cash, diamonds, and gold. The grass and shrubs planted by the Sonderkommando were completely torn up, along with the charred ground where the grills once stood.

The locals had no idea the Wachmen were still on premise as Vlad flung the door open and shouted, "You miserable Pollack's, get the fuck out of here or I will shoot every one of you. I will burn down your houses and kill your families if you dare to come back here. Do you hear me?" Vlad continued to shout. "Is there no simple decency or humanity left in this world? Leave this place alone." The locals dropped their tools and scurried off. They would be back after the Wachmen left for France.

The train left promptly at 7 a.m. with First Platoon on board, including two SS handlers to keep an eye on them. Even though the men faithfully murdered over a half million Jews, they were still not trusted. The temptation to put on civilian clothes, blend in with the population, and talk about what happened at Belzec lingered as a worry for the SS.

The train left the station bound for France, and a black-eyed Orlov glowered at Vlad while gesturing a knife slit across the throat. Vlad looked away, sunk into his comfortable chair and closed his eyes. He hadn't thought about his parents or brothers in months. Nor had Vlad processed the magnitude of what happened at Belzec, and his personal role in all of it. Vlad began to realize his complete disconnection with God and the Catholic faith.

Vlad suffered heavy moral damage on many levels, and it would take time to be functional without constant alcohol dulling his mind. How Vlad would live with himself, if he could, would play out over time. France awaited.

Chapter 26
Minneapolis, Minnesota
Present Day

Max arranged dinner for Dane Atkinson, Carl Jeffries, Father Grant Moudry, Vlad and himself at Murray's Steakhouse. Murray's is a dining institution, serving the upscale and those celebrating special occasions with its delicious steak for years. Other outstanding and trendy steakhouses dot the landscape, but Max enjoyed seeing a Murray family member behind the bar or reservation kiosk every visit. James Murray warmly welcomed Max, seated the dinner party, and comped the first round of drinks.

Father Moudry picked up Vlad and drove him to the restaurant at Max's request. Vlad considered Father Moudry his priest for the last 60 years, sharing a mutual deep spiritual bond and genuine friendship. Vlad held Father Moudry with high regard and followed him to different parishes during his distinguished career. Grant Moudry was retired for over 20 years and in his mid-eighties, but remained a towering figure in the area. Respected by all, Grant Moudry served as a voice for those who had none, regardless of religious affiliation.

Vlad smiled as Sandra placed the first round of drinks in front of each person. Sandra worked at Murray's seemingly forever, a professional server in the truest sense of the word. Not many servers in the state earned six figures working four nights per week. People came in for the steak, but they stayed for Sandra. Reservations at Murray's are hard to come by, and requests to be in Sandra's section are even more difficult to accommodate.

"Cheers!" Vlad started to say as he lifted his glass in a toast "To my son, Max, and to all of you at this table. I give humble thanks for all you have done, and are doing for this old man." Vlad started to choke up and cry.

Father Moudry took over and said "Dear God, we thank you for Vlad, and the friends and family seated here tonight, which are symbols of your love for us. Amen" All gently clanged their cocktail glasses and took a drink. Different conversations broke out among the friends and acquaintances. Every table at Murray's had guests and chatter filled the room, which is what Max wanted. They could speak freely, without people listening to their private conversation.

Sandra took dinner orders and brought the second round of drinks. She turned away to help another table, and Max asked Dane for an update on Vlad's case status to the group. Dane leaned in, "I want to remind everyone that anything said tonight stays within the group. We are discussing sensitive information, which will cause us headaches if there are loose lips."

All nodded in the affirmative and Dane continued looking at Vlad. "Washington wants to crucify you. Young guns looking to make a name at Justice view you as the last opportunity to nail a Nazi. Everyone must understand this is being discussed around the world, and to win a conviction will make careers for some of my younger colleagues. Max and I discussed at length the legal procedures and appeals that he can employ. This is the first I have told anyone outside the US Attorney's Office, but I recused myself from the case this morning. Otherwise, I would never be here at dinner with you all. This move will free me up ethically to be a quiet guardian angel, rather than an adversary for Vlad. Quite frankly, I don't have it in my heart to prosecute him. I have four more years before my official retirement and a deep well of contacts within the department. What are they going to do, fire me?"

Everyone laughed and gave a short round of applause. Max smiled at the group "If they fire you, come work for Chayka, Kimo, and Gust. Use your prosecutorial experience to defend the rich and well connected in this town. Finally, make some money for once in your life."

The group again laughed, and Dane said "Seriously Vlad, the best lawyer in town represents you. But the Department of Justice also wants a conviction. I can say with a fair amount of confidence that Israel will ask for extradition and want a trial. You have two big dogs fighting over the same bone. That bone is you."

Dane continued after taking a sip of his Manhattan. "I am not saying this will be easy or a walk in the park. You are in good hands with Max, let him do the worrying and leave the rest to us." Vlad quietly nodded and said thank you to Dane.

Carl Jeffries spoke next as Sandra finished carving the steaks tableside, and made sure all had fresh drinks. "I appreciate being included in this dinner but have the feeling I am invited so Max can stick me with the bill. Even though the guy makes about ten times more money than I do."

Father Moudry chimed in "Then make it one hundred times more money than I make." The table again erupted in laughter. Vlad wanted everyone together for an informal session, and to thank all involved for their help. He hoped it would touch on the serious, but be light enough for all to enjoy themselves in the company of each other. He was most pleased and spot on.

Carl continued in a more serious tone. "I have watched the videotapes Max has made thus far of Vlad. I am beginning to formulate a series of articles spanning three or four Sunday newspapers. I must say it's an incredible journey to view the footage and listen to Vlad. Not sure if there has been a more compelling story in my 40 years of journalism. It has it all; deep historical significance, self-preservation, greed, murder, rape, hate, redemption, survival, love, and everything in-between. I have told the bosses about my exclusive access to sources the rest of the world wishes they had, and about my intention to write this piece.

They are eagerly awaiting, believe me. I must reemphasize Dane's point about this being a bona fide international story. It strikes the human soul in ways other stories can't begin to touch. My hope is if we ever come in contact with aliens, they will read about Vlad's life. It displays the best and worst that humanity has to offer, and tells much about who we are as a people."

As dinner wound down, Dane asked Father Grant Moudry a question. "Father, as a non-Catholic, I need some guidance on the whole concept of the Sacrament of Reconciliation or confession as many call it. It's confusing for me. With all due respect Father Moudry, many non-Catholics don't understand the church forgiving a person for their sins. I think many people feel that is God's domain, not mans. I mean, can a murderer and a rapist be forgiven if they are sorry? What about justice?"

All at the table leaned in to hear father Moudry except Vlad, who discussed many times the exact question with him. The concept of making horrible choices in a hard world morphed into a cornerstone of their friendship. Father Moudry finished the last of his wine, set the empty glass down on the table and wryly replied "What about justice? Isn't that your department?"

The whole table laughed, as did Dane, realizing what he just said. Father Moudry gave Dane a 'gotcha' smile, looked around the table and continued. "Reconciliation is an ancient sacrament that has evolved over thousands of years in the Catholic Church's history. Go back to Medieval Europe. People would only confess on their deathbed fearing harsh penances and judgment by others. Some would be put in locks and chains, others forced to wear clothes made of the itchy and most uncomfortable rucksack. Some poor souls during that time would be banished from society, or condemned to hell. The focus on punishment was entirely wrong. "

Max looked at Dane "Sounds like the ancient church and your first two ex-wives have a lot in common, focus on punishment."

Dane smiled and replied, "The punishment continues with alimony paid every month!" The whole table erupted in laughter. The group was enjoying some good-spirited fun and learning something about the faith that meant so much to Max's dad.

The group quieted down, and Father Moudry continued, "We are all sinners. When a person is a member of the Catholic faith, the sin not only reflects upon the individual but on the entire community as a whole. As the leader of a particular community or parish, I represent the people in saying the community absolves you if you are truly sorry, seek to change the behavior that led to the sin, and make amends. We come together in Holy Communion every Sunday at Mass. We are one body of Christ, and if a member of the body is not well, we work to remedy that."

Father Moudry finished by saying "For most Christian denominations that I know of, The Lord's Prayer is a guiding principle. The Lord's Prayer states most clearly "Forgive us our trespasses, as we forgive those who trespass against us." There is not much ambiguity there, and Reconciliation is an extension of that. It brings us closer to God, our faith and ourselves. It's a positive examining of one's conscience, which in my opinion we all should do more often. We are not living in ancient Mesopotamia under Hammurabi's 'Eye for an Eye, Tooth for a Tooth.' Our God is a loving God who also gives us free will, and that free will enables us to make good and poor choices. If a poor choice distances us from God and damages grace from within, the Sacrament of

Reconciliation is exactly that. Reconcile oneself with God, the community and with those who are closest to us."

All at the table nodded, not necessarily in agreement but in understanding. Carl Jeffries then spoke up "What about penance?"

Father Moudry smiled and said "As Saint Francis said, 'In pardoning, we are pardoned.' We do give the person who is seeking absolution a good work to perform. That is correct. Reconciliation requires an effort of their part too. Normally it's not that tough of an assignment, and hopefully, leads to reflectiveness on life and what's important. A few prayers or acts of kindness are penance 99% of the time. God forgives, we just need to forgive ourselves and do our humble best to lead undamaged lives. Penance helps with that."

Father Moudry graciously drove Vlad home after Max paid the bill and goodbyes said. Carl, Dane, and Max stayed behind and ordered a nightcap at the bar. They discussed the upcoming Vikings season. No talk about Vlad and his situation. They left at midnight grateful to God in their private way for the ties that bind. All commented walking out the door about Father Moudry's insight. True friendship is indeed a symbol of God's love for us. Max couldn't help but think about Pavel. A man he never met, but felt extreme gratitude for the friendship he showed Vlad during those years. Max owed Pavel a debt that could not be repaid. His emotions overtook him. Max gazed into the night sky with grateful tears, and simply said thank you.

Chapter 27
October 1943
Drancy, France

Vlad and First Platoon were stationed in Drancy, a suburb 10 miles north of Paris. It was a beautiful autumn in German-occupied France. Despite rationing, the cafes bustled with wine, food, and women. Vlad and Pavel enjoyed their 48 hours leave per week immensely. They were free to visit the city and do as they pleased. The other five days per week were dedicated to Drancy and the deportation of French Jews to Auschwitz.

Vlad felt his favorite writer Charles Dickens described his time thus far at Drancy. "It was the best of times, it was the worst of times, it was the age of wisdom, it was the age of foolishness, it was the epoch of belief, it was the epoch of incredulity, it was the season of light, it was the season of darkness, it was the spring of hope, it was the winter of despair, we had everything before us, we had nothing before us, we were all going direct to Heaven, we were all going direct the other way."

They were in Paris, the most refined and culturally advanced city in Europe, if not the world. Paris had museums, cinemas, galleries, beautiful hotels, and restaurants. They also were assigned to Drancy, guarding Jews bound for certain death. Betrayed by their fellow French citizens, the Jews were interned at a makeshift camp waiting their turn to Auschwitz.

The camp was a five-story U-shaped building with a large courtyard in the middle. A place easily mistook for a multi-family housing complex in any advanced city. But this housing complex was surrounded by barbed wire, floodlights, armed guards, attack dogs, and watchtowers.

Drancy was a concentration camp for Jews in The City of Lights. Vlad and Pavel were used to remote stretches of Poland or Ukraine, where evil committed was concealed from the larger population. Drancy was in plain view. Buses, taxis, and pedestrians passed by daily. People in nearby apartment buildings saw into the courtyard, with its condemned inhabitants.

This was a world war between great powers that spanned multiple continents, but Vlad also understood it was also a total war on the Jews. The war on the Jews consumed all of Europe. It was complete with no respite. French Police, French gendarmes, and local authorities handed over 70,000 Jews to the SS to be murdered. 11,000 were French children. The large majority passed through Drancy Transit Camp in route to Auschwitz.

When newly arrived Jews entered Drancy, Orlov would greet them. His usual first words were "Jews, welcome to Drancy. Conditions are crowded, and the food is scarce. If you want to do us a favor and hang yourselves tonight, please write your filthy names on a piece of paper and stuff it in your mouths. It will make our record keeping easier. That is all."

The fear those few sentences struck into the Jewish people at Drancy was palpable. Orlov loved watching their faces fill with dread. He would approach the most vulnerable and harangue them until many physically collapsed. Orlov couldn't strangle a Jewish child each morning, so this was the next best thing for him.

The SS ensured Drancy offered no toilet facilities, little food, no running water, severe overcrowding, humiliation and rough treatment from the guards. Forcefully tearing apart Jewish families was a constant fear. For many months, adults were sent to Auschwitz while children stayed behind. The French reconsidered and decided keeping families intact on the train ride to Poland was more humane. The entire family policy was adopted by the SS in deference to local sensitivities.

The housing complex at Drancy was originally designed to comfortably accommodate 500 people. It held close to 7,000 at any given time. Some Jews were at Drancy for a few hours, some for a few days and some for a few weeks. Very few were interned more than a few months. Transports bound for Auschwitz departed two times per week with 1,000 men, women and children.

Vlad and First Platoons job was the orderly loading and unloading of transports and general guard duty of Jewish families. Vlad noticed the hatred against French Jews was more subtle and refined than anti-Semitism back east. No significant pogroms or Babi Yar type massacres, and open violence was rare. But the French fed the insatiable SS appetite for Jewish flesh and blood.

Orlov's grudge against Vlad continued to simmer. The feud between them had not boiled over as of yet, but Orlov's constant jabs at Pavel in front of the others were taking a toll. "Jew lover" was how Orlov would address Vlad on a normal basis. It caught on with some other men and became a nickname that began to stick. Vlad didn't mind the name, as much as the disrespect and embarrassment it garnered him daily. The resentment between them could be felt by all.

Pavel warned Vlad to be careful of Orlov. "Kid, stay clear of that psychopath. We both know his history of strangling children, rape, and love of torture. Of all Wachmen to have punched, he is probably to most volatile. Watch your back and try not to provoke him."

Vlad responded, "I can't stand that uneducated murdering pig. The crap he pulled at Belzec, and here at Drancy, defies all norms on how human beings treat each other. Yes, I am part of it too, but I try to do the minimum. I am doing it to save my skin, and I hate everything about this goddamned business. He is doing it because he is a homicidal maniac and loves every minute of it. That scumbag enjoys knowing these Jews are heading for death. I despise it."

Vlad and Pavel sat at a Paris cafe on a warm Saturday Fall afternoon. They were due back Sunday and had some time to relax. After their meal and a bottle of wine, they walked to a local bar for beers and hopefully French women. They ordered their first round, and a shout came from the back.

"Look, the Jew lover and his buddy are here. What a pleasant surprise." Orlov stumbled up to Vlad and Pavel and slurred "What are you drinking, Chayka? Is that Manischewitz kosher wine from America?"

Vlad rolled his eyes at Orlov "No. I am drinking beer, how about you? Is that a cup of Jewish blood or is it wine in your hands?"

Orlov looked at Vlad with bloodshot eyes. "You know Chayka. I went and saw The Eternal Jew at the cinema today. Great movie, explains much about these rats we are getting rid of. Believe me. The SS is doing the world a favor. You need to go see it."

Vlad took a sip of his beer. "I have always enjoyed Hollywood movies, not a fan of German ones."

Orlov sarcastically replied, "Hollywood is controlled by Jews, Chayka. Figures you would enjoy them more. Just who exactly do you think you are? You are just as much a part of this as I am. You walk around acting like I'm the devil and you are some saint. Does your shit smell different than mine? Were you at Trawniki, Rabka, and Belzec? How many Jews did you drive into the gas chambers? You are worse than these rats. They don't deny being Jews, but you deny who you are."

Vlad took another long sip of beer and questioned Orlov. "Who do you say I am?"

Orlov replied "You are the same as me, sacrificing others to save yourself. I was at Chelm, same as you. I am happy to be drinking in Paris, instead of dead in some POW camp. Vlad looked at Pavel who was listening intently but staying quiet.

Vlad then looked at Orlov. "I am nothing like you. Yes, I was at Trawniki, Rabka, and Belzec. You know that. But it wasn't me who needed to strangle a kid before breakfast. That was you. That, Orlov, is one of many things that set us apart."

Orlov laughed, "Saint Jew lover standing before me in the flesh. Let me tell you something Chayka. There will be a reckoning between us. Don't think for a minute that sucker punch during our last night in Belzec will go unanswered. I would like to kill you right here, just don't want to spend ten years in Dachau on account of your sorry self."

"Feeling is mutual Orlov," Vlad replied visibly agitated. "I will see you in hell when this is all over and will be happy to send you there first. Now get out of my face before I smash this beer glass across your head."

Pavel stepped in "Unless you two want to get arrested, put your dicks back in your pants and settle the hell down."

Orlov shouted back "Why are you always protecting him, Pavel? This guy is a pussy and isn't one of us. Never has been, never will be."

Pavel, who was much stronger than Orlov, grabbed him by the collar. "Orlov, I grew up with his older brother in Kiev, and he probably froze to death at Chelm. I knew his parents. Chayka is from a good family. If he doesn't get out of line or cause any problems for the platoon, I have his back. Quite frankly Orlov, you deserved to get punched back at Belzec. If that's all you have coming after all the crazy bullshit you've pulled since Trawniki, I'd say the penance has been light. So back off and leave the kid alone. Also, cut the Jew lover crap. We are all sick of hearing it."

Pavel let go of his shirt and grabbed his beer. "Now if I can finish my beer and maybe get laid, that would be nice. So buzz off, you're killing my chances with any women here."

Orlov straightened his collar and gave Vlad a dirty look. "Okay, Pavel, no problem, but I'm telling both of you now, this is not over. Chayka will pay. Not today, not tomorrow, but before I die, he will go first. Have a nice night ladies."

First Platoon reported back for duty at Drancy the following morning. Vlad's difficulty trying to adjust increased each time he returned to Drancy from leave in Paris. The Jews in transit to Auschwitz looked, dressed, and spoke like any other person in France. It may have been some innate mild anti-Semitism on Vlad's part, but the Jews back east were not assimilated into the larger population. They spoke Yiddish, dressed different, looked different, wore their hair and beards differently, and usually kept to their own. Vlad did not witness much social interaction between Jews and others in Ukraine.

Jews in France were fully assimilated. They spoke French, were patriotic, stylish, artistic, and educated. It wasn't that Eastern European Jews were easier to kill. It was just different in France. Vlad had a hard time explaining because it didn't make sense to him, none of it did. Right or wrong, Drancy was almost harder on Vlad. Especially painful was watching the children shipped off to certain death at Auschwitz. Vlad had enough and vowed to regain control over his life and actions.

Chapter 28
Drancy, France
June 1944

Living conditions deteriorated as Drancy eased into summer. The apartments had no glass or screens in the windows. Birds, bugs, and rabies carrying bats infested the already filthy quarters. Floors were bare concrete, and rotten straw was used as bedding. Not a single piece of furniture was available. Toilets consisted of overflowing coffee cans of human waste. Lice covered children roamed dark hallways begging for food and clean water. Cockroaches and mice were rampant. Electricity was turned off, water as well. Vlad knew the people of Paris were aware but turned a blind eye to the plight of their fellow citizens.

A group of Jewish children were found hiding at an orphanage in Izieu, a village outside of Lyon. Klaus Barbie gave the authorization to send all 44 of them to Auschwitz via Drancy. Vlad was at the loading ramp when they passed through. The tormented faces and pleas of mercy from these French children gave him renewed nightmares. He constantly replayed what Christ said about kids. "Let the children come to me. Do not stop them. For the Kingdom of God belongs to such as these."

To regain his sanity and a small measure of redemption, Vlad smuggled food and medicine inside the wire. When Vlad returned from leave, he covertly brought meat, cheese, wine and medicine hidden on his person. Few SS or Wachmen wanted to patrol inside the housing complex, due to the awful smell and conditions. This gave Vlad opportunity to enter the complex as part of guard duty and hand off his goods to a confidential source.

Vlad was taking a huge risk by helping these people, anyone giving aid or comfort to Jews was subject to immediate torture and certain execution by the Gestapo. If caught, he would experience the most severe punishment that could be meted out. Vlad felt it was the least he could do after Belzec and was happy to be an undeserving martyr if caught. He was also attempting to find some semblance of grace, and emerge out of his personal hell.

Vlad quietly befriended a Jewish prisoner he could trust to distribute the meager smuggled goods to those most in need. The prisoner was a respected poet and close friends with some of the most celebrated artists in the world. He was gifted, famous, and respected in France and throughout Europe. He converted to Catholicism 20 years prior, but was classified Jewish by the SS and thus deserved nothing less than death. Vlad was able to keep him off the transport list because the prisoner was too sick to travel. Vlad also kept him updated on the news from the outside, which was passed along to the imprisoned Jews. Pavel knew of his actions but kept quiet to Vlad and everyone else.

Pavel and Vlad guarded the courtyard at Drancy on a beautiful June afternoon, when Pavel confided. "The Americans and British have landed massive forces in Normandy. They are bogged down in hedgerow country but are breaking out. The Wehrmacht does not have the strength to push them back, and the Luftwaffe is diminished to the point of ineffectiveness. Once the Allies get into the open country, it's only a matter of time before they're here. Hang on kid. I have the feeling Germany's days are numbered. The Russians are advancing in the east, and the Americans are advancing from the west. No way these bastards can win a two-front war."

Vlad gave him a worried look. "What will the Red Army do with us? We will be considered collaborators and traitors. Stalin's henchmen will shoot us on the spot. Plus we are still sending trainloads of Jews to Auschwitz, even though the Allies are on French soil and fighting this way."

"Exactly, Chayka, keep your head and stay calm. If anyone is going to capture us, it's going to be the Americans or British, not the Red Army. Keep up what you are doing to help these people. I will protect you as best I can."

Vlad gave Pavel a surprised look "You know?"

Pavel responded "Yes I do, and must say it's a brave but stupid thing to do. Be careful. If Orlov or any SS find out, it's your neck, and I won't be able to help you."

Pavel gave Vlad a serious look and continued. "When the time comes, we will set a plan in motion that prevents us being deployed east to fight the Russians. You are right. If they capture us it's the firing squad for sure. Keep it quiet."

Knowing the end of the war may be near, Vlad allowed the Holy Spirit to re-enter his life and started having daily meditations with God.

Normally before bed, he would silently beg God for forgiveness for what he had done.

Unable to say confession to a priest, Vlad quietly admitted his weaknesses, grave sins, and selfishness. He much preferred to speak with another human being with training in divinity, which is why he enjoyed the Sacrament of Reconciliation. Vlad took great pleasure in receiving absolution, and his soul felt cleansed after confessing. It was solid and tangible, but Vlad was very apprehensive how a priest or his Catholic faith would react to the mortal sins committed since Trawniki. He wanted forgiveness and absolution, but felt wholly undeserving of both.

A transport in late June carried some Christian women who fell in love with, and married, Jewish men. They did not convert to Judaism, or raise their kids Jewish. According to Nazi racial laws, these women were not supposed to be passing through Drancy in route to Auschwitz. They made the most difficult decision to accompany their husbands on the journey east. When Vlad questioned their status, Orlov said with a smile. "They are Jew fucking whores. I hope they are gassed and roasting in the next day or two. They have spread their legs for snip cocks, and deserve what's coming to them." Vlad never heard the obscene slur before and was visibly shaken by the depravity of Orlov. It was another vulgar display of crudeness that highlighted the chasm between them.

Orlov forced the humiliated women to dance for his entertainment during their one-day layover, before continuing to Auschwitz. The prettiest Christian wife caught Orlov's eye, and he kidnapped her at knifepoint in the middle of the night. Orlov forced the French woman to a quiet corner of the camp and suddenly threw her to the ground. With a knife to her throat, he made her say "I am a Jew fucking whore" hundreds of times as he viciously raped her.

When Orlov was finished with the attack, he said to her. "You will be on a train tomorrow for a three day trip to Poland. Upon arriving at your destination, you will be separated from that Jew husband and have your head shaved. After the barber, you will get undressed and told to take a disinfecting shower. The shower room is a gas chamber, the doors will slam shut, and you will die a horrible death within 15 minutes. Your beautiful face will have any teeth ripped out that have gold fillings, and your sexy body will be tossed in an oven. Your ashes will be dumped in a local river."

The terrorized woman lay speechless as Orlov stood and zipped up his pants. "When you are writhing on the gas chamber floor in a few days and unable to breathe, I want your last memory to be of me raping you, and how good it felt. Now get back to your Jewish husband, you foul whore."

The women were shipped out the next day with their families and husbands, Orlov blew a kiss to the woman he raped as the train departed for Poland. The terrified look in her eyes gave him an instant erection.

Vlad and Pavel heard new rumors the SS needed assistance in Hungary. There were 500,000 Jews somehow yet untouched. Jews had been slaughtered in Europe for almost five years, and Vlad couldn't believe so many were still alive in one place. Even though Germany was on a clear path to defeat, Himmler and the SS wanted every single Hungarian Jew dead. The SS would come close to achieving their heinous task, in an orgy of summer violence.

The usual help of anti-Semitic locals helped speed an astonishing slaughter. 12,000 Jews per day were packed on trains and sent to Auschwitz from Hungary. The death camp was overloaded during the summer of 1944 with Hungarian Jews to kill, and crematoriums could not keep up with the number of dead. Word around Drancy was First Platoon would be called upon to help facilitate the murder. Vlad and Pavel had no intention of letting that happen.

Chapter 29
Drancy, France
Mid-August 1944

The Americans, British, and their Allies fought to the outskirts of Paris. The final transport to Auschwitz left Drancy on July 31st, and no more Jews arrived. A small detachment of SS stayed behind at Drancy with First Platoon, burning all documents relating to arrests and transports of Jews. The SS were trying to hide crimes committed during the occupation. Mounds of paperwork and other evidence burned for days in the courtyard. It reminded Vlad of the corpse burning during the final months at Belzec.

The last major issue for the SS were the remaining 1,000 Jews at Drancy. It was now impossible to get them by train to Auschwitz, and a forced march to the east was out of the question. Before evacuating, the senior SS Commander gave orders to set the Jewish prisoners free the next day. However, the remaining SS junior officer left in charge had no intention of following such an outrageous demand. He considered it sacred duty to murder the remaining Jews, and was happy to face an SS court martial because of his beliefs.

The junior officer reversed orders and informed First Platoon that every Jew would be shot the next morning. Time was of the essence. The Allies were expected to enter Paris within 24 hours. First Platoon was to rendezvous with the SS in Reims after the Jews were shot, and the Junior SS officer planned on surrendering there to his superiors. First Platoon was to be deployed to Hungary from Reims, assisting with the roundup and deportation of Jews to Auschwitz.

The next morning only five SS and First Platoon were left at Drancy with the Jews, everyone else evacuated to the east. The Allies liberated Paris and were within a few miles of the camp, all that remained was the liquidation of the remaining prisoners. Three German transport trucks were loaded with First Platoon's gear and room for all to sit. They had engines running, ready to take the men to Reims after their work was finished. The SS set up two tripod-mounted heavy machine guns facing into the courtyard, and First Platoon was busy assembling Jews in 10 rows of 100 to be murdered. If done correctly, this action would be over within 30 minutes and the men on their way.

The Wachmen had their loaded rifles neatly stacked in pyramids near the machine guns. They were ordered by the junior SS officer to finish off any wounded Jews after the machine gun fire ceased. If time permitted, a search for hidden valuables among the dead was possible. The assembled Jews were trembling with fear and anxiety. They knew their fate. Time for deception had passed, and a violent death was soon at hand. Orlov was in the back having the Jews undress, searching for any hidden valuables. Upon realizing the reason for the delay, the annoyed junior SS officer ordered Vlad and Pavel to pull Orlov up front with the rest of First Platoon and the SS gunners. Vlad and Pavel walked to the last row of 100 Jews and saw Orlov putting diamonds in his pockets.

"Orlov," Pavel said in an agitated voice "The SS officer wants you up front, he is nervous and upset about the delays you are causing."

Orlov pouted. "This is bullshit. I know these goddamned Jews are hiding jewels. There must be pounds of gold and diamonds. We are going to shoot them, and the locals will get the loot, just like Belzec."

Vlad looked at Orlov "Do what you want Orlov, I will report that you are not coming. I promise he will open fire with you still in here. Have a good day."

Orlov gave Vlad a worried look. "Okay. I am coming with you."

The three walked to the front where First Platoon and the SS waited. Assembled were 1,000 crying Jews beginning to say the Kaddish. Orlov spoke to the junior SS officer in charge "Sir, don't you want them undressed and double checked for valuables?"

The SS officer replied sharply "No, we have no time. We shall liquidate these vermin as they are, and move out to Reims." The officer looked around. All was ready. Vlad and Pavel could feel within seconds, the officer would give the order for the two machine gunners to open fire.

Vlad and Pavel gave each other a nod and pulled out their service pistols. Per their plan the night before, Vlad was first to squeeze the trigger and shot the junior SS officer in the chest. Pavel quickly followed with two shots, one in the head for each SS machine gunner. Vlad rapidly turned his weapon and delivered two head shots to the remaining SS men. Within ten seconds, all five SS were dead.

The Jews stood frozen, and First Platoon was trying to process what happened. Nobody moved or said anything. Pavel had his pistol at the ready and was watching Orlov. Vlad was looking at the others, making sure nobody ran for their rifles or side arms.

"Kill the Jew lover and his friend" Orlov screamed to First Platoon breaking the silence. One Wachman went for his pistol, Vlad shot him dead. Another two made a run for their rifles. Pavel shot them both in the back.

"Kill them" Orlov shrieked. Vlad ran to Orlov and pistol whipped him above the ear, he dropped to the ground like a stone, knocked out cold.

Pavel looked at the rest of First Platoon. Both he and Vlad had their side arms pointed at them, cocked with fingers on the trigger. Pavel shouted "Get the hell out of here if you don't want to die. If anyone reaches for a weapon, it will be the last thing you do."

Most of First Platoon turned and scurried out the front gate of Drancy, running into a full company of battle-hardened and well-armed American soldiers of the 4th Infantry Division. All Wachmen were immediately taken prisoner of war, including an unconscious Orlov. Vlad's slow spiritual and personal rebirth had begun. America awaited.

Chapter 30
Early September 1944
Western France

The American 4th Infantry called in the International Red Cross to care for the Jews. As they were French civilians, it was considered a French humanitarian matter. Vlad sensed the Americans found it curious that 1,000 people were assembled in the courtyard, with dead SS lying next to machine guns. The large group looked ragged, but were in decent health and no danger of imminent harm.

The SS Vlad and Pavel killed at Drancy were a non-issue for the American soldiers, who considered dead SS a good thing. The Waffen SS were fierce and fanatical combat forces, who inflicted heavy casualties on the Americans as they advanced through France.

Under heavy guard outside the gates of Drancy, Vlad was searched for weapons or contraband and disarmed by the GIs. The 4th Infantry Division landed at Utah Beach in the first wave on D-day and fought the entire way up to capturing First Platoon. Despite the dehumanization of war, the Americans treated Vlad with respect. He was allowed to keep personal effects, such as pictures of his family and a gold cross carried since Confirmation.

Vlad and First Platoon began the 150-mile march to the French coast near Normandy. It was a chaotic few days with thousands of Allied troops pouring into France driving east, while thousands of German prisoners marched west towards the coast. The number of well supplied and well fed American soldiers, passing the ever-growing column of POWs, was an impressive sight. The Americans looked like a formidable foe, and Vlad was relieved he didn't have to fight them. It eerily reminded Vlad of being force marched with his brothers out of Minsk, and towards the hellish German prison camps. The brutality Vlad experienced as a Soviet POW made him extremely apprehensive to be captive of yet another foreign power.

First Platoon became dispersed among thousands of other POWs during the march to Normandy Beach. The Americans separated the POWs into manageable sized groups of 500. Vlad, Pavel, and Orlov stayed grouped together to the embarkation point. Orlov physically recovered from being pistol whipped, but couldn't remember who did it, nor recall the events from the entire day of capture. If and when his memory did recover, Pavel promised he would protect Vlad.

Vlad's group was told through American interpreters they were being transported to the United States via Liberty Ship. Vlad, Pavel, Orlov and the rest of the group were relatively well treated and decently fed since capture. Vlad wanted to believe the Americans were different, but he actively participated in the Nazi deception of keeping Jews calm until it was too late. Vlad worried the Americans had a version of the tube for the German POWs and would be herded into gas chambers at the last minute. His actions at Belzec were constantly at the forefront of his thoughts as the POWs marched west.

Vlad wasn't sure of his fate until they reached the French coast at the English Channel after six days of marching. The group arrived near Omaha Beach, where the Allies landed on D-Day three months earlier. The enormity of the continuing Allied operation was unreal to him and the other POWs. Hundreds of ships stretching to the horizon were in port or waiting their turn to unload supplies, soldiers, and war material. Tens of thousands of fresh-faced, well-armed troops walked off the ships and headed towards the front. Thousands of jeeps, trucks, tanks and heavy weapons poured in. Barrels of fuel amounting to a million gallons stored near the beach were stacked on a scale hard to imagine. Vlad knew the Americans meant business. They were here to win, and they were here to stay.

A Liberty Ship finished unloading more American soldiers and supplies and was ready to receive 750 POWs bound for Norfolk, Virginia. Vlad, Pavel, and Orlov boarded the ship and were escorted to the crowded, but sufficient lower cargo hold. There were enough makeshift bunks for all POWs aboard, sleeping in shifts would not be necessary for the Germans. Much to the chagrin of their American hosts, who shared bunks with at least one other shipmate. The cargo hold was ventilated, but still hot and smelled like a men's locker room. The bathroom facilities and general sanitary conditions were adequate. It would make do for the Atlantic crossing. When all were aboard, a tugboat maneuvered the ship out of the man-made Mulberry pier and into the English Channel. Another vessel immediately took the spot of Vlad's Liberty Ship. Refueling for the voyage back to Norfolk took place in the channel. Time was not to be wasted.

Vlad wasn't sure about the rest of the men, but this was his and Pavel's first time on a ship. The yawing of the vessel made them nauseous, and Vlad was the first POW below deck to vomit. As the ship reached the open Atlantic, she rolled and pitched in the choppier seas causing a majority of the men to become sick. The stench of vomit in the cargo hold was so overpowering, the Americans entered with hoses and sprayed the lower deck with seawater pumped from the outside. It had been four hours into the journey. The POWs on board were not sailors, and it showed.

The captain ordered the POWs onto the main deck for an announcement after dinner was served, which few of them ate. Vlad never saw the open ocean before and was startled by the idea of not being able to see land. It was a foreign feeling he would never get used to. Above the assembled men stood American sailors manning mounted machine guns pointed down at the POWs. Other sailors stood on the catwalk holding Thompson submachine guns at the ready, in case anyone decided to revolt and rush the American crew.

Once all were on deck and assembled, the Captain played a recording in German over a loudspeaker. "You are prisoners of war in custody of the United States Army. You are being transported to Norfolk, Virginia courtesy of the United States Navy. You will be fed regular rations three times per day and receive fair treatment. If any of you need medical attention, please speak with our liaison officer, and he will have you see the corpsman. The journey should last ten days provided good weather, which we expect. No problems with previous POW transports have occurred, and we expect the same on this voyage. You will be allowed on deck three hours per day for fresh air and exercise. There are enough life vests for each POW in the bunk area. If we are torpedoed by one of your U-Boats, put on a life vest and pray the sharks stay away until rescue. Any further questions can be directed to your senior officer. That is all."

The second night at sea, the POWs started talking amongst themselves in greater numbers. Many remained sick, quiet and personally reflective on the finality of the sudden life change. By the third day, most got their sea legs, were feeling better, and accepted their fate as POWs. Some were content to be there, others not. By this point, Vlad, Pavel, and Orlov learned enough German since Trawniki to speak with, and understand the men in the cargo hold. The men were already dividing into three different groups, based on their view of Hitler and National Socialism.

The first group comprised of ardent Nazi's committed to Hitler's murderous treatment of Jews and other undesirables. This group consisted mainly of SS and very anti-Semitic Wehrmacht soldiers. Although they viewed him with less worth because he was Ukrainian, Orlov gravitated towards them. They gave him grudging credit for the Wachman uniform, knowing what it meant.

The second group was by far the largest and consisted of regular soldiers who answered the call to fight for Germany. They were relatively apolitical and didn't feel strongly one way or another about Hitler and the Nazis. When their country needed men to fight, they enlisted and served with honor. Their feelings towards the Jews varied, some were anti-Semitic and others less so. They all had strong attachments to Germany and its defense. It's where they were born and raised. Most had families to worry about back home and didn't want harm to come to them. It's why they fought.

The third group, about the same size as the first, were mostly conscripted into the Wehrmacht and forced to fight Hitler's war. They were anti-Nazi, felt Hitler hijacked Germany, and would lead to their homeland's destruction. They resented being forced to fight, but the alternative was most likely jail, a concentration camp or worse. This group was not all made up of Germans, as many people from conquered European countries were coerced into the military to fight on the side of Germany. They felt the treatment of Jews was wrong, and in some cases privately knew of Jews being hidden.

As they observed groups forming onboard the ship, Pavel pulled Vlad aside. "I don't like how these POWs are dividing up based on views of Hitler and the war. It is dangerous and could easily lead to violence between them. We need to stick together as usual and avoid being drawn into any of these groups of people. Who knows how this will play out, but I feel the tension rising between them. Stay neutral and keep quiet."

Some in the three groups rearranged bunks and seating for meals so that they could socialize together. No one had voiced loud feelings to the entire ship one way or the other about where they stood. They were quiet conversations at the beginning. That would change as the days onboard passed.

The Liberty ship was at sea for eight days under sunny fall skies and calm winds. The Captain kept his word on decent treatment, adequate food and three hours daily above deck. The men all needed a shower and change of clothes, but otherwise were fine. The POWs were on deck for exercise and fresh air, when Navy guards on duty heard a commotion from the stern of the ship.

Orlov was with the group of Nazi loyalists having a cigarette and talking loud at the rear of the ship when Vlad and Pavel walked by. "Hey, Jew lover" Orlov barked out "I finally remember it was you who pistol whipped me, and both of you killed five Waffen SS at Drancy." The Nazi loyalists all looked at Orlov like he was crazy "It's true, this Jew lover and his buddy shot an SS Officer and four other SS. They did it to save a bunch of Jew pigs in France. They would rather see SS die than Jews. They are guilty of high treason and should be shot or thrown overboard. Goddamned disloyal bastards they are. Your days are numbered Chayka, you too Pavel."

Pavel had been waiting for this and was prepared. He ran up to Orlov and smashed him with his fist in the same spot where Vlad pistol whipped him earlier at Drancy. Orlov screamed and crumpled to the deck writhing in pain. He tried to stand up but lost his equilibrium, fell again and hit his head on a steel winch as he went down. Orlov lay motionless on the deck, and his breathing became shallow. The American guards above fired their Thompsons on full automatic into the air. All of the POWs dropped to their stomachs and stayed motionless as whistles blew and sirens wailed.

Pavel looked at the group of Nazi loyalists as they lay on their stomachs and shouted, "This guy has been trouble for three years. Both Chayka and I served at Belzec and helped kill hundreds of thousands of Jews. We did things to them you can't dream of, and anyone questioning his loyalty or mine has no clue what they are talking about. The two of us have done more damage to the Jews than all of you combined, times 100." Pavel then stood up with fists clenched and said "Orlov is mentally ill and should be either in an institution or gassed. He's a lying bastard and loyal to Russia. The asshole is trying to deflect any problems onto us. Don't listen to a word Orlov says. He's a habitual liar and bad alcoholic. He must be going through withdrawals and hallucinating because there isn't booze for him on this ship."

The Nazi loyalists looked puzzled but believed Pavel. After a brief silence, one of them said "You are all Ukrainian dogs, loyal to whoever feeds you. Stay away and tell your friend Orlov not to come near us when he recovers. None of you would ever be able to kill an SS Officer and get away with it. We would have received word if it happened. We don't care how many Jews you claim to have killed, but if Orlov is telling even a shred of truth, you are both dead."

Pavel gave them a hard stare and walked away with Vlad. "Pavel," Vlad said with a worried expression "I haven't felt this unsafe since the prison camp at Chelm. Those SS would kill us without blinking an eye. The Americans lock us in for the night. If the SS decide to believe Orlov, we could easily be killed in our sleep. No POWs would intervene in to stop it, nor would they testify against any of them. I can't have survived all of this madness only to die on my way to the United States."

Pavel gave Vlad a reassuring look. "Nobody is going to die. We will sleep in shifts and wake the other person if there is a problem. You are right. We are on our own. The Americans are not going to come down here and keep the peace in the middle of the night. Just watch my back, and I'll do the same for you. We should be in America in a day or two."

Chapter 31
Mid-September 1944
Norfolk, Virginia

The Liberty Ship was docked for 45 minutes on a perfect fall morning when the POWs were allowed to assemble on deck for the last time. Vlad and Pavel squinted as they looked out and surveyed the massive naval station. Endless rows of piers jutting into the harbor lined with battleships, Liberty Ships, aircraft carriers, troop transports, cruisers, submarines, oilers, and destroyers. A gentle breeze blew as the POWs were ordered to disembark from the ship, and march to a large brick building a mile away for interviews and processing.

As Vlad stepped off the pier and onto actual American soil, the moment was not lost on him. He turned to Pavel "This is the land of the free, where people can worship as they please. Let me say this quietly to you my friend. It's something I haven't uttered in almost four years. 'I look forward to the resurrection of the dead and of the life of the world to come. Amen.' It's the ending of a prayer we recite at Mass. It applies to me, my near dead spirituality and what lays ahead for us in this country. I wonder if God has given me a chance to somehow become reborn. If the Americans were to punish us, it would have happened already. I hope God forgives me Pavel, and maybe allows me to live a normal life before I die. Is that too much to ask?"

"Look, kid," Pavel whispered "I hope God will forgive you, but these Americans may not. You are right. A person has freedom of religion here. But if they uncover our role at Belzec, we could face a firing squad, who knows? Crime is crime, and we could be punished. My understanding is that America is a nation of laws. I am quite certain they have laws against murdering hundreds of thousands of innocent people. When they start asking questions, say you were drafted into the Wehrmacht and fought in the east before being transferred to France to fight off the invasion. It's straightforward and believable, keep your nerve and stay close to me."

The group walked for a mile under guard along a dirt road towards an administration building, recently converted to a processing center for POWs. Almost 20,000 POWs per month would pass through this place, overwhelming the Americans doing the actual interviewing. Most of the fluent German speaking American army interpreters were in Europe near the front being used in urgent battle situations. They served as cryptologists, interrogated captured German soldiers for real-time battlefield intelligence, interpreted communiques from secretly decoded Enigma machines, and communicated with German military units dictating surrender terms. Interviewing POWs at Norfolk and elsewhere stateside was not a high priority for the US Army, and the low quality of information gathered was apparent.

The POWs were escorted into the building by groups of 50. Vlad and Pavel waited their turn, and Orlov appeared with his head bandaged. His eyes were swollen, and the entire side of his face was black and blue. He was coherent enough to understand the Nazi loyalists were avoiding him and stood alone near a group of men waiting to be interrogated. Pavel waved him over.

"What are you doing?" Vlad asked.

Pavel raised his hand as if to shush Vlad. "Hang on kid, let me talk to him." Orlov hesitated for a moment and then walked over to see what Pavel wanted.

"Listen to me, Orlov. Keep your mouth shut with these Americans. They could react most negatively if they find out we murdered Jews at Belzec. I am not sure what will happen if you tell them, but it won't be good for any of us. Chayka and I are saying we were drafted into the Wehrmacht and fought in the east, then were transferred to France to help fight the invasion. If you have any brains left in your thick skull, do the same and avoid trouble. If the Americans take us individually, our stories will match and make sense. Got it, Orlov? Or am I going to smash you again in the head right here?"

Orlov looked at them both and nodded. Pavel continued. "By the way Orlov, your SS buddies said to stay away from them, or they will kill you. They didn't believe a word you said and think you are a crazy alcoholic. If you don't believe me, just walk up to them and see what happens."

Orlov looked like a cornered and wounded mean dog. He lashed out, "Chayka, you are the biggest pussy I have ever met in my life. I should have killed you when I had the chance. You may have Pavel protecting you now, but that won't last forever. Who knows what the Americans have in store for us. If you are unprotected, and I get the chance, I will strangle you like the Jew lover you are."

Pavel looked at Orlov in disbelief and said "Would you shut the fuck up for once in your miserable life? Did you hear a word I said? Are you going to cooperate so we can get out of this place without getting shot by a firing squad, or are you going to act like your stupid self and wreck it for all of us?"

Orlov let out a sigh. "I will go along with this, purely for the sake of myself, not either of you. We were all forced to join the Wehrmacht, fought in the east and were transferred to France to help fight the invasion. That sound about right?" Both Vlad and Pavel nodded in agreement.

An American Officer with five armed guards took another group of 50 men which included Vlad, Pavel, and Orlov. They marched into the administration building where 50 desks with chairs and 50 American interviewers awaited. "Remove your shirts" a voice called out in bad German "Set them on the ground in front of you, then raise your arms towards the ceiling."

The 50 POWs did as requested and stood shirtless in front of the large open brick room. A medical doctor with two assistants and three armed guards quickly inspected each man. Anyone with a blood type tattoo near the armpit was deemed to be SS and forcefully removed from the room. Five men out of the 50 were escorted out of the area to a holding cell.

"Put your shirts back on, proceed to an open desk and sit down to be interviewed." The same American sergeant said in his terrible German accent. He studied German for only six months, and it was painfully obvious. This was his assignment, and Vlad could tell he hated every minute of it.

"Fill this out." He said to Vlad in broken German. It was a questionnaire in German asking name, rank, branch of service, birthplace, and date of birth. It asked if the person was a member of the Nazi party and other questions regarding attitudes towards Hitler and the war. The questionnaire also asked about the POWs work history, and if they possessed any trade skills. It was designed as a first step separating the fanatical Nazi's from the rest, and to determine future work assignments.

Vlad was done filling out the form in five minutes. The American sergeant looked it over and stamped it with the word Algona. He took a picture of Vlad facing front and profile. Vlad was given a temporary paper I.D attached to twine, worn like an oversized necklace. American military police came into the room and removed three more fanatical men, based on their questionnaire answers.

Vlad, Pavel, and Orlov remained with the group that now numbered 42 men. "This way," a corporal said to the POWs as he motioned to the door. The men entered a large warehouse with tables staffed by American enlisted men ordered to outfit each POW. Vlad received socks, boots, underwear, pants, shirts, a light jacket and a winter coat. He also received a belt, gloves, and a winter hat. All articles of clothing had "POW" emblazoned on them.

Vlad thought about his first day at Trawniki when he received clothes from slave laborers. Most were Jews and destined for a grisly death after their servitude with the Nazi's was completed. He remembered the first person he shot in the courtyard almost three years prior, it seemed like a lifetime ago, and in fact, it was. Vlad promised himself to somehow atone for what he had done to his first victim and countless others.

Vlad's thoughts were interrupted by the same corporal who shouted in German, "To the trains." Vlad and Pavel gave each other an apprehensive look, but the expression on Orlov's face was priceless. It was like the angel of death entered his body and scared the life out of him. Vlad burst out laughing at the sight. It enraged Orlov and drove the tension between them even higher. The men waited on the platform for the train to arrive. All were expecting cattle cars to take them to their next destination. None of them had the slightest idea what awaited.

Chapter 32
Norfolk, Virginia

The POWs initially refused to believe the Pullman cars were for them. All assumed they would be at least riding with the luggage in the rear. They boarded the cars, and everyone took a seat in the plush recliners with armrests and built-in pillows. Vlad estimated there were 15 to 20 of these passenger cars with 70 men per car. At either end of each car, one army enlisted man sat with a rifle. The other security measure on board was for POWs to raise their hand if a bathroom break was needed. Only one POW at a time was permitted to use the restroom. Vlad recalled trains arriving at Belzec, with numerous SS on the roof of each boxcar holding automatic weapons guarding a harmless people doomed to death. The flashbacks to Belzec continued unabated.

The train pulled out of Norfolk Naval Base and headed east. An African American Porter entered Vlad's car with a silver platter of finger sandwiches and glasses of cold milk. He walked over to Vlad and Pavel who were seated next to each other and lowered the plate to chest level. The porter smiled and gave a nod, motioning them to take a sandwich and milk. Vlad and Pavel looked at each other in astonishment and gladly helped themselves. Vlad gave the porter a smile and said thank you in Ukrainian.

The porter laughed and said "I'm used to you boys sayn' danke, what language you speakin'? That Russian? We have Russians on this train? Good lord! What's this war comin' to? You boys enjoy your sandwiches and let me know if you want more." He had no idea what this Porter was saying in English, but Vlad flashed a smile he had not done in years. It almost hurt his face but felt great. The porter was the first black person Vlad and Pavel had ever seen, probably the same for most of the POWs on board.

After the porter left and moved onto the next car, Vlad let out a deep breath and set down his empty glass of milk. He cocked his head to the right, looking out the window and at Pavel. Pavel gave him a knowing nod and Vlad was first to speak. "I am having a hard time reconciling how the Americans are taking care of us, versus how we were treated by the Germans, and what we did to the Jews. Here we are riding in luxury, but the Jews were packed into cattle cars like sardines. We are offered milk and sandwiches. They were offered cruelty and death. The Jews froze in the winter and suffered heat exhaustion in the summer. They begged for water, and we answered with violence and spite."

Vlad started to cry as he continued to speak. "I remember when I was with my brothers at some hell on earth Nazi POW camp. We were starved, and those Nazi bastards threw a dead dog over the fence for us to eat. Our fellow countrymen beat each other to death over the goddamn thing. When there wasn't a dead dog, they fed us rancid soup made from grass and horse bones. We are separated by an ocean, but it feels like a different planet here. Are we that much different how we treat each other and how human life is valued? Do you think God loves this country more than He loves ours? What's the matter with us? We forced these people to come across the Atlantic Ocean and fight a war. They treat us with respect and show everyone on this train kindness. It's hard to fathom."

Pavel was teared up as well. He was about to reply when Orlov turned around. Orlov was perched on his knees and looked over the back of his seat into the next row, where Vlad and Pavel sat. "Are you crying Chayka? You damn Jew lover. What's your problem now? The only reason I would be crying is that there are no Jews to kill. While our SS brothers shoot or gas every Jew in Europe, we sit here on a train to God knows where. If I am going to cry, that's the reason. By the way, I saw you smiling at that black monkey. I suppose you are a black lover too? Jews and Blacks, huh Chayka? Is that your thing now?"

Vlad turned around so that he and Orlov were almost nose to nose. Orlov continued in a hushed and menacing voice. "You shot SS men and pistol-whipped me." He looked at Pavel "You blindside punched me on the ship." He looked back at Vlad. "But you sit and smile at the Negro. Your true colors are coming through loud and clear, Chayka. You will never leave America alive. I can tell you that right now. I swear to God, if there are any SS or Nazi loyalists wherever we are going, you are a dead Jew Negro lover."

"Sit down" the American guard yelled in bad German. Both Vlad and Orlov turned around and sat in their respective seats.

"Next stop, Richmond." the conductor yelled as he passed through the Pullman car. They arrived in Richmond, Virginia soon after. Vlad and Pavel saw armed soldiers on the platform, forming a perimeter with

American civilians behind them. The civilians were both black and white, many young men in uniform not part of the guard detail also waited for trains.

"Off the train," the guard said again in bad German. The POWs all stood, took turns to leave their seats, and exited the Pullman car. The train ride lasted about an hour and a half. They stepped off the train and onto the platform.

Orlov blurted out, "America is not that big, we are here already." When the POWs cleared the entire train, they marched under guard to a separate and isolated wing in the station. The POWs split into different groups, according to the tags given at Norfolk worn around their necks. Different trains came and went, and different POW groups boarded them. Vlad saw trains with lighted signs in the upper corner of the locomotives displaying strange names of destinations.

POWs were divided into much smaller groups and boarded trains to places like Texas, Kansas, Nebraska, New Mexico, Florida, and Tennessee. Vlad saw the Nazi loyalists from the Liberty Ship escorted towards a train that said Oklahoma on the front engine window. They were under heavier guard than normal and scowled at Pavel and Vlad as they walked by. The Americans attempted to quarantine those who believed in, and were committed to, National Socialism. The danger of Nazi radicalization spreading throughout an enclosed camp and intimidation of fellow POWs was a major concern.

The Americans tried to put all the rotten eggs in one basket, and Vlad understood the main camp for them was in Oklahoma. The method was far from perfect. Many POWs simply lied on the questionnaire they filled out in Norfolk. Or upon realizing the American interviewer spoke little German, feigned ignorance and spoke in ways the interviewer couldn't understand. Others pretended to speak Russian, Polish, Italian or Hungarian to try and outwit their new captors. There were many instances of Nazi loyalists infiltrating camps, causing mayhem and creating hazardous atmospheres for inmates and guards. Even though he was just a Wachman and Ukrainian, Orlov would covertly play the future role of an adherer to Nazism.

Vlad's train said Chicago. A place he knew due to gangster stories during prohibition in America, tales that reached all the way to Kiev. He imagined a city filled with Tommy Guns, bootleggers, and Al Capone types walking the streets. Vlad found it curious that his POW camp was in such a big city with a huge civilian population. He was unaware of three more transfers before reaching their main camp, and it wasn't in Chicago.

Vlad, Pavel, and Orlov were grouped together with 300 other men. They all noticed their ID tags were stamped with the word Algona. It was a place none of them had heard of, nor had many Americans unless they were from Iowa.

While Vlad, Pavel and the rest of the POWs waited for their train in Richmond, the same guard who accompanied them from Norfolk walked in. "Come with me, and line up on the platform, your train is almost here." The group walked into the early afternoon sunshine and watched their train roll up to the platform. It was considerably shorter than the first train, only seven passenger cars with a few freight cars in the rear. The POWs were ready to board but were delayed by commotion on the train. They heard shoving, shuffling of feet, and loud voices. Vlad didn't understand the language, but it was evident the people inside were arguing.

A large group of black sailor recruits from Atlanta, headed to the Great Lakes Naval Station for boot camp, occupied one of the passenger cars. There was not enough room for the POWs and young black sailors, as someone failed to couple more passenger cars to accommodate both groups. No other passenger cars were available in Richmond, and there was no time to waste if the train was to depart as scheduled. The conductor and two white naval officers stood on the platform discussing what looked like a serious and heated matter, in front of all to see.

After a few minutes of tense talk, the conductor yelled at the two Naval Officers "This is my goddamned train. If you don't like my decision, then have your niggers walk to Chicago for all I care." He pointed to Vlad and the other POWs exclaiming, "They sit up front in the Pullman cars, and the niggers sit with the luggage in the rear. Have General Eisenhower call me and complain. This train leaves in exactly three minutes whether your niggers are on or not, so get moving and quit wasting my time."

None of the POWs spoke English, but all understood when they saw black sailors exit the Pullman car. Vlad immediately recognized the humiliation and shame on their faces. They heard about Jim Crow laws and racism in America. The Nazi's used it as effective propaganda to justify their treatment of the Jews. Vlad remembered reading about Hitler's disgust at the 1936 Olympics in Berlin. The black American athlete Jesse Owens won four gold medals and smashed numerous world records. It exposed the absurdity of Hitler's Master Race.

The black sailors walked off the passenger car and past the POWs towards the back. A crowd of civilians gathered near the train to witness the spectacle, and word spread fast around the station. There was an uneasy silence as black men in uniform, who were expected to fight and even die for their country, were treated as second class citizens to the enemy they fought. The sailors eyeballed the POWs and muttered profanities under their breath, the unfairness and complete hypocrisy of the situation showed on their faces. The last black sailor exited the Pullman car, and the American guard ordered the white POWs on board. Orlov was first to board and made a monkey sound as he passed the last black sailor. The conductor was the only one in authority within earshot and heard the epithet. He did nothing.

Chapter 33

The train ride brought the POWs through the heartland of America. Rolling in and out of states like West Virginia, Ohio, Illinois, Indiana, Missouri and finally Iowa. Vlad and the rest of the POWs were surprised at the abundance of cars on the roads, food on the train and the vastness of America. All POWs were astonished at the general quality of life people were living during the greatest war humanity had ever seen. Compared to where they came from, the United States was far wealthier and much different from propaganda the Germans consistently produced. Abundance was everywhere.

Orlov and some other POWs were convinced the train took a specific route, avoiding cities bombed by Hitler's Vengeance weapons. Josef Goebbels' Nazi propaganda machine promised vengeance on the United States for bombing and laying waste to Germany. As the train rolled through Middle America, it was apparent even to Orlov the industrial and agricultural might of the United States. America possessed unmatched output of ships, planes, trucks, tanks, bombs, artillery and other weapons.

The food produced and distributed was on a scale the POWs found incredible. Trains regularly passed them heading towards the east coast, full of supplies and soldiers for the war in Europe. One thing they did notice as they passed from town to town was the shortage of men from 18 to 40 years old. They were simply nowhere to be found.

Vlad thought about the black soldiers back in Richmond. Unknown to him, they got off at the next stop and transferred to another train headed to Chicago in passenger cars. Nazi propaganda depicted America as mongrel people ruled by Jews. Americans were portrayed as people corrupted by black music, racist, money hungry, lazy and soft. That picture all but vanished for every POW on board. America was a hardworking, industrious and polite society sending millions of its sons and massive amounts of supplies to fight Nazi Germany. However, the incident with the black sailors showed all was not perfect in the land of the free and home of the brave.

Vlad witnessed how black American sailors were forced to make way for white enemy POWs. For him that meant race relations superseded war and the enemy they fought, which astonished him. Vlad learned about the American Declaration of Independence in his youth. He recalled the famous words 'all men are created equal.' A noble concept, but easier said than done he thought to himself. He thought about the dreadful Nuremberg Laws, a critical first step in launching the Holocaust. "At least the Americans strive for an ideal" Vlad muttered to himself.

Vlad gave Pavel an inquisitive look. "America seems like a complicated place. Why do black people fight to liberate Europe when they are not treated as equals at home? Could you imagine Jews fighting for Germany? And these porters on the train taking care of us are all black, but they treat us with kindness and look happy living in here. It makes me wonder about the Jews."

Pavel turned to Vlad with a surprised look and said "Are you comparing the Jews to the Nazi's and blacks in America? Because if you are, that is way off my young friend. I saw what happened at the train station, and it bothered me also. There is a separation between them, and it must go back to the days of slavery. I remember reading about the American Civil War in history class. Many white men died to end slavery and keep this country together. Black people must believe life will continue to get better in America. Otherwise, they would never fight for a country they didn't believe in. Look, kid, you were at Belzec and saw what happened to the Jews. That is not even close to what is going on here. You know that."

Vlad replied "Of course it's not Pavel. I guess no country is without its bad sides, with fear of people who are different. It's just a case of how out of control it's allowed to go. I remember pogroms as a kid. Christians committed acts of arson, rape, and violence. Nobody did anything about it, and now look what's happening to the Jews back in Europe. I hope America never lets that happen. It is too great of a country to do so."

Vlad then whispered to Pavel. "I never want to leave here."

Pavel gave Vlad a smile and said "I understand, and if that's what you want, I hope it happens. For me, I will go home, even if it means the firing squad. My heart and head are in Ukraine, but you are different, Vlad. I could see you staying here somehow, just keep that thought to yourself. Escape is impossible. We sailed across an ocean and are on a train heading deep into America. You will need to figure out a way to make it so. I do know we are here until this war is over, maybe longer.

Enjoy the stay and watch out for Orlov, he's meaner and crazier than ever. He is like a caged animal waiting to lash out at someone or something, and it will most likely be you or me. Just be careful."

The train entered the State of Iowa, and the men were restless after three days and nights of travel. They were given playing cards and magazines by the porter, which helped pass the time and alleviate boredom. Two American guards with loaded rifles at either end of Vlad's passenger car slept in shifts, so one was awake at all times. Had they truly wanted to, the POWs could have easily overpowered the guards.

Orlov was quietly trying to organize a revolt, and escape from the train before it reached a camp where security was sure to be tighter. Word reached Pavel and Vlad about the plan, which Orlov wanted to hatch after dark that evening. Pavel stood up in the aisle and spoke in Ukrainian to Orlov so that the guards couldn't understand. "Where are you going to go after you leave this train? You don't speak English, you don't know the people, you don't know the terrain, you don't know where we are, and you don't know where we are going. You have no food, no money and are wearing clothes that have POW printed on them in big white letters. You are a stranger in a foreign land who crossed an entire ocean to get here. If you try to escape, all you're going to do is get every one of us shot. Don't do it, and if I see you making a move, I will knock your ass out cold again. Got it?"

Orlov gave Pavel a dirty look and turned away in defeat. Pavel was right, and Orlov knew it. No escape attempt would be made, at least not on the train. Suddenly, they were interrupted by the conductor who had been relatively absent to this point.

He walked through their car and shouted: "Algona in 15 minutes."

The guards stood up, and the one who barely spoke German raised his voice. "We are almost there, gather your belongings and prepare to get off the train." Some of the POWs clapped and whistled, most were ready to disembark and see what awaited them.

The train came to a stop, and the men exited onto the platform. It was early evening with dusk approaching. The land was flat, and corn was growing as far as the eye could see. The growing of food in this place was almost magical to all of them. Vlad felt like they were in the middle of nowhere, and in fact, they were. The Army set up Camp Algona on purpose. It was removed from large populations or defense industries. The closest town of any size was Mason City about 50 miles away. The POWs stood in North Central Iowa, thousands of miles away from where they were born. They couldn't have been further from home.

Chapter 34
Algona, Iowa
October 1, 1944

The POW camp covered 280 acres of former farmland, surrounded by two chain-link fences and topped with barbed wire. Eight watchtowers and 170 heated wooden buildings occupied the inside. It was the largest POW camp in the upper Midwest and housed 2,500 prisoners. The camp was well light, tidy, and inside the city limits of the small town of Algona. Camp Algona also had many branch camps on a much smaller scale in the Dakotas and Minnesota. In all, nearly 10,000 German POWs were under the authority of the Camp Algona system.

The POWs were escorted on foot from the train station by armed soldiers to the large wood framed gates of Camp Algona. An American officer who spoke excellent German met the newly arrived POWs. "Welcome to Camp Algona. For you, all hostilities are over. The United States Army has brought you to me until the shooting war in Europe is finished, and the Allies are victorious. You will be well cared for, and all rules of the Geneva Convention followed regarding your treatment. You will be allowed to write home and earn camp currency by working. We are expecting another 500 POWs tomorrow and 500 by the end of the week. Some of you will stay here, but most will be transported to our branch camps in states nearby."

The American officer let the din quiet down from the assembled POWs. "We have reviewed your records and determined where each of you will be assigned. The camp assignment is based on your skill sets and will coincide with work needed. If you were a farmer, then you will be assigned to a camp near farms that need labor. Most of you who do not have farming skills will be assigned to forestry duty in camps to the north. You will now be divided into groups based on the camp which you are assigned. Please listen for your name to be called and barracks number. For those assigned to a different camp than Algona, you leave tomorrow to make room for more of your countrymen. Dinner will be served at 6 pm after everyone showers, followed by taps and lights out at 10 pm. That is all."

Vlad, Pavel and Orlov's name were called with 50 others and assigned to barracks number 20. The group entered the well-built wooden structure, furnished with 30 bunk beds and a potbelly stove for heat. Each bunk had a mattress, two sheets, a wool blanket and a pillow. The showers were warm and badly needed after two weeks on a boat and three days on the train. Vlad and the rest of his barracks group showered, shaved, and then escorted to one of the four large mess halls inside the wire at Algona.

The meal consisted of chipped beef on toast, which the American GIs affectionately called 'shit on a shingle.' Creamed corn, bread with butter, and cherry gelatin rounded out the meal. The POWs were taken aback by the presence of butter. Vlad thought back to the last time he had tasted it. To the best of his memory, he ate butter during the first week at Trawniki and had none since. It also made him think of his brothers. Vlad missed them deeply and still felt most guilty about surviving up to this point. The reason he lived and they didn't, haunted him on a regular basis. The unholy choices made to survive were always at the forefront of his mind.

Regardless, the butter tasted great. Chipped beef on toast tasted good to him also. The cherry gelatin was a curious dish. He had never seen it before. The wobbly texture was strange, but he liked the flavoring. Compared to what Vlad ate as a Soviet POW and Nazi Wachman, he was eating like a king. Again, the abundance of America was never ending.

The next morning, the men were up at 5:30 am and ordered to the central assembly area by 6 am. After all had been assembled, an army bugler stepped forward and played reveille as the Stars and Stripes were hoisted up the flagpole. The American soldiers faced the flag and saluted. The POWs stood silently with arms at their sides. Two POWs who arrived on the train with Vlad's group, but in a different passenger car, suddenly gave the Nazi Salute and shouted "Heil Hitler." Four guards immediately approached the two and sent them on the next train to Oklahoma. Algona and its branch camps were not designed for ardent Nazis.

After breakfast, Vlad's group marched out of the camp to the same train station from the night before. The train left promptly at 8 am and headed north. Vlad had a window seat and saw the sign "Minnesota" about an hour into the trip. The train continued north making stops in small towns with strange names like Blue Earth, Winnebago, and Mankato. The group changed trains under guard in Minneapolis.

They continued north from Minneapolis, and Vlad noticed the change in topography. The flat plains and farms turned to woods. The woods continued to thicken until changing into forests. Lakes big and small were everywhere, with scatterings of small fishing boats enjoying the sunny October day. The war seemed a long way away.

About seven hours into the trip since leaving Algona, the conductor called out "Deer River in 15 minutes." The guards motioned the POWs to gather their belongings and be ready to disembark. The men exited the train and stood in front of a small station with 'Deer River' painted on it. The wooden structure was big enough to hold 25 people, had two small bathrooms and a dirt parking lot. Two buses waited for them with engines running. Vlad and the other POWs noticed a considerable chill in the late afternoon air as they walked to the awaiting vehicles. They were definitely north.

The buses drove through town and headed north on a two-lane paved road. Vlad saw a sign that read "Now entering the Chippewa National Forest." Vlad had no idea what the words meant, but was struck by the density and variety the trees, and the fall colors awed him. Although the trees were past peak, many leaves remained and were incredible shades of red, yellow and gold. Vlad saw deer, bear, eagles, and moose during the short trip. America's abundance of seemingly everything was noticed by all.

The two buses took a left-hand turn on a dirt road and drove a short distance until they reached their destination. It was an abandoned CCC camp from the depression era days, with ten large cabins connected by dirt pathways. An eight-foot tall wire fence did surround the camp, but would have been easy to climb if someone was motivated. No guard towers were present.

A man in an army uniform stood inside the camp. He waited for the POWs to unload and assemble in front of him. He began to speak "I am Lieutenant Stokes. You are in my care as prisoners here at camp Cutfoot Sioux. You will do forestry work six days per week, eight hours per day. The War Department needs lumber, and you will assist in that effort. You will be paid in camp currency that can be spent on cigarettes and other items in the camp canteen. If you work hard and don't cause any problems, your treatment will be fair but firm. These cabins have not been used in seven years. They need to be cleaned, which is the first order of business. I expect you to form your own leadership council and abide by military discipline. Lights out and bed check is at 10 pm. For those of you contemplating escape, you are in the middle of a remote wilderness with many wolves, bears, and tribes of wild Indians who love scalping white men. You will learn the rest as you go. That is all."

Lt. Stokes was unfit for combat because he didn't pass the psychological exam with the army. He wasn't dangerous, just wholly incompetent. But he possessed strong family connections. His father was the 20 year elected sheriff of Itasca County. One of his brothers was a rising political star in St. Paul and the other brother a high ranking intelligence officer in Washington. The family had deep political, military, and law enforcement connections. The reason Stokes became an Army Lieutenant, and put in charge of this far-flung POW camp, was due to his family.

The POWs spent the first-week cleaning, clearing brush, organizing the mess hall, digging a new outhouse and getting the bunkhouses in order. By the end of week one, the cabins were warm, and the camp was homey and comfortable. Orlov was surprisingly quiet and worked along with rest of the men. Pavel was on the leadership committee and promised to maim Orlov if he messed with Vlad. Being stuck in the deep woods of Northern Minnesota had a calming effect on all of the men. Stokes kept to himself and left the men more or less alone.

The camp was called Cutfoot Sioux because of the lake it was located near. Unlike most other lakes whose shorelines are totally developed, Cutfoot Sioux is inside the Chippewa National Forest. Development was very restricted, and the area looked much like it did before European settlers arrived. The POW camp could not be situated in a more picture-perfect natural setting. People from all over the Midwest would pay money to stay at one of the three resorts on the lake, and enjoy the world-class Walleye fishing. The POWs got to stay for free. Camp Cutfoot Sioux soon earned the nickname "The Fritz Ritz."

Chapter 35
Camp Cutfoot Sioux

The work available for the POWs to perform was endless. This was due to the trifecta of the American Army needing food and supplies, few American men of working age left on the home front, and a massive influx of healthy young POWs able to fill the gap. It was against the Geneva Convention to have POWs work in munition factories, or anything directly tied to the war effort. But many farms, mills, and non-direct war manufacturing facilities were desperately short on help. This occurred around the country and in Northern Minnesota.

Camp Cutfoot Sioux POWs were put to work cutting down trees in the Chippewa National Forest. The men were divided into teams of 20 and driven to various areas in the forest to harvest timber. Each group normally had one armed guard and a foreman from the lumber company giving direction. The foreman would choose different Pine, Ash, Maple, Birch and Oak for the men to cut down.

After pruning the branches, the huge logs were loaded onto horse drawn carts or sleighs and pulled to the nearest logging road. Trucks arrived with log loaders, and the trees went to local sawmills for processing. The lumber coming out of timber country would feed an insatiable demand for the military, and for the housing boom to follow after the war.

Vlad and the POWs were initially isolated from the local population. They got up at 6 am, ate breakfast, and set out to the forest in army surplus trucks driven by guards. They spent the day logging and returned to camp by 4 pm. It was hard work and days were long, but the men enjoyed the experience for the most part. Work got them out of the camp confines and into the wilderness. It was great exercise and gave the men a sense of belonging, accomplishment, and meaning.

Sundays were always a day of rest for both the POWs and guards. Vlad and the rest of the men noticed the peculiar habit of no headcounts on Saturday nights. The guards counted the POWs after work was completed on Saturday afternoon when they arrived back to camp. Many of the guards then drove into Deer River, or nearby Squaw Lake, to drink and carouse at local bars. With most able-bodied men off fighting, the availability of lonely women was a big draw. Even though many of the guards were older World War I vets or men not fit for duty, the drought of young men had many women lowering their standards. Headcount did not happen again until Sunday night.

Late autumn was in full force, and like all people and animals in the North, much work needed to be done before winter set in. A few miles from camp was a resort on Lake Cutfoot Sioux called Williams Narrows. It was located on a peninsula, surrounded by water on three sides. The water on the tip of the peninsula was a narrow channel where Walleye, Muskie, and Northern Pike migrated each spring and fall. Rustic guest cabins dotted a dirt road that formed a circle around the resort. Williams Narrows was in the unique position of being privately owned in a National Forest, a very rare occurrence.

The owner of the resort needed help with fall cleanup. Taking docks out of the water, winterizing cabins, and staging shanties used for ice fishing during the winter were some of the necessary chores. Tommy Williams was the patriarch and owner of the resort. He was also well connected and knew the Stokes family for 50 years. Williams only son was fighting the Nazi's in Europe, which left his only daughter Betty at the resort to help out. The work to be done was far too much for them to handle alone, and they required extra help.

Lt. Stokes and the rest of the regular guards returned after a night of heavy drinking at the Hill Bar in nearby Squaw Lake on Sunday afternoon. They relieved the older, part-time guards at the camp. Tommy Williams arrived unannounced at the main gate of Camp Cutfoot Sioux at 4 pm in his Ford pickup truck. Lt. Stokes was summoned out of his quarters, ordered the gate open and greeted him with a warm handshake.

Lt. Stokes father, Sheriff Stokes arrived soon after, and the three ate dinner together discussing ways POWs could be of service at the resort. Williams needed two men for a few weeks of work. They would be returned to camp for continued logging in the forest afterward. Both Lt. Stokes and the sheriff were concerned about the risk of escape, but Williams gave assurances they would be watched. $250 cash under the table to both of the Stokes' helped assuage any fears regarding security. The deal was consummated, and Williams would return the next day to pick up the selected prisoners.

As one of the four chosen leaders to represent their fellow camp POWs, Pavel was in a position of strength and influence. He spoke with

Vlad after receiving the order for two needed POW workers when Williams left. Vlad was eager to leave the camp, and explore somewhere else besides the forest. Orlov was relatively quiet since arriving at Camp Cutfoot Sioux. His power was marginalized because he had no one to strangle, rape, murder, or abuse. Pavel was Vlad's firewall. Orlov knew as much and bid his time to strike during a future moment of weakness for Vlad.

Williams waited at the front gate Monday morning. Pavel and Vlad were let out of the camp and climbed into the back of his pickup with bags packed. It was a sunny, mild October day and the ride from Camp Cutfoot Sioux to Williams Narrows was enjoyable for them both. Vlad was again impressed by the vastness of the national forest and the beauty of its animal inhabitants. All of the deciduous trees had lost their leaves, and he was able to see deep into the woods. These were not just cosmetic stands of trees along the road to give the impression of a forest. They were deep woods seemingly without end.

Williams took a right turn off the highway onto a gravel road aptly named after him. His resort was about 3 miles down a road canopied by trees and lined with marshes. Vlad felt the presence of God in this place. It was a mixture of nature and spirituality that grabbed him and didn't let go. Suddenly, Williams downshifted as they approached a decline and entered the resort.

The resort was empty of guests, as was normal this time year. Kids were back in school and the moms back at work, filling jobs their husbands left to fight in Europe and the Pacific. They parked in front of the main lodge, and his daughter Betty walked out of the front door to greet them. Vlad was astonished to see a beautiful woman standing on the stairs waiting for them to get out of the truck. She was tall, had long dark hair, and a perfect brown skin tone. Her eyes were a deep brown. She had high cheekbones, perfect lips, and gleaming white teeth. He was instantly taken by her beauty, and even more surprised when she greeted them in German saying "Guten morgen."

"Good morning," Vlad replied in broken English with a smile.

"Tell them I expect 10 hours of work per day. They will get plenty to eat and be well treated." Williams said to Betty. "But if they try to escape, I will gladly shoot them both. These goddamned German sons of bitches are the reason your brother isn't here, and the fact they are standing in front of me is maddening as hell. They work, eat, sleep and never leave the grounds of the resort. Now please show them to cabin number four, that's where they will be staying. Then meet me at the docks." Her brother wanted to fight the Japanese, but that duty was left the Marine Corps. Instead, he was sent to Europe aboard a Liberty Ship and landed at Omaha Beach in France about the same time Vlad and the others left the exact spot.

Betty Williams was as smart as she was beautiful. She attended the first two years of medical school at the University of Minnesota, but left to help with the resort when her brother joined the Army after Pearl Harbor. Betty earned her undergraduate degree at the University of Minnesota with a major in biology and a minor in German. She was also conversational in the Ojibwe language. Betty was looked upon as a doctor and healer by many locals, including Native Americans from Leech Lake Reservation.

She held great weight in a community void of medical doctors. Broken bones to be set, babies to be delivered, wounds to be treated, and infections to be cured were all part of her unofficial duties. There were constant whispers by the locals in Deer River that she was part Indian. The rumor was her mother had an affair with, and got pregnant by, a Native American. The social stigma and general shunning that accompanied a "half-breed" in Northern Minnesota was very prevalent. But when people were in need, they all turned to Betty for help.

The mistrust, fear, and hate between whites and natives were as strong in Northern Minnesota as whites and blacks in the south. It just didn't receive the attention that white and black race relations did. Native Americans were an abandoned, marginalized and almost forgotten people. They were also politically unorganized and chronically impoverished. But Tommy Williams always loved Betty as his own, and never spoke to her about the rumors.

Her mom and his wife passed away ten years prior. Betty had a healing quality about her that surpassed two years of medical school. It was also spiritual in nature, and Betty combined many effective traditional native healing methods with modern medicine. Her knowledge of plants and their medicinal qualities surpassed any white person back at medical school. Everyone who knew Betty could sense the unique aura surrounding her. It was a gift many local whites grudgingly admired.

"This will be your cabin for the next two weeks, get unpacked, and dad wants you at the dock soon," Betty said to Pavel and Vlad in cheerful German. Betty flashed them a smile Vlad felt was worthy of movie star status. She simply was one the most beautiful women Vlad had ever seen. Vlad checked himself mentally and quickly determined her beauty and aura were not a case of him being void of women for the past four years. When some men are absent from women for an extended period, anything looks good. This was not the case with Betty Williams.

The cabin was small and rustic, but most adequate. It had two bedrooms, a private bathroom, a galley kitchen and running water. The walls were knotty pine and the floor carpeted. There were mounted deer heads on the wall and a large fish mounted above one of the bedroom doors. The cabin had electricity, heat, and a radio. Vlad and Pavel had not listened to the radio in years. It was punishable by death in Nazi-controlled Europe.

They all met at the wooden docks in the back bay of the resort. Thousands of tall plants grew about five feet directly out of the water, and Vlad had never seen anything like it. "Wild Rice," Betty said in German with a gentle laugh, as she noticed Vlad staring at the plants. "You will have to try it during your stay here. It's wonderful food, healthy and delicious." She gave him that Hollywood smile again, Vlad couldn't resist smiling back. It had been a very long time since a permanent grin graced his most handsome face. It would be a nice change over the next two weeks.

Chapter 36

Betty introduced Vlad and Pavel to fishing during the ensuing days after work was done, and before lights out. They went to the narrows and cast lines baited with leeches, in search of the elusive Walleye Pike. The Walleye is the most sought after fish in Minnesota, and thrive in the cool lakes for which the state is well known. It has the distinction of being the official state fish and is considered to be one of the mildest and delicious on the planet to eat. Walleye can be notoriously finicky eaters and hard to catch. The fish typically feed at dawn and dusk, when they come up from the depths to more shallow water. The Williams family depended on Walleye to make a living, many small businesses in Northern Minnesota did.

Pavel didn't particularly enjoy fishing, but Vlad took to it right away. Betty fished since she could walk, and gave Vlad many pointers on how to catch, clean, and cook Walleye. She taught Vlad to feel for the famous subtle bite of the fish, and correctly set the hook. If the hook were set too hard, it would tear through the mouth of the Walleye. If set too lightly, the fish simply stole the leech. Tommy Williams grudgingly allowed Betty and Vlad to fish at the Narrows, and even let Vlad borrow some of his most prized rods and reels.

Tommy sensed a friendship forming between Betty and Vlad, which he watched carefully. Vlad was friendly, polite, handsome, and normally had a big smile as he worked hard around the resort. Tommy wouldn't admit it to Betty, but he actually liked him. The only problem was that Vlad was the enemy. A fact Tommy Williams had a very hard time accepting.

As the days passed at the resort, Vlad and Betty started to talk while they fished together after work. Between her German and Vlad's improving English, they communicated fairly well, and their mutual attraction to each other grew. The way Betty smiled and her general body language left no doubt she found Vlad very attractive. But any romantic relationship was forbidden between POWs and the local population. It was dangerous and illegal.

The physical attraction between Vlad and Betty was certainly there, but it ran much deeper as well. Betty was quietly marginalized due to her mixed ethnicity and belonged to a native people hunted and killed as an official government policy for many years. Her people were ghettoized onto reservations, starved, and robbed. They were considered subhuman, and as General Phillip Sheridan famously said, "The only good Indian is a dead Indian."

Even though the war against the Indians ended as an official United States government policy almost 70 years prior, the negative attitude remained for many. The fact that 20,000 Native Americans were serving with great distinction in both theaters of war did not deter bigotry, much like their African American counterparts. Betty experienced cold silence from most local people beginning in grade school, but never from the Native Americans at Leech Lake Reservation.

Vlad did not possess the ethnically mixed background or experience the bigotry Betty contended with on a daily basis. But he certainly related to a people deprived of their way of life and hunted to the point of extinction. Vlad understood the Indian Wars and Belzec were far different in scope and brutality, but he recalled the SS officer during training relate the robbery of the Jews to the robbery of the Native American people. Neither of them understood it at the time, but two lives from very different worlds were more interwoven than anyone expected.

Their last day of work at the resort ended early, and Tommy Williams invited Vlad and Pavel to dinner at the lodge prepared by Betty. Pavel and Vlad showered and got dressed inside their cabin. "Pavel, Betty is the girl I am going to marry."

Pavel gave Vlad a look of incredulity "Did you hear what you just told me? Marry this girl? I understand it has been nice working at this resort, and yes, she is beautiful. But you are a POW living in a prison camp. Don't forget that small detail, kid." Pavel stopped himself, took a deep breath and said calmly "Look, I don't mean to pee in your army boots and I'm sorry. There is most definitely a connection between you two, but how exactly do intend to do this? "

Vlad smiled "I have no idea Pavel, but I have never felt like this before about a woman, and I have had plenty."

Pavel laughed and replied "Your way with women has followed you from Kiev to this place. You are unbelievable! Look, just be careful and don't set yourself up for some serious heartbreak. Keep in mind your place, and where we are. Have you also considered you feel this way because of the lack of women over the years?'

Vlad nodded his head yes. "I have, but this is different Pavel. I think I love her, and she feels the same about me."

Pavel raised his eyebrows. "You two fish and talk every night, has she said anything about being in love with you?' Vlad shook his head no, and Pavel continued. "Kid, don't say a word to her about what we did to the Jews back in Poland and France. If she were to tell her dad, we could be shipped to that camp in Oklahoma where the SS are held. That would not be good for either of us. I swear to God, Chayka, don't say a word. One other thing, if you start getting too close to this girl and her dad doesn't like it, he could have Lt. Stokes transfer you off to another camp, and you will never see her again. So if you love her, play it smart and keep your head. Don't do or say anything stupid at dinner tonight. By the way, we are late, let's get going."

Vlad and Pavel walked out of cabin number four, and towards the lodge. The sun was setting on Cutfoot Sioux, the lake was calm as glass, and both could hear Loons calling in the distance. They had gotten used to the most unusual and beautiful call of the bird. Neither of them heard anything quite like it before in their lives. The natural beauty of this place was awe inspiring to Vlad, and he silently promised himself to figure out a way to marry this woman he had known for two weeks.

They sat down for dinner, and Tommy and Betty Williams did the sign of the cross before saying grace. Vlad surprised them both by naturally following along. Betty smiled at her dad, and then looked at Vlad, "Katholisch?"

Vlad smiled wide and said in English "Yes."

Tommy Williams let out a huge laugh, breaking the slight tension at the table. "A Catholic Nazi at my dinner table while my son is over in Europe fighting. What a world!"

Vlad understood some of what Tommy said and replied in broken English "Mr. Williams, I am not a Nazi. I hate the Nazi's. They came to my country and destroyed it. They killed many people. They killed my brothers and probably my parents. They murder, rape, and kill for fun."

Tommy Williams looked at Betty, then at Vlad. "Then what the hell are you doing here? Why were you fighting on their side? You were taken prisoner by our GI's, correct?"

Vlad looked at Betty "In German please?" They spoke back and forth for a few minutes at the dinner table, making Pavel nervous and Tommy somewhat bewildered.

Betty looked at her dad when she and Vlad finished their back and forth conversation. "They were both taken prisoner by the Germans, then forced to fight against Russia. Otherwise, they would have died at a prison camp, just like his three brothers. Neither Vlad or Pavel like the Germans, but they are afraid you will say something to Stokes and get them in trouble."

Tommy looked at Vlad and said "Don't worry, I won't say a thing. Both of them have been excellent workers and complete gentlemen. Anyway, Stokes said I could use either of them around the resort, for a fee of course."

Betty smiled at her dad and Vlad saying excitedly "Please dad, have Vlad come back and help."

Tommy gave her a smile "I will, but I do sense the attraction between you two. Promise me I don't have anything to worry about, and yes, we will set up an arrangement with Sheriff Stokes. It has to be through the sheriff, his kid running that camp is too stupid to deal with."

Vlad smiled and said thank you to Tommy. Pavel smiled and shook his head as if to say 'I can't believe this kid.'

Betty got up and returned with dinner. Fried Walleye, potatoes, wild rice, bread, butter, and jam. Tommy had a beer in his hand and noticed Vlad glancing at the bottle. "Beer?" he said to Vlad making a motion of offering his hand.

Vlad gave a big smile. "Yes, please."

Tommy looked at Betty with a smile. "I did say the boy is polite." He proceeded to hand Vlad and Pavel each a bottle of Grain Belt Beer. Vlad had not drunk any sort of beer or liquor since Paris, and the beer tasted great. He was mindful of how much he drank over the last three years, and promised himself to be careful with alcohol from this day forward.

After dinner, Pavel offered to help with dishes so Vlad and Betty could walk to the narrows and fish for Walleye. Tommy Williams again allowed Vlad to use his fishing gear and watched from the lodge kitchen window as Vlad baited Betty's hook with a leech. Betty baited her hook since she was five years old, and Tommy never saw her let someone else do it. It was yet another small, but telling sign of their mutual feelings.

Tommy shook his head in disbelief as the actual thought entered his mind of an enemy POW and his daughter forming a friendship, or even more. "Of all the guys in the world, she picks this one" Tommy Williams muttered to himself as he looked out the window and finished his beer. He lightly chuckled and ironically smiled.

Suddenly he saw Vlad's fishing rod bend in a fashion that indicated a fish of sizeable weight was hooked. Tommy was at the narrows in under a minute and watched in excitement with Betty as Vlad reeled in the fish. The state record for an individual Walleye was 17 pounds, and Tommy figured Vlad had something close to it on the other end of the line. Betty observed her dad putting his hand on Vlad's shoulder as he fought the fish, it was the same thing he did with her brother. Tommy didn't realize what he was doing. It was a natural reaction when fishing with people he liked. Betty had a knack of sensing nonverbal actions and emotions in other people. She understood a connection was made between Vlad and her father at that moment.

When the fish surfaced, Betty and her father looked at each other in happy surprise at the length and girth of the Walleye. Tommy still had his hand on Vlad's shoulder and shouted out, "That could be a state record, my boy. Holy smokes what a fish!"

The importance of landing an actual Minnesota state record Walleye was not lost on Betty or her father. The person who held the record was a famous and celebrated personality. He also designed a fishing rig for Walleyes bearing his name and made a small fortune as people bought it in hopes of repeating the feat. It would be locally akin to a golfer winning The Masters, or a boxer winning the heavyweight championship. Breaking the state record Walleye in Minnesota would be front page news across the region, even during a time of epic battles in the Pacific and Europe.

Vlad's heart raced as the Walleye took a run for deeper waters and snapped the line. His fishing rod recoiled back to its straight position, and the loose fishing line fluttered in the wind. All three let out loud expletives, both in English and Ukrainian. Tommy looked at Vlad and said out of breath "You fought that fish perfectly, it's my fault. I gave you a rod and reel with only six-pound test line. That fish must have weighed 20 pounds, almost three more pounds than the state record. Don't worry. These fish tend to stay fairly close in the back bays and narrows this time of year. We will try again when you come back and work for me. It's getting late, I am heading to bed and will let you two say good night. Betty, I want you in the lodge in ten minutes."

Tommy gave Vlad a smile and pat on the back as he left. Betty smiled and said to Vlad "He likes you, and so do I. You leave in the morning back to your camp. I will miss you, but we will see each other soon." Betty leaned in and gave Vlad a kiss on the lips. Vlad wrapped his arms around her and kissed her passionately, with Betty responding in kind. This moment had been building up since they first laid eyes on each other two weeks ago. A spark ignited the fuse. Life and love were suddenly on an undetermined path.

Chapter 37
St. Louis Park, Minnesota
Present Day

Max turned off the video equipment in stunned silence. Vlad spoke uninterrupted for almost four hours, and Max was processing all of the information has dad related. He refrained from the natural inclination to cross-examine and get deeper into the story. Vlad was tired, and it was close to 10 o'clock at night. There would be time in the coming days to hear more and ask questions. Vlad slowly rose out of his chair and headed for the stairs. Max simply gave him a hug. "I love you, dad, and thank you for everything you have done for me."

Vlad gave him a tired smile and said "Let's talk tomorrow. Let me know if you can make it over, or if the following day works better. I am very proud of you son." Vlad turned and wearily climbed the stairs for a much needed night's sleep.

The next day Max was at the law office during another busy afternoon, when his secretary announced Carl Jeffries was waiting in the lobby to see him. Max found it very unusual that Carl wouldn't just call, email, or text. Max quickly finished filing a continuance motion for the NFL player whose girlfriend was claiming physical abuse and seeking damages. These were the cases that paid the bills, and Max needed to balance them with the needs of his dad.

Max decided to walk to the well-appointed lobby and greet Carl, instead of having him sent back to his office. He needed to stretch his legs, and also show Carl the respectful action of greeting him personally. "I'm sorry to visit unannounced Max, but felt we should discuss this in person," Carl said shaking Max's hand. "I have some information that you need to know. Is there somewhere we can speak privately?"

Max gave Carl a nod of the head and said "Of course, come back to my office. Can I get you anything, Carl? Coffee, water or soda?"

Carl shook his head "No thanks, Max, but I appreciate the offer." The fact Max didn't have one of his many employees ask Carl if he needed anything was yet another display of respect and humility that hallmarked Max's reputation.

They sat down in Max's office, and Carl started "Max, I know you are busy, and I have a deadline for tomorrow's paper due in 90 minutes, so I will keep this brief. I received a call from a reporter who works for VGTRK in Russia. It's the biggest media company in Russia with too many TV and radio stations to count. I think it's state owned, but that's not important here. Anyway, this Russian reporter said he was contacted by a 95 year old Ukrainian named Mikhail Chayka who claims to be your dad's brother. He said Mikhail heard about Vlad's case on TV at the retirement home where he lives. The reporter told me he is in good health with his mental faculties fully intact."

"Can this story get any crazier? I was with my dad last night, and you wouldn't believe the stuff he's telling me. I didn't press him, but I have the feeling that my mother may not have died in Europe during the war. It's unbelievable. I was just starting to wrap my mind around it and form some questions that I could ask him tonight or tomorrow. Now this? His brother Mikhail is alive? Holy shit Carl. Does anybody know about this? Is it being reported?"

Carl shook his head no. "That's part of the reason I came to you personally. This guy wants ten grand as a finder's fee."

Max rolled his eyes "How do we know he is telling us the truth?" Carl handed him an envelope with Mikhail's address, phone number, and picture. Max looked at the picture. He immediately recognized the resemblance to his dad.

"Look, Max," Carl said breaking the silence, "This reporter says he will keep quiet to let us do our due diligence, and determine if he is your dad's brother. He made a veiled threat that something bad could befall Mikhail if payment is not received. I don't know how business is conducted in Russia, but I do understand that it's corrupt as hell over there. Russian Mob, bad government actors, criminals and the like. He also said for another ten grand, all documents would be in order for Mikhail to leave the country and visit the United States."

Max set down the photo and looked at Carl. "20 grand to bring my dad's brother back from the dead and meet him face to face is dirt cheap in my opinion. Tell your Russian reporter that if Mikhail is alive and can come visit my dad, he will have is 20 grand within a week."

Carl stood from his chair. "Sounds good Max, and thanks again for dinner at Murray's last week. I love that place, especially when you are picking up the tab."

Max smiled "It always tastes better when someone else is paying, doesn't it? Okay, let me think through this and figure out how I present this to my dad. I was going to take the night off with him and meet Dane for a few drinks, but maybe I will cancel and go over to his house."

Carl walked to the door and said as he was leaving. "Go and meet Dane, he might have some insight on how to proceed with this new revelation. Or meet your dad and tell him the news. Both sound good to me."

Max stood up, gave Carl a look and said kiddingly "Get the hell out of my office. I swear you writers are more fickle than the direction of the wind. Make a decision for once in your life."

They both knew it was friendly needling and Carl laughed as he walked out of the office. Max sat back down and looked at the picture again. He didn't want to get his dad's hopes up, only to have them dashed if this were some scam. The news for Vlad could wait a day, drinks with Dane were on.

Max met Dane on the sprawling deck of Lord Fletcher's on Lake Minnetonka. It was now early summer, and the lake action was in full swing. Lake Minnetonka is by far the most desirable to live, boat, be seen on, and drink next to. It's a combination of money, power, partying and showing off. Keeping up with the Jones's has no match in the upper Midwest than Lake Minnetonka. Max sat at the outdoor bar and watched a divorced couple sit on opposite ends of the bar. They were showing off their respective younger arm candy, trying to piss each other off. It perfectly captured part of the lifestyle that can be found on the lake.

For their part, Max and Dane enjoyed the women at the bar and stiff summer drinks. Max had vodka lemonades, and Dane was knocking back Long Island ice teas. Boats designed for Lake Superior or the Gulf of Mexico gaudily paraded through the private channel of Lord Fletcher's, looking for a place to dock or just seeking attention. The bikini-clad ladies on the bows of the awkwardly large vessels were always a fun sight to behold for both of them.

Dane finished his second Long Island, Max wrapped up his latest update and let Dane take some time to form an opinion on the matter. After Dane checked the behinds of two beautiful women half his age walking past he spoke "Make sure your dad's brother is indeed alive, and pay them if they can prove it. It may seem like a strange way of doing business in this country, but my understanding it's fairly standard procedure in that messed up part of the world. Anyway, what's 20 grand to you? It will take 20 billable hours at your rate to make it up, big deal. But one question for you my friend, how do you plan on confirming it's him? How will you know?"

Max looked at Dane through his sunglasses. "I won't. My dad will have to make that determination. The details of his story have not been released, even though Carl is excited to get it out there. This guy claiming to be my dad's brother would have to corroborate his early life with Vlad. The thing is, I don't want to get my dad's hopes up only to have it be either the wrong guy or some total scam."

Dane sat back on his bar stool and watched as a 50-foot yacht slowly passed by. Driven by an overweight guy in his mid-60's with four women half his age front and center on the bow. "Man I need to start making more money," Dane said with a laugh as he shook his head. Then he focused on Max and continued, "Look, I think your dad is tougher than you give him credit. The crazy times he's been through has probably caused him to develop a fairly thick skin. I would be just as honest with him as he is with you. That's the least you owe him."

Max nodded in agreement and was suddenly approached by a woman his firm represented in a high profile divorce four years ago. He had not spoken to her since, and the attractive woman asked if she and her three beautiful divorced friends could sit with Max and Dane. They readily agreed, and four women about 20 years their junior sat down and ordered a round of beers with tequila shots. The evening would again end well for both of them, as one of the friends lived less than a mile away from the bar and invited the group back for drinks. The party lasted until midnight, with Dane cabbing it back to Minneapolis and Max spending the night. Max was late to the office the following morning.

That evening Max brought dinner to Vlad's house. He decided to tell his dad about the call from the Russian reporter, but not about the money. It was the truth, just not all of it, and Max felt comfortable with his decision. Max had the video equipment rolling. "Dad, you mentioned that the nightmares were bad all the way through your time at Drancy, but haven't mentioned them since being captured by the Americans. Did they just stop?"

Vlad responded quickly and looked directly into the camera for the first time since Max had recorded him. "No, they were horrible, but your mother cured me." Max was so taken aback by the revelation that he was speechless. News about Mikhail would wait.

Chapter 38
Late March 1945
Camp Cutfoot Sioux

Vlad and Pavel worked sporadically for Tommy Williams over the winter, but there was less to do during the cold weather months at the resort, and the visits became less frequent. The reduced work visits to Williams Narrows during winter did not deter Vlad and Betty from growing closer. Vlad took full advantage of lax camp security by sneaking out on Saturday night and returning before sunrise on Sunday morning. Numerous other POWs did as well. They took in a movie at the small theater in Deer River or even grabbed a cold beer at one of the local taverns. Everyone knew but no one cared, some of the local women frequented certain bars on Saturday night knowing a few handsome POWs may be there.

Sheriff Stokes ensured his incompetent son never got into any trouble with the Army, and occasionally provided POWs rides back to camp before sunrise on Sunday morning. He now realized how inept his son, the Lieutenant, truly was. Had he not been the sheriff of Itasca County, camp mismanagement would probably have made the local paper. But the publisher was a childhood friend, and the POWs didn't cause trouble that was newsworthy, so a quiet detente ensued. Money changed hands among the locals, cheap labor was available from the POW camp, and for the most part, things ran well. Most in Northern Minnesota and the rest of the world believed the war would be over soon. Many didn't feel the need to rock the boat.

One thing Pavel and Vlad noticed was Orlov never made an attempt to leave the camp, nor did a group of POWs that gelled around him over the winter. They rearranged bunkhouses and dining hall shifts, so Orlov's group could all eat and sleep together. Neither Pavel nor Vlad knew what to make of it, and frankly, neither one cared. If Orlov was quiet, well behaved and occupied, that was all right with both of them. Maybe life in this remote prison camp had soothed his twisted soul after all.

Tommy Williams met with Sheriff Stokes and requested Pavel and Vlad for two weeks of spring cleanup, and opening the cabins at Williams Narrows. He wanted to take advantage of winter's early end and get a jump start on the many chores needing attention. The sheriff obliged and arranged to have both of them ready the following morning at the camp's front gate. Cash was passed onto the sheriff and the Lieutenant, it worked out for everybody, and no one was the wiser.

Vlad and Pavel climbed into the back of Tommy Williams's pickup truck the following morning. Orlov purposefully got close as possible to the fence and gave a menacing stare as they drove off. Orlov glowered at Vlad and simulated a knife slit across his throat, while Vlad flipped Orlov the middle finger. It was something the POWs picked up on from local logging truck drivers.

Vlad was unaffected by it, but Pavel looked worried and said as they drove away from camp, "I just got a strange sense from Orlov that something has happened, did you two get into an argument or something? I haven't seen that crazy look in his eyes since Belzec when he would be looking for a Jewish kid to strangle."

Vlad shrugged his shoulders. "I haven't spoken to that jerk in months. Not sure what his problem is, I am just looking forward to working at the resort and seeing Betty."

Pavel replied with a smile. "You see her every Saturday night, what the hell do you two do anyway."

"We talk about the future, I love her Pavel, and she has told me the same thing. We speak of escape and moving away where nobody knows us and growing old together."

Pavel gave him a hard look. "Be careful kid, and remember what I said last fall about creating a scenario where you do something stupid and wreck it for the both of you. By the way, do you talk about the past?"

Vlad got teared up and shook his head no "I haven't had the guts to tell her, but she suspects something. We fall asleep together in her truck, and when my nightmares kick in, she holds me and helps me through it. Betty thinks they are bad dreams from combat and watching buddies die. She has no idea my dreams are visions of hundreds of thousands of innocent people we helped slaughter. My fear is if I tell the truth, she will never want to see me again."

When Tommy Williams arrived at the resort with Vlad and Pavel, Betty stood next to the front door of the lodge. She ran down the steps and greeted Vlad with a giant hug and kiss on the lips, Tommy gave them a smile and walked inside. He knew for months Betty was leaving on Saturdays after he went to bed, and returning to the resort early Sunday morning. They went to Mass, ate breakfast in town, and both acted like nothing happened.

It was a quiet detente, much like the rest of Northern Minnesota over the past year. Tommy trusted Betty to make wise choices, and always told her to follow her heart in matters of love. She was doing as he asked, just in a most unusual way. He decided not to intervene as long events didn't force his hand, which to this point they had not.

Pavel and Vlad settled into the same cabin from the previous fall and quickly made themselves at home. Tommy had a long list of chores to get done. Regardless of any relationship, Vlad was expected to work ten hours per day and equally hard as Pavel. One pleasant surprise for Vlad and Pavel was Tommy invited them into the lodge for meals every night, complete with a few beers. Vlad's English had gotten much better, a result of spending Saturday nights with Betty. Pavel's English improved slightly, and he communicated well enough to convey what he needed to say.

Tommy and Vlad hit it off right away at dinner the first night. Pavel and Vlad worked hard all day, and Tommy was at ease knowing the two would complete chores that needed doing. Tommy treated Vlad like a respected friend and trusted worker. He also gave tacit approval to date his daughter. It was the first man in Betty's limited dating life that Tommy approved.

After work on the second night, all four were in the lodge eating dinner when it started to rain. The after dinner fishing would have to wait. The inclement weather gave them a chance to talk at length, and for Pavel to ask a question of Tommy that was on his mind since last fall. "Mister Williams." Pavel asked in the best English he could muster "Why do you and other Americans treat us so nice? It is a much different experience for Soviet POWs in German camps."

Betty looked at her dad as he answered Pavel. "My son and Betty's brother is fighting a war in Europe, and it's my understanding he has entered Germany. He fought near Bastogne during the Battle of the Bulge, where over 23,000 Americans were taken POW. If he were taken prisoner, my sincere hope would be that he would be treated the same as you are being treated. I do know for a fact word has gotten back to Germany that we are following Geneva Convention rules regarding their

POWs in the United States. If we are following the rules and taking care of Germans in America, then hopefully Germany is taking care of American POWs as well. Do unto others as you would have them do to you."

Vlad, Pavel, and Betty all nodded their heads in agreement at the simple profundity of Tommy Williams as he continued. "I fought in France during World War I, and believe me when I tell you that I hate war. War solves nothing and actually makes matters worse. Yes, Hitler is evil and needs to be defeated, so does Japan. But I promise there will be other enemies to fight when this is all over, and it will most likely never end. There will be people in this country and other countries who will sound the drumbeat for war, and drag the people along. We need to understand this is a fight among leaders of nations, not the people."

Vlad then asked, "What do the American people think about Germans?"

Tommy looked a bit confused as he pondered the answer. "Honestly, I think most Americans hate the Germans, but they hate a people they have never met. You two are the first Germans, or at least people who fought for Germany that I have met, and I like you both very much." He then looked at Vlad and said "I think people have a fear of others who are different. If a leader of a country wants to use fear to divide people against one another, then it tends to be an effective way of that leader staying in power. But here we are in my lodge at this beautiful resort sharing a meal, drinking a beer, and my guess is that my daughter loves you. Are you my enemy? I think not. We share the same faith, we are both Catholic and so is my son. Should Catholics be killing each other? Again, I think not."

Vlad reached out and grabbed Betty's hand. He looked at Tommy Williams. "I do love her and want nothing more than for her to be happy. I want to spend the rest of my life with her and would like your permission to do so."

Tommy took a deep breath. "Vlad, you are a POW, you have no legal rights. You are not a citizen of this country, and you will be shipped back to Germany once this whole God-awful mess is over. The Army keeps a close count on the number of POWs housed in these camps, and they cannot be a man short. I have spoken with Sheriff Stokes and his other son who is a Major in military intelligence in Washington D.C. They both told me that every German POW is going back. No one will be allowed to stay. How do you plan on marrying and taking care of my daughter if you are in Germany and she is here? I like you and would approve under different circumstances, but I can't give you my blessing given the situation. I hope both of you understand."

Betty started crying. Vlad was still holding her hand and said, "I will figure a way for us to be together. I love you, and one thing I have learned over the past few years is that love is more powerful than fear and hate." Vlad paused and asked, "Do you have a Bible?"

Tommy gave him a quizzical look. "Of course, it's right here."

He handed the Bible to Vlad who paged through it and began to read aloud in English "Love is patient, love is kind. It does not envy, it does not boast, it is not proud. It does not dishonor others, it is not self-seeking, it is not easily angered, it keeps no record of wrongs. Love does not delight in evil but rejoices with the truth. It always protects, always trusts, always hopes, and always perseveres." Vlad stopped reading, skipped to the end of the passage and finished. "And now these three remain: faith, hope, and love. But the greatest of these is love."

He looked at Tommy who was welling up with tears. "There was a time not so long ago when I truly believed that faith, hope, and love were dead in the world. If you had seen the things I have seen and done the things I have done, you would understand. Betty has shown me that faith, hope, and love are alive and well. The Holy Spirit brought her to me. I have faith and hope that our love will find a way for us to be together."

Tommy looked at Vlad and Betty and said "How can I argue with that? Let me put some thought into this over the next two weeks and see what I can do. I will tell you one thing. If it can happen at all, it is going to take a miracle and cost a fortune."

Pavel was on his fifth beer and spoke again after listening to, and mostly understanding what was being said. The rain was coming down harder as darkness fell. The soft leather chairs, beers and fire inside the lodge created a setting for truths being told. Pavel spoke his best English so all could understand "Vlad, if you believe that telling our story will help you stay in this country, then go ahead and do it. I am concerned if others find out we will be sent back to the Soviet Union and executed upon arrival. But I trust Mr. Williams and Betty, so feel free to speak. You have my blessing."

Vlad gave Pavel a look of astonishment. "Thank you, Pavel, I owe you my life."

Two hours and another few rounds of beers later, Vlad told Tommy and Betty the truth about their experiences since they were both POWs at Chelm. They also discussed Orlov and his tumultuous relationship with Vlad. Both Tommy and Betty sat in disbelief, shock, and horror at what the Germans were doing to the Jews. Vlad spared no details and explained their entire murderous experience since the summer of 1941. He verbally walked them through Trawniki, Rabka, Belzec, and Drancy.

Tommy spoke first when Vlad was done. "I guess some wars need to be fought, and this is one of them. In this country's history, I would say World War II and the Revolutionary War are the conflicts that truly represented a clear and present danger to our nation and needed to be fought. I am proud that my son is over there helping defeat those Nazi sons of bitches. How could the German people be duped into following a maniac like Hitler, and give him the power to commit such horrible crimes in their names?"

Vlad shrugged his shoulders and said, "I don't know, if the Americans elected a gangster as president instead of Franklin Roosevelt, then you may be in the same spot as Germany." Tommy gave a light chuckle and understood the wisdom of Vlad's comment.

Betty accepted the terrible choices Vlad made to sacrifice others to save himself. Had he chosen to refuse the SS officers demands and die at Chelm, someone much less deserving would have taken his place. She understood the possible criminal implications and heavy spiritual damage caused by his decisions. Had events unfolded differently, Vlad would never have exhibited such homicidal behavior, and she knew as much.

Tommy sensed Betty's feelings and agreed with her. He continued, "Who am I to judge you? I have not walked a mile in your shoes, and very few people in the history of the world have faced such maniacally evil choices. However, most people in this country will not be as forgiving when word of these atrocities gets out. If what you say is true, it's a crime too big to cover up and will make world headlines."

Betty, like many people, encapsulated the massive scope of the Holocaust into a few details she couldn't shake mentally. For Betty, the bear pit at Belzec was the most inhumane and barbaric story she ever heard. Forcing a father to watch his son mauled to death by a bear and then himself thrown in afterward was something Betty felt could only happen in another dimension. It was unfathomable cruelty and a disgustingly painful way to perish.

Betty was also extremely disturbed the SS used a wild animal in their attempt to wipe out the Jewish people. A bear was even more upsetting and offensive, as the animal took on great significance for the Ojibwe. Bears in the Ojibway culture represented motherhood and protection of the young. They were considered great spirits of power, knowledge, and life balance. Betty understood how Vlad, fellow Jews, and even Barry the dog were forced to perform their murderous task at the behest of the SS.

But to coerce a bear to do the same thing was incredibly hard for her to accept. It reflected the heinous delegation of murder the Nazi's employed. Vlad and Pavel told Betty about Orlov's jealousy when the Commandant would toss the last Jewish boy in the bear pit, denying Orlov the opportunity to strangle the child. Betty's revulsion at the Nazi's and Orlov was cemented, and she now fully understood Vlad's past.

It was getting late, Tommy got up from his chair and made the nonverbal gesture that it was bedtime. As Vlad got up, Betty hugged him and whispered in his ear "Keep the cabin door unlocked."

Tommy approached both Vlad and Pavel. "Thank you for sharing your story. It makes me feel better my son is fighting a war that is actually worth it. They said the war I fought was 'the war to end all wars.' Boy, were they wrong."

Tommy embraced Vlad. "God bless you, son." He grabbed Pavel's hand, gave him a warm handshake "God bless you also." Vlad and Pavel thanked them for the hospitality and walked back to cabin number four, where Pavel fell asleep when his head hit the pillow. Vlad stayed awake waiting for Betty, who arrived quietly 30 minutes later after Tommy was sound asleep. They made love again. It was getting much better since the first time months ago on a cold January Saturday night inside Betty's truck.

Pavel and Vlad worked hard around the resort putting in ten hour days. Tommy was happy that all spring cleanup chores were completed, and was at ease knowing the resort would soon be open for business.

The docks were put in, cabins cleaned, the lodge was fully stocked, and grounds immaculate. The war seemed to be winding down, and Tommy hoped his son would be back in time for some late summer fishing.

He also thought about Vlad and Betty and repeatedly wondered how he could make it work so Vlad could stay. He wanted it for Betty, but he wanted it for himself also. Tommy felt a deep connection with Vlad, but also felt premonitions that Betty was pregnant. She wasn't showing, but Tommy noticed a glow he only saw when his wife was expecting both children.

Chapter 39

On their last Sunday working at Williams Narrows, Vlad and Pavel were due back at camp by 5 pm. Betty knocked on the cabin door early in the morning, Vlad sleepily answered and saw the love of his life holding a change of regular clothes. Betty handed them to Vlad. "My dad wants you to come to Mass with us this morning. These are my brother's clothes, but they should fit. Be at the lodge in 15 minutes. She gave him a kiss and turned around. Vlad watched her walk away and admired her backside. He couldn't believe how perfect she was. Beautiful, kind, smart, and even Catholic. Best of all, she loved him, and he loved her.

Mass started at 9 a.m., and Tommy deliberately showed up five minutes late to avoid introducing Vlad to his lifelong friends. They sat in the back of the church, and Vlad was overcome with the emotion of seeing Americans worship in the open. Back in Ukraine, Mass was held in secret, and his religious education was mainly done at home. The freedom Americans enjoyed by worshiping as they pleased was symbolic of the overall strength of this country. Vlad felt a people free to choose how they worshiped would be more likely to protect their way of life. Even if some were treated as second class citizens, like black people and Native Americans, they still fought for a country they believed in and saw hope for the future.

The outside of the small church was white clapboard with a modest bell tower on top. Inside were wooden pews with an aisle down the middle. As Mass progressed, Vlad understood what was happening, but missed some words as the young priest spoke in English. The beauty of Mass, Vlad thought to himself, is that it's the same throughout the world. For almost two thousand years, Catholic Mass consisted of three parts; the Bible readings, the homily, and ending with Holy Communion. The language was different of course, but the Order of Mass was the same on every continent in the world. It made Vlad feel at home.

The first reading was from the book of Luke, Vlad recognized it right away as the lector began to read out loud and sat spellbound listening to the words. "He also told this parable to some who trusted in themselves that they were righteous, and treated others with contempt. Two men went up into the temple to pray, one a Pharisee and the other a tax collector. The Pharisee, standing by himself, prayed thus. 'God, I thank you that I am not like other men, extortionists, unjust, adulterers, or even like this tax collector. I fast twice a week; I give tithes of all that I get.' But the tax collector, standing far off, would not even lift up his eyes to heaven, but beat his breast, saying, 'God, be merciful to me, a sinner!' I tell you, this man went down to his house justified, rather than the other. For everyone who exalts himself will be humbled, but the one who humbles himself will be exalted."

Betty held Vlad's hand after the reading, and both silently felt that it was handpicked, which of course it wasn't. Vlad felt like the tax collector, undeserving of forgiveness for the decisions to save himself by committing horrendously evil acts.

If the public became aware of his actions at Belzec, they would be the Pharisees and Vlad, the despised tax collector. But what would these modern Pharisee's have done if they were in Vlad's shoes? They would indeed cast judgment, much like those back in biblical times. Hopefully, Vlad thought, there would be a modern day disciple of Christ who would act like Jesus and ask those without sin to cast the first stone.

Vlad's mind wandered back as the priest, who was probably younger than he was, began to read the Gospel. Vlad mentally missed the second reading altogether and was a bit embarrassed by it. The priest held the Bible for all to see. "The Holy Gospel according to Luke." The entire congregation along with Vlad signed themselves with the cross on the forehead, lips, and heart replying "Glory to you O Lord."

Vlad sat in awe as the priest began reading aloud the Gospel that again seemed to be handpicked for him "There was a man who had two sons. And the younger of them said to his father, 'Father, give me the share of property that is coming to me.' And he divided his property between them. Not many days later, the younger son gathered all he had and took a journey into a far country, and there he squandered his property in reckless living. And when he had spent everything, a severe famine arose in that country, and he began to be in need. So he went and hired himself out to one of the citizens of that country, who sent him into his fields to feed pigs. And he was longing to be fed with the pods that the pigs ate, and no one gave him anything.

"But when he came to himself, he said, 'How many of my father's hired servants have more than enough bread, but I perish here with hunger! I will arise and go to my father, and I will say to him, "Father, I have sinned against heaven and before you. I am no longer worthy to be called your son. Treat me as one of your hired servants." And he arose and came to his father. But while he was still a long way off, his father saw him and felt compassion, and ran and embraced him and kissed him. And the son said to him, 'Father, I have sinned against heaven and before you. I am no longer worthy to be called your son.' But the father said to his servants, 'Bring the best robe quickly, and put it on him, and put a ring on his hand, and shoes on his feet. And bring the fattened calf and kill it, and let us eat and celebrate. For this my son was dead, and is alive again; he was lost, and is found.' And they began to celebrate.

"Now his older son was in the field, and as he came and drew near to the house, he heard music and dancing. And he called one of the servants and asked what these things meant. And he said to him, 'Your brother has come, and your father has killed the fattened calf because he has received him back safe and sound.' But he was angry and refused to go in. His father came out and entreated him, but he answered his father, 'Look, these many years I have served you, and I never disobeyed your command, yet you never gave me a young goat, which I might celebrate with my friends. But when this son of yours came, who has devoured your property with prostitutes; you killed the fattened calf for him!' And he said to him, 'Son, you are always with me, and all that is mine is yours. It was fitting to celebrate and be glad, for this your brother was dead, and is alive; he was lost and is found."

Vlad related to the Prodigal Son as if he were him. He deserted God and lived a life of depravity and sin. Vlad remembered in shame how he told Pavel "Fuck God," and felt the Trinity didn't exist for a few years in his life. He now realized the footprints in the sand during that time were not his, they were God's. Vlad returned from life in the wild to the warm embrace of both his faith and the Williams family. Tommy Williams reminded Vlad of the Father in the story, and he wondered how Betty's brother would react to his presence upon returning from Europe. It fit the moment perfectly. Vlad was not sure if he were just so spiritually thirsty that any Bible reading would seem designed for him, or if this were another sign of the Holy Spirit back in his life.

At the end of Mass, Vlad stood in line for Holy Communion and attempted to recall the last time he took the sacrament. He figured it was a week or two before he and his brothers traveled to Minsk with their new-found friends. He thought about how lucky he was to have found Betty and prayed to God for peace and guidance in finding a way to stay with her.

His thoughts were interrupted by the young priest offering Holy Communion to him. "Body of Christ."

"Amen." Vlad took it in his hands and placed the host in his mouth. At that moment, Vlad felt the Holy Spirit wash over him. It was like being baptized and receiving First Communion at the same time. It could have been psychosomatic, but Vlad chose to believe and promised God that he would never question his faith again. After Communion, most Catholics return to their pews to pray, listen for announcements, sing a closing hymn and receive the benediction. Tommy instead walked out of the back door and motioned Betty and Vlad to follow. Tommy didn't want to gather and chat with friends after Mass as he normally did. They got into Tommy's pickup truck and drove off before anyone else had the chance to inquire about Vlad's presence.

On their way back to the resort, Betty sat in the middle of the front seat touching Vlad with her right hand and Tommy with her left hand. She wanted to feel the energy running between them and announced in a calm but sure voice "Dad and Vlad, I am pregnant. I believe that I am about four months along, and am euphoric that I am carrying the child of my soul mate. Dad, I have thought this through and have a plan that will not cause you any embarrassment or shame. You have been the best father a daughter could ask for, and I want you to understand this is in no way a sign of disrespect. I know about my heritage and Mom's affair with a man from the Leech Lake Reservation. I also love you for accepting me as your own, and never questioning our relationship. Regardless how I came into this beautiful world."

Vlad sat in silence holding Betty's hand, as Tommy drove on the highway towards the resort. Betty continued, "Dad before you say anything, please hear me out. I have rendered medical treatment to many people around here, both Native and white. The elders on the reservation gave me permission to move before I start showing. I will live there until the baby is born, then return to you. I can spiritually feel this child will do great things. He will be smart, loyal, and a leader among his people. It's a boy, and he will make us all proud."

Tommy looked at Betty and replied with kindness and sympathy. "I love you, Betty. Everything will turn out fine. You are welcome to stay at the resort during your pregnancy."

Betty shook her head. "No, it will be better this way. You will have Vlad and Pavel to help around the resort while I get ready for my time to pass. There will be fewer questions from guests and people in town. I want this summer to be a success for you. I know the last few years have been hard financially, and you need to do well. Please let me do it my way."

Tommy smiled "Have I ever had a choice? When will you be leaving?"

Betty replied, "I will be here for Walleye opener weekend, soon after I will quietly enter the reservation where a small house on Leech Lake is waiting for me."

The three pulled into the resort and parked in front of the lodge. They got out of Tommy's truck, hugged each other and walked inside to eat their last breakfast together before Vlad returned to Camp Cutfoot Sioux. Tommy and Betty would drop off Vlad and Pavel that evening to Lt. Stokes for continued duty in the forest. It would be the last time all of them would be together alive.

Chapter 40
Mid-April 1945
Camp Cutfoot Sioux

The war was far off, but news on both fronts was freely given to the POWs. Most of them believed what they read and were being told, but a small faction led by Orlov still felt it was propaganda. Every country knew World War II was coming to an end with the Allies victorious. Instead of the violence abating, Vlad watched it eventually reach a crescendo with nuclear weapons unleashed on Japan. The violent events unfolding on the world stage were reflected in a microcosm at Camp Cutfoot Sioux as well.

On Monday, the work details were sent into the forest for the regular eight-hour shift of cutting down trees, trimming off the large branches and hauling them to the main dirt road. Vlad and Pavel were split up into different details. Vlad noticed Orlov and some of the other POWs in his group seemed agitated. It wasn't the usual relaxed atmosphere as they drove to their work site. The day progressed normally, it was warm, and the men were given extra water breaks to keep hydrated.

The older guard watching Vlad's group walked out to the road to be picked up and driven back to camp for lunch. Lt. Stokes slacked off to the point of allowing the POWs to remain unguarded in the forest during the afternoon. The guards ate lunch back at camp and stayed there until 4 p.m. when it was time to pick up the POWs. The guards willingly gave ten percent of their army pay to Lt. Stokes for the privilege of working half days but getting paid full time. There were no problems to this point, as the POWs produced enough timber for the lumber company's quota on a daily basis. The locals were content and happy.

This was the opportunity Orlov waited for. He separated Vlad and Pavel into different work details and made sure they were a few miles apart in the forest. Both work details were laced with Orlov's loyalists, who felt everything the Americans said about the war's progress were lies. They believed Hitler's Vengeance Weapons would lead to ultimate victory, and wanted to be on the side of the Nazi's when it was all over. Orlov had twisted visions of being welcomed back into Germany as a hero who never lost the faith. Orlov believed he would be rewarded with land in the United States by a victorious Germany, maybe even named a governor of a state. A few of his minions at Camp Cutfoot Sioux believed his fantasies and decided to follow him blindly.

During their lunch break, Vlad got up to urinate and tripped over a log and landed on his back. Orlov stood up and screamed to the others pointing at Vlad "I think the Negro Jew lover is afraid of his own shadow and can't even piss or walk without his buddy Pavel around. Get up you stinking swine, or I will drive this ax into your Jew loving skull." Vlad got up on his feet and was taken aback by Orlov's sudden explosion of fury. He was caught completely off guard and starting to process what was happening when Orlov rushed him with a wooden ax handle tightly gripped in his hands. Orlov swung the sturdy handle like a baseball bat and delivered a wicked blow to the side of Vlad's face. Blood flew out of Vlad's mouth and nose as he spun around and landed face first in the cool mud of the forest floor.

Orlov looked at his hand-picked group and shouted "Don't forget this warning. I will do the same to any of you who say a word. I'm sick of this Jew loving maggot being protected by Pavel and running off to work at that goddamned resort. He is weak, spoiled, and thinks his shit doesn't stink. This disloyal worm pistol-whipped me in France, and sucker punched me back in Poland. He killed as many Jews as me but thinks he is the Pope or some fucking saint. He even believes the endless propaganda the Americans have fed us about Germany losing the war. He rejoices in the news. I swear he probably is happy when the Americans claim to be winning. I have sworn revenge on this little bastard and now is the time."

Orlov walked over to Vlad who was moaning on the ground and shrieked "Get up you filthy Jew Lover." Vlad rose up on his knees and looked at Orlov with blood and dirt covering his face. Orlov screamed "From here forward, you are a rotten Jew Lover. I will kick the shit out of you every day until you finally die. You will do both my work and yours, and hand over your camp currency to me every week. I swear to God, I will kill you before we leave this camp and make your life a living hell. Until then, your ass is mine!"

Orlov clenched his fist and delivered a near knockout blow to the side of Vlad's face. Blood again flew into the surrounding trees and sprayed the other men as they stood by and watched. Vlad lay motionless in the dirt as Orlov began to spit on and curse him. He repeatedly screamed "Heil Hitler" and "You worthless piece of shit" as he wildly kicked Vlad in the side, breaking ribs and other bones. Some men could have died from the severe trauma.

Vlad somehow managed to stagger with Orlov's work detail to the logging road at the end of their shift. Vlad's face was swollen, bloody and he could only open one of his eyes. His cheek had deep gouges, and his hair was matted with blood and mud. Vlad walked buckled half over, instinctively covering his broken ribs using his right arm. The transport truck pulled in sight to pick up the men, and Vlad got a strange feeling in the pit of his stomach.

The truck stopped in front of the group, and nervous silence permeated the scene. Frequently Pavel's group was talking about the day and upcoming dinner back at camp. The men even sang German drinking songs on occasion. This time was noticeably different, and as Vlad stepped up into the back of the truck, he immediately knew why.

Pavel lay dead wrapped in a blood-soaked blanket in the middle of the floor. He suffered a massive head wound from an ax.

"What happened?" Orlov asked with a smirk.

"Pavel's double-edged ax bounced back when he hit a knot in a pine tree." A voice inside truck called out. "The back of the blade hit him square in the forehead. He was killed instantly. It happened 15 minutes before the end of our shift."

"That's horrible, poor bastard," Orlov said sarcastically. Vlad painfully dropped to his knees over his dead friend, pulled back the sheet, and inspected the wound. It looked like someone split his forehead in two, no different than splitting a log for a campfire. Vlad tried to cry out, but was in so much pain himself, found it impossible to do so. Tears streamed down his face as he looked at Orlov in full rage.

"Sit the hell down so we can get back and eat dinner." Orlov barked out at Vlad. "He's dead, and you're lucky to be alive, you Jew loving dog."

Orlov was almost drunk on the violence he orchestrated. He had not felt this way since Belzec, and it was an incredible emotional high for him. Visions of commanding a camp like Belzec deep in the woods of Northern Minnesota, and killing American Jews raced through his mind. Orlov was sexually aroused as he fantasized about murder and rape. His thoughts were interrupted when the truck pulled up to the front gate of Camp Cutfoot Sioux.

The Itasca County Sheriff and county coroner waited to greet them, along with Lt. Stokes. The truck driver radioed ahead to notify Stokes of the tragic accident. The sheriff pulled himself into the truck and uncovered Pavel's face. He took a recoil step back and almost threw up at the sight. Copious amounts of blood pooled around the body, brains oozed out of his forehead, and Pavel's skin tone looked ashen.

Sheriff Stokes had very few homicides in his 20 years. He needed a simple and straightforward story that satisfied the Army and his constituents in Itasca County. The county coroner was a drinking buddy and old high school friend. He too was inexperienced with homicides. It was ruled an accident on the spot, no autopsy would be performed, and burial was approved for the next day. Pavel's death was an open and shut case. The Itasca County Sheriff, camp commander, and county coroner said so. Sheriff Stokes wanted no negative attention on him or his sons, and there would be none in this matter.

Pavel's body was buried the next morning in the woods outside Camp Cutfoot Sioux. A wooden marker made by some of the men was given to Vlad to be placed on Pavel's grave in the future. Vlad first needed to recover from his wounds at the hands of Orlov. He would spend four weeks in the camp infirmary. The only available medical person to set his broken bones was Betty. Sheriff Stokes made the call to Tommy Williams informing him what happened, and his confidential need for Betty's medical expertise. They arrived 30 minutes later.

Chapter 41
May 1, 1945
Camp Cutfoot Sioux

By the time Vlad was released from the infirmary, Orlov had asserted total control over the POWs. The number of Nazi sympathizers was grossly underestimated by the US Army in many of the camps. Orlov exploited that fact by gaining the blind obedience of a few to intimidate the many. Pavel was murdered by one of Orlov's henchmen in the work group. The rest were scared into submission and silence by the real threat of retaliation by Orlov and his Nazi loyalists.

Orlov previously held secret meetings after lights out giving hate and fear filled speeches. There were no SS at Camp Cutfoot Sioux. Orlov claimed to represent them and was not shy bragging to the men about his exploits at Belzec. The anti-Semitic, the impressionable, and those who were sympathetic to Hitler gravitated to Orlov. It was during those secret meetings that Orlov and his group conspired to kill Pavel at the end of their logging shift.

Orlov's main follower was placed in Pavel's work group and agreed to carry out the murder. He walked over to Pavel and drove an ax into the middle of his forehead, splitting his face in two. Pavel was dead instantly. None of the other POWs did or said anything. It affirmed the plague that had befallen Germany and the Jews as said by Edmund Burke. "The only thing necessary for the triumph of evil is for good men to do nothing."

The rest of the POWs quietly submitted or face the wrath of Orlov's men. Lt. Stokes was somewhat unaware of the situation, and wouldn't have intervened if he fully were. He looked the other way as Orlov and his small group menaced the other POWs. Lt. Stokes had no desire to interfere with the POWs provided the logging work got done, no escapes were attempted, and the camp operated with quiet efficiency. Orlov afforded him all of that. In return, Orlov now ran the inmates with an iron fist and complete fear.

Beatings of the men were commonplace, especially if they did not relinquish camp currency and do the bidding of Orlov's loyalists. Vlad's fate was in Orlov's hands, and he suffered terribly because of it. Not so much from the beatings, but because Pavel was dead.

Betty set Vlad's broken ribs and bandaged his wounded face. She never saw someone take such a beating. It took great strength not to reveal her feelings as she rendered medical aid to the father of her unborn child in front of Lt. Stokes and the sheriff. Sheriff Stokes promised a future favor to Betty and Tommy for helping Vlad and keeping quiet. Tommy Williams began thinking through how he could take up the sheriff on his offer, while helping Vlad realize the dream of staying in Minnesota and marrying his daughter. It would take much more than Betty's medical care to make that happen.

When Betty was done tending to Vlad's wounds, Tommy pulled the sheriff aside. "Please do me this small favor. Keep the kid safe from Orlov, and keep him confined or whatever it is your son needs to do. The kid knows his way around the resort, and I will need him to help out this summer with my son still in Europe. His buddy Pavel is dead, and I accept your finding that it was an accident. Don't let it happen twice." Sheriff Stokes nodded in agreement.

Germany officially surrendered on May 8th, igniting blissful pandemonium in large cities and small towns all across the United States. Events were sobered somewhat because Japan still needed to surrender, which would occur on August 15th. Demobilization of 12 million uniformed American military personnel proceeded slowly at first, but sped up considerably as every politician was under intense local pressure to bring home the troops. It would take almost 24 months to get most of the soldiers home, which still left an immediate labor shortage stateside.

Timber needed to be harvested and fields needed to be planted. The postwar economic boom was beginning to unfold quickly. Many POWs remained in the United States for another year to work, and all returned to Germany by 1946.

Betty left Williams Narrows for Leech Lake Indian Reservation in Late May after the Walleye opener as promised, and Vlad remained separated from Orlov on orders from the sheriff. Vlad recovered from his wounds and bided his time to determine whether he would be returned to Germany or somehow stay in America. It all would soon come to a head.

Chapter 42
August 1945
Camp Cutfoot Sioux

Orlov was ordered by Lt. Stokes to leave the camp alone, and walk a mile down the dirt road to retrieve tools his group had supposedly left behind. Before leaving alone out the main gate, Orlov impotently cursed his crew for making him take a walk. Orlov's hold over the people who conspired against Pavel and Vlad had diminished significantly. It was now clear the war was indeed over, with America and her allies victorious. Lt. Stokes threatened Orlov a $20 fine in camp currency if the tools were not back in an hour, further increasing his anger and agitation.

When Orlov was out of sight and sound of the camp, a pickup truck approached from the oncoming direction on the dirt road that he walked. Betty slowed down, and Orlov saw her with two other Native American men riding in the front cab.

Betty stopped the truck, and her two half-brothers stepped out of the vehicle. They were tall, muscular, and both carrying sturdy wooden clubs with claws from a black bear attached to the end. The three-inch razor sharp bear claws were affixed to the club by short leather straps and simulated a bear paw when swung. These two sturdy bear claw weapons were hand-made by Betty's grandfather 40 years prior and were ceremonial in nature. However, if used in battle were sure to inflict massive damage on the unfortunate victim.

Orlov looked confused as the two men approached him. He walked backward attempting to distance himself and fell on his backside after tripping over a branch inadvertently lying in the road. Orlov tried to yell for help but was in shock looking at the two large Native American men standing over him carrying the unusual weapons.

Betty stepped out of the truck and was splattered with blood as one of her half-brothers began the attack on Orlov. Her muscular brother swung the club at a speed of 60 miles per hour, and the attached but free moving bear claws struck Orlov in the head with massive force. Betty was unfazed by the blood and watched her two brothers reign down bear claw blows on Orlov's face, back, stomach and legs. Orlov howled in pain, much like his victims in the bear pit at Belzec. Betty thought it spiritual and natural justice for him to die in the same manner.

She suddenly asked her brothers to stop and walked up to a half-conscious and broken Orlov writhing in pain on the dirt road.

Orlov recognized her from the time she set Vlad's bones but had not seen her since. Betty calmly walked behind Orlov, sat on his back and began to strangle him. Orlov started to turn blue, just like all of the Jewish children he strangled as they lost consciousness. Betty squeezed as tight as she could until she felt a damaged spirit pass out of his body, then let go with her hands full of blood and stood above his corpse. Her brothers dragged Orlov to the roadside, got in the pickup and quietly left the scene back to Leech Lake Reservation. The entire episode lasted under five minutes, and there were no witnesses.

Orlov was retrieved by camp personnel after not returning on time. The telltale claw marks made it easy for all involved to determine the official cause of death as a mauling by a black bear. Photographs were taken by the sheriff as proof. It was most plausible and occasionally happened in Itasca County. Orlov was quickly buried. Sheriff Stokes officiated the brief investigation, and the county coroner signed off on the death certificate. Lt. Stokes lost two POWs under his watch. His brother, the Major in Washington DC, assured all involved there was nothing to fear. With so many POWs housed in the United States, deaths from accidents and natural causes at the camps happened from time to time.

That night, Lt. Stokes, Sheriff Stokes, and Tommy Williams met at the resort long after the guests had gone to sleep. Tommy walked them into the back area of the lodge where he kept live minnows. It was a large tub with a pump that circulated cold water, keeping the bait fish alive for weeks at a time. Tommy removed the minnows into a temporary cooler, and in their place was a sight no one could believe.

The state record Walleye Tommy quietly caught one day prior splashed angrily in the large tub. Lt Stokes and the sheriff looked at an amazing 18-pound Walleye with beautiful golden color, a huge belly, enormous eyes, and the largest tail any of them saw on that species of fish.

Williams Narrows was an official weigh station of the Minnesota DNR. Tommy weighed the fish, took Lt. Stokes fishing license information, and filled out the proper documentation. It was official. Lt. Stokes just broke the Minnesota state record for Walleye. It would be front page news in two days, ensuring Lt. Stokes instant celebrity and admired outdoorsman status. His name became synonymous with the most sought after fish in the state, and he held the record for generations to come. At the end of his long life, his tombstone acknowledged the most amazing accomplishment. No one but Tommy and Betty knew Vlad almost caught the very same fish in the Narrows the previous fall. Tommy tried to catch it ever since and finally did. Thus, guaranteeing Vlad's ability to stay behind with his daughter.

Tommy offered the fish as payment to the Stokes family for Vlad to stay in the country and to kill Orlov. 3,000 dollars to the sheriff also sweetened the agreement. Betty's half-brothers, who took Orlov's life, were happy to have the opportunity to kill a white man without any recourse. Sheriff Stokes gave them his word using Tommy Williams as an intermediary that no prosecution would result from the murder. The Native American brothers felt it was a small down payment on a debt owed to generations of their oppressed ancestors, and considered it an honor to kill such a worthless human being. Tommy Williams became a modern fisher of men in a most unusual way. Saint Peter, he was not, but Tommy understood the symbolism and irony that a fish was used to save one good man.

The deal was cemented. Vlad would be officially listed as dead from kidney failure, and a coffin partly filled with dirt and rocks was buried in the patch next to Pavel and Orlov. Vlad was secretly driven to the Leech Lake Indian Reservation with a legal identity and $5,000 cash. It was a hefty sum of money for Tommy Williams, enough to buy a car and small home. The driver's license and social security card even had his original name. The documents were covertly provided by the sheriff and the Stokes brothers in St. Paul and Washington DC.

They were all comfortable their dad, the sheriff, vouched for Vlad's character. Their inept brother being self-sufficient for the rest of life by holding the state record was also a relief. One POW staying behind wouldn't hurt anybody, and the price of not having worry about their incompetent brother was well worth it.

Vlad spent the first night in Betty's home on the reservation. Her time to deliver was soon at hand, and they both fell asleep in each other's arms. He awoke the next morning in a small bedroom lined with quilts hanging on the walls. The smell of cooking food, mixed with smoke from a wood-burning fire permeated the room. Upon looking out the window, he saw a huge lake lined with evergreens and other deciduous trees whose leaves were slowly beginning to turn color. Vlad walked out of the tiny bedroom and entered a small main room to find Betty kneeling next to a wood burning stove. She was cooking meat, vegetables, and native fry bread.

The small living space had a picnic table, an old sofa, handmade cupboards, and old countertops. The walls were covered with colorful handwoven blankets, for both insulation from the cold and decoration. Deer antlers were mounted to the wall, and a Walleye was prominently displayed above the door. Many unfamiliar religious artifacts were neatly assembled on tattered shelving as well. The floors were dirt and covered by uneven planks of wood. It was the poorest dwelling he had ever been in, but it was warm, dry, clean, and tidy. It would certainly make do for the birth of their son.

Betty's time for delivery had come to pass, and three native women that helped birth many children on the reservation entered with blankets. They politely asked Vlad to boil water on a fire they made outside and to keep it coming. He was excused from the home, as Ojibwe tradition called for women only during this time. Vlad continued to pull water from Leech Lake and boiled it over the fire. The women kept bringing out pots and pans, while Vlad refilled them.

Six hours into the process, a worried woman helper came out of the house needing more water. "Baby boy is healthy. Betty is not well and asking for you." Vlad ran into the bedroom to find his healthy son safely wrapped in blankets and tended to by one of the women. He was in good hands. Betty bled profusely during, and after the delivery, something very wrong had happened, and the women were powerless to correct the situation. If Betty were in a medical setting, the outcome might have been different, but it did not matter now. They were one hundred miles from the nearest hospital and had no phones. The women had seen this before. Uncontrolled hemorrhaging during childbirth was not common, but not unusual either.

Betty was in the process of bleeding to death, every heartbeat from Betty brought new flows of blood from her birth canal. She slipped into unconsciousness and never recovered. Vlad was called in by the women too late to say goodbye. Vlad saw plenty of death at his young age, and he knew death when he saw it. Death enveloped Betty and would not release its grip. Betty Williams died as a despondent Vlad held her hand, leaving him a single father with a newborn son in a foreign land. Even though he was legal to stay and had money, his life ahead seemed like an overwhelming task. It was agreed upon that he could not return to the resort and needed to leave the area. A job was pre-arranged for him at a metal fabricating company in a new first ring suburb called St. Louis Park. A suburb that was beginning to experience a post-war building boom, and a large influx of Jewish families migrating out of North Minneapolis to the new development.

Chapter 43
Deer River, Minnesota
September 1, 1945

Vlad stayed on Leech Lake Indian Reservation, living in the small
shack for another week. He got to know his son and received valuable
tips on caring for an infant from the native women. Betty was given a
traditional native ceremony. Then her body released to a devastated
Tommy Williams. Tommy had her cremated and the ashes spread on
Lake Cutfoot Sioux. There was no funeral Mass for Betty due to his utter
despondency.

Tommy was notified by an Army Chaplain in October that his son
was shot and killed by a drunken American soldier at a vehicle
checkpoint outside Frankfurt. The army was learning quickly that
millions of idled armed soldiers, combined with copious amounts of
alcohol, led to tragic results. His death spurred faster demobilization, and
tighter weapons controls on soldiers waiting to return home.

Vlad left the reservation mid-afternoon on Saturday and was expected
at his job in the Twin Cities on Monday. His yet unnamed son
accompanied him as he drove through Deer River, before turning south
towards Minneapolis. Vlad decided at the last minute to take a left off
the highway and drive by the church where he celebrated Mass with
Tommy and Betty. It was a warm fall day, and the front doors were
propped open. Mass did not start for another hour, but the young priest
was available to hear confessions for any Catholic that wished to receive
the sacrament. It's common practice for the Sacrament of Reconciliation
to be celebrated before Saturday evening Mass.

The church was empty as Vlad walked in with his infant son, using a
handheld carrier the native women made for him. The young priest was
lighting candles when he turned around and saw Vlad. The priest walked
over to Vlad and said welcome, Vlad looked at him with sunken eyes and
a damaged soul the priest could clearly see. The priest extended his hand.
"I am Father Grant Moudry. I am here to help in any way, what can I do
for you?"

Vlad shook his hand. "Will you please hear my confession?"

Father Moudry helped Vlad with the baby by having Sister Gemma
hold him and gently escorted Vlad to the confessional.

Vlad started to speak in a hushed tone, "Forgive me, Father, for I have sinned, it has been five years since my last confession. My sins are terrible and many." Vlad began to break down and cry, Father Moudry gave him time to compose himself, and Vlad continued "Father, you have heard stories about death camps the Nazi's used during the war?"

Father Moudry was puzzled at the question and replied "Yes I have. What does this have to do with you here in Deer River?"

Vlad proceeded to tell Father Grant Moudry about his time at Trawniki, Rabka, Belzec, and Drancy. He confessed about his murderous role and his spiritual void, how he abandoned God because Vlad felt God abandoned him.

Vlad took over twenty minutes to divulge his secrets, which only Pavel, Betty and Tommy Williams knew about. Betty and Pavel were dead, and he would never see Tommy again. Tommy Williams sold the resort soon after hearing about his son and died brokenhearted that winter.

When Vlad's confession was over, Father Moudry absorbed the enormity of the situation and sat quietly for a few minutes. He finally simply asked, "Are you truly sorry for your sins?"

Vlad replied, "Of course I am Father."

Grant Moudry then said, "Are you ready to receive your penance and absolution?"

Vlad replied yes with tears streaming down his face.

"Is that your child that you brought to church this evening?" Father Moudry asked.

Vlad again said yes and explained Betty Williams was the mother and he the father. Vlad told the priest about her death. Suddenly it clicked with Father Moudry. He remembered Vlad from Mass, and now it all made sense. He was at the POW camp on Cutfoot Sioux and met Betty. He got mixed up at the horrific death camps and somehow made it here. Father Moudry knew Betty had fallen in love and was expecting a child, but didn't know the outcome. Tommy Williams had not yet informed Grant Moudry of her death.

This was young Father Moudry's first parish, and by far the most demonic confession he would hear in his long life. It was a monumental test for the young priest, and he responded well. "You will receive absolution from this church and community if you follow this penance now and for the rest of your life. The Jewish people have a saying in Hebrew that is 'Tikkun Olam' or in English 'Repair the World.' You cannot undo what has been done, but you can try and repair the world beginning with this child. You shall take this child and give him a Jewish first name. You shall devote the rest of your life raising this child in the Jewish faith, lovingly observing all customs and traditions. You shall never take a wife, for she will most likely be Christian and thus interfere with your penance. You are a young man, and this is a penance that will last a lifetime, but you must accept and agree out of love. It's your decision, but if you seek absolution, this is what you must do."

Vlad said through tears of joy "I accept Father, and I want us to stay in touch, so you can watch me perform my loving penance. It is something I truly desire, please do this for me."

Father Moudry agreed.

Vlad then asked, "Does God forgive me?"

Father Moudry was again taken aback. "I cannot speak for the Almighty, but I think our God is a loving and forgiving God. You are going to need to forgive yourself for what you have done. If you love this Jewish boy, never reject God again, never bring harm to another person, and try to live a Christ-centered life. Then it's my hope and belief God will have Mercy on your soul at the hour of your death." Vlad sobbed uncontrollably.

Father Moudry again asked, "Do you accept this penance out of love?"

Vlad said yes.

Father Moudry then asked Vlad to recite the Act of Contrition with him as a closing prayer. "My God, I am sorry for my sins with all my heart. In choosing to do wrong and failing to do good, I have sinned against you whom I should love above all things. I firmly intend, with your help, to do penance, to sin no more, and to avoid whatever leads me to sin. Our Savior Jesus Christ suffered and died for us. In his name, my God, have mercy."

Father Moudry then said to Vlad, "As Jesus said to the woman who was about to be stoned to death for adultery 'Neither do I condemn you. Go and sin no more.' "

Vlad left the church after giving Father Moudry his new address in St. Louis Park. They formed a bond that would last a lifetime. He walked to his car with his son a transformed person. The damaged Vlad Chayka walked in, and a reborn Vlad Chayka walked out. The Sacrament of Reconciliation changed his life, changed the way he would raise his son, and gave him tools to attempt to repair the world. He was spiritually intact, emotionally healed, and in good standing with his church.

What the rest of society would have to say was a different matter altogether. It would be determined over time, if ever. He hoped to serve his penance out of sheer love and take his secret to the grave. The truth is hard to contain, and almost always shines through the darkest of clouds. Vlad's truth would be no different.

Chapter 44
Present Day
Minneapolis, Minnesota

Max sat at his home early Sunday morning, the mid-summer sun was rising, and he watched runners making their way around the three-mile circumference of Lake Harriet. The carrier was late with the newspaper, which was usual. Despite a generous tip at Christmas, the guy could never seem to deliver a Sunday paper on time. Max was eager to read Carl Jeffries first article on Vlad. The series would span three weeks of Sunday editions. Max offered his suggestions and secretly viewed a rough draft. But per their agreement, Carl had final say on the content and editing.

Max did agree to include the part about his mother and Vlad's penance. Vlad gave permission to retell his confession to Father Grant Moudry almost 70 years ago. It was such a beautiful testament to love over hate that Max figured it might positively impact people. Even though Max was not Catholic, he understood the power of forgiving those who many in the world felt unforgivable. Max also believed it could help repair the world, even just a little bit. Tikkun Olam.

Max and Vlad discussed at length his mother and her life. He fully understood that he was born out of love, and Vlad told him the truth, but not all of it. His mother indeed died during the war, just not how Max envisioned. It was after formal hostilities ended World War II, but it was still a war for Vlad. Vlad's war ceased when he walked out of the church in Deer River.

A few weeks after Vlad finished his life story, Max drove to Northern Minnesota visiting Williams Narrows and the little Catholic Church in Deer River. He rented a boat and fished for Walleye on Lake Cutfoot Sioux. While he fished alone, Max prayed the Kaddish for his mother and burned sage in her memory. Max tossed the burnt sage into the lake and beseeched God to consider him worthy of what others sacrificed on his behalf. For a wealthy man like Max who traveled the world, he never visited Deer River.

Deer River was only a four-hour drive from his home. Vlad brought him fishing on many weekends to other lakes in the state, and they camped in the Boundary Waters Canoe Area at least 20 times during

Max's youth. Max loved the outdoors, and Vlad encouraged him to earn his Eagle Scout. Max happily accepted the award earned during freshman year of high school. But they never visited Williams Narrows Resort or Lake Cutfoot Sioux. Max never questioned why, and Vlad never had to explain.

Before he left the area, Max stopped by the Leech Lake Indian Reservation and spoke with elders who recalled Betty's story with great fondness and respect. It was a healing experience for all. Max was warmly welcomed and felt his mother's presence during the visit. He was a quarter Native American and most proud of a newfound heritage. The tribal leaders said he was welcome back anytime. Max hoped to oblige that fall.

Max had the most unusual heritage of his parents being both prey and predator. Each of whom filled both sides of the unending cannibalistic human food chain. Both were worlds apart, but it was most symbolic of God giving humans free will, and the ability to choose therein. For those who believe and for those that don't, the eleventh commandment that Jesus taught was to 'Love one another as I have loved you.' Max found that most fitting as a smart Jewish kid, and now he understood what it meant as an even smarter adult. He had a mother and father that loved him as they were loved. Max was American, Jewish, Ukrainian, Ojibwe, loved, blessed, and lucky.

Dane was due to arrive shortly and drive Max to the Minneapolis\St. Paul International Airport. Max happily paid the $20,000 to a well-connected Russian extortionist for Mikhail to travel and see his brother Vlad. It had been almost 70 years, and the reunion would be epic. Max received word that Mikhail somehow survived Chelm, fought against Germany during the Battle of Berlin, and was a decorated war hero. How that came to pass would be quite a story and one that Carl Jeffries already spoke to Max about writing. Carl felt that Vlad's story already in print, combined with Mikhail's yet unpublished life, could win him a Pulitzer Prize. Max agreed and wanted Carl to write the piece once Vlad and Mikhail had time to reunite.

Vlad was delighted to hear that his brother was alive, and would be living with him as the legal case proceeded.

Dane was informed that Israel was requesting extradition for Vlad to stand trial for crimes against the Jewish People. How it would play out was anyone's guess, but Vlad had Max to defend him. The irony of a Jewish son defending his father who was a guard at Belzec would continue to make world headlines. Max felt if it went to trial, it would be one for the ages. Vlad fully understood and accepted that God's forgiveness and absolution from the church were one thing, human justice was quite another.

Vlad spoke on the phone with Mikhail, Vlad's Ukrainian was rusty, and the conversation was choppy, but the deep longing to meet was apparent. Both agreed the most fitting way to mark the momentous occasion would be to celebrate Mass privately. Vlad waited at his home in St. Louis Park with Father Moudry for Mikhail's arrival. The only attendees would be Father Grant Moudry, Vlad, Mikhail, Max, Dane, and Carl. Max felt the Mass would be intensely spiritual and personal. He was excited to be a witness.

The carrier arrived with the Sunday paper at the same time Dane pulled in the driveway. On the front page were the large bold words "Unholy Choices." Max gave a wry smile at the appropriate and clever title. The first line of the article was a quote from novelist Raymond Chandler "Down these mean streets a man must go who is not himself mean." Max welled up with tears and set the paper on the kitchen table. He knew the article would be a fair recounting of Vlad's early life. Max would have time to read later. A whole new chapter in all of their lives waited.

Made in the USA
Columbia, SC
16 December 2017